**Seattle Ghost Story** ... is his best book yet. This time, its Ravenna Park that is the source of the trouble. There are complex family relationships and a very charming offbeat love story in addition to some real chills. The ending is satisfyingly dramatic.

Hilary Carkeek, *All Hallows No. 18*
The Ghost Story Society

DiMartino writes again in his vein of expertise: the tradition of the Victorian ghost story ... **University Ghost Story** ... locally intriguing plot ... there are secrets and all that spine-tingling stuff.

*The Seattle Weekly*

He continues to pull audiences to the edge of their seats with the same intriguing and gripping style ... **University Ghost Story** ... will undoubtedly follow its predecessor's footsteps to the top of the University Book Store's bestseller list ...

Jill Tamane
*Footnotes*

Last year DiMartino scored with another thriller called **Christmas Ghost Story.** This year he'll entertain you with our very own **University Ghost Story.**

*UW Weekly*

**Christmas Ghost Story** ... set on Beacon Hill. The season is Halloween through Christmas. And the ghost is real. The Rossi family disagrees about nearly everything. But one thing they do concur on: Nana's back from the grave and she's not happy.

Joe Adcock
*Seattle Post-Intelligencer*

# SEATTLE GHOST STORY

by

Nick DiMartino

*Nick DiMartino* (signature)

Cover and Illustrations

by

Charles Nitti

## ROSEBRIAR PUBLISHING

Lynnwood, Washington

*Seattle Ghost Story*
Copyright © 1998 by Nick DiMartino

Cover art and illustrations © 1998 by Charles Nitti

Rosebriar Publishing
820 195th Place S.W.
Lynnwood, Washington 98036
(425) 776-3865

ISBN  0-9653918-2-5

Library of Congress cataloguing-in-publication data is available.

for my mother

**Mamie Lombard DiMartino**

Thanks to

Jolene Lennon, Chuck Nitti, Siobhan Wallace, Jody Aliesan,
Robert Carlberg, June Miller, Sherry Laing, Lori Morgan, Jason Deetz,
Roger Kim, Antoinette Wills, Pauline Twitchell, Molly McGee,
Aaron Fitzgerald, Hilary Carkeek, Carla Rickerson,
Don Sherwood, Alice Burgess, Elaine Woo, Janine Van Sanden, Paul West,
Allan Davis, Kit O'Neill, Mark Hafs, Catherine Anstett,
Brian Murray, Crispin Stutzman, Scott Cline, David Chew, Don Mizokawa,
Jonas Taylor Siegel, Jared Paul, Antoinette Wills, Liz Fugate,
Kent and Jena Schliiter, Geoff Wright, Meredith Jones, Ruth Lewing,
Mark Mouser, Judith Chandler, Debbie Kilgren, Stephanie Wolfe,
Tony Tomassi, Robin Williams, Jim and Mike Morishima, Tetsuden Kashima,
Sylvia Riveland, Kim and Whitney Ricketts, Aaron Rabin,
Cynthia Gilbert, Diana Olson, Barbara O'Neill, Jonathan Day, Mark Todd,
and all the others

# SEATTLE
# GHOST STORY

# CHAPTER ONE

# The Morning It Happened

## 1
## Crows

Nothing in particular about that dark September morning seemed ominous or unusual. Pepper Merlino had run through the ravine for years, ever since eighth grade, following the main trail through the trees as it twisted along devotedly beside the shallow, gleaming trickle of Ravenna Creek. She had passed through those same twists and turns hundreds of times a year, and never tripped or stumbled or felt herself in danger.

She set out on her morning run shortly before seven o'clock that Saturday. She slipped quietly out of the house in the dark without waking her mother or Grandma. The crisp breeze was chillier than she'd expected. It cut through her heavy red sweatshirt as though it were a T-shirt. She hadn't switched over to her winter sweatpants yet, still enjoying the mobility of jogging shorts. She paid the price now in gooseflesh. She gritted her teeth, and increased her speed.

Pepper was twenty-seven, lanky, athletic. Two months ago she had chopped off most of her shoulder-length black hair, wearing it now in a short, layered boyish cut that radiated feistiness. It was a whole new look for her, after years of long, seductively feminine hair. It gave her a confident, straight-forward, assertive look, a look she found refreshing, a look her mother hated. She always stood up to her full height of five-nine. She had a short Roman nose, arched, questioning eyebrows, eyes that were big and expressive, cheeks that got red easily.

She had run through the park often enough that she looked forward to seeing all her favorite places and special trees every morning. She liked to watch them change through the seasons, to see the maples stripped of their leaves in the fall, the ravine overgrown with flowering undergrowth in the spring. She dreaded the thought of living somewhere else permanently, of no longer running through it.

She was an overworked, underslept graduate student in the College of Forest Resources. Her emphasis was on Ecosystem Analysis. She was midway through writing the first draft of her thesis, "The Reforestation of Ravenna Park," in her second year at the nearby University of Washington. She had sent out applications for doctoral programs to Oregon State, the University of British Columbia, and the School of the Environment at Duke. By next year she could be living anywhere. The thought of actually moving away from her mother and Grandma made her ache. She loved Seattle, the lakes and trees and moody skies. She loved the ravine.

The bends and curves of the trail created blind spots, and Pepper knew them all. She knew each and every place where she went temporarily out of sight, wherever the reinforced rock-chip trail swung out and around so broadly that vision was cut off both in front and behind. A bicycle could come whizzing around the bend out of nowhere. A man could step out of the salmonberry thickets. At that hour of the morning, with barely enough light to see, any shadow could become suspicious.

Crows were making a ruckus up ahead at one of the trail's dark turnings. Something was really bothering them. Or else delighting them — it was hard to tell with crows. The air rang with their loud, outrageous cawing, shattering the peacefulness of the morning. Pepper found crows amusing. They always seemed much smarter to her than anyone suspected. She was convinced they had a sense of humor.

"That's because you're part crow yourself!" her mother was fond of responding. "That's the part of you that drives me crazy." Pepper's intense eyes and thick mop of hair were both as black as the feathers of the crows screeching and swooping through the branches ahead. She wondered what was getting them so agitated.

How her mother hated crows!

"For crows I swerve out of my way and try to hit them," Rose Merlino had said often enough, clutching the steering wheel like she meant it, back in the days when the State of Washington had trusted her with a driver's license. Grandma's little joke, whenever Rose started driving crazily, was "she's trying to hit crows again."

"Mom, they're just birds," Pepper would say. "They're not evil. They just do what birds naturally do."

"They're vicious killers," her mother would hiss. "Remember how they attacked the poor little baby robins in the back yard. They pecked them to death. They went at them again and again with their beaks. They ate them!"

She remembered the one time her grandmother had dared to oppose her mother. Grandma quietly said, "Crows don't do anything human beings don't do."

Her mother's cheeks had flushed red. She had glared at Grandma, who had glared right back. Those two! Always a little war of love raging between them. Always chewing over issues of the past. Always locked together in combat, still guarding and hurting each other after all those years. At times the thought of escaping from Seattle into a rigorous doctoral program in Oregon was very appealing.

Pepper came around the turn, and her pace slowed nearly to a stop. Crows — the trees were full of them, the sky was full of them. Crows, by the dozens! Over the ravine loomed an agitated whirlwind of flapping black feathers. What were they doing? She squinted up at them in awe. The ravine echoed with their cries. Before her swarmed a squawking cloud of wings, darting and weaving over and under each other in a complicated choreographic knot, plunging and soaring through the ear-splitting ruckus. Their dizzyingly-complex flight patterns occupied her thoughts for longer than they should have.

The man and his dog appeared unexpectedly.

No one else was anywhere in sight. The crows were suddenly silent. She couldn't quite see the man's face. He froze, staring. The dog displayed a huge set of jaws, released a park-rattling bark, and lunged.

Her foot came down on an uneven dip in the trail, and twisted out from under her.

Gone was the sky full of crows. She hit the ground hard. The breath was knocked out of her. Suddenly all she could see were rock chips and fir needles up close on the muddy trail. All she could hear was barking. She looked up as brown, hairy jaws with a giant tongue loomed over her. The dog's enormous face filled the dark morning sky. Then the man stepped into her vision, looking down at her.

She was stretched out on the trail. Every bone in her body had been thoroughly rattled. The edges of sharp rocks cut into her palms, her stomach, her legs. She blinked in confusion.

"You all right?" He reached out a hand to her.

"No, I'm not all right!" she snapped, dodging any contact with his hand, getting up onto her knees, eyes bright with pain. "Keep away from me."

That was all the farther she got before his energetic dog bounded forward, assaulting her with enthusiasm, tongue in her ear, tongue in her eye.

"Get him off me!"

"Down, Bobo, down!"

Bobo had some loud things to say in return. He said them inches away from her face.

"Come on, Bobo, shut up." He approached her. "I'm so sorry. He's really friendly. He's trying to say hello. He just says it very loud."

She wasn't in the mood for humor. She scrambled up onto her feet, shaking off the shock, brushing off her scraped hands. Then she recognized him. "Wait a second, I've seen you before."

He was one of the neighbors who frequently walked their pets at that hour. They'd never talked but she had noticed him before, a fortyish man with big shoulders and time-battered Old World features. He had short-cropped, salt-and-pepper hair and an olive Mediterranean complexion. His teal-green parka flapped open unbuttoned. He wore a black turtleneck under his flannel shirt. He had big, dark eyes, a neatly-clipped mustache in a black-stubbled jaw.

He was accompanied by the largest Airedale she had ever seen. At the moment, the dog was charging in a zigzag around him in all directions, a hundred and twenty pounds of lively, curly-brown, big-footed snoopiness, lunging one way and another across the trail like a giant wind-up toy out of control, sniffing every tree, every bush, every plant.

"You ever heard of a leash? You ought to be using one!"

He grabbed at the dog's collar, yanked the reluctant dog toward him long enough to hook the leash he held in his hand onto the collar clip. "I usually do. It was just so early—"

She massaged her shoulder, flexed her elbow. She gently shook out her ankle, glaring at him, her eyes bright with indignation. "Why would anyone train their dog to attack?"

"He was just being a loyal dog," said the man. "He was acting out of love."

"Right." She laughed in contempt. "You call that love? I call it open jaws."

He seemed to be thoroughly embarrassed. "You see, well, it's just that — Bobo responded to you that way because, well — he knows when I'm afraid."

"Afraid? You?" She wasn't sure she'd heard right. "Why would you be afraid? I'm the woman alone."

He chuckled awkwardly. "To tell you the truth, with that haircut I couldn't tell — it was too dark. You could have been anyone. You see, I — well, I've been mugged before. I was afraid when you came out of nowhere. Bobo could feel my fear. He was protecting his master. Hope you're all right."

"I'll live." His story was plausible, possible. "Although I'm certainly not as good as I was before your dog tried to attack me. I'm in pain, for one thing. And slightly embarrassed. I've never fallen here before. Ah, look, here's the reason. With a hole like that—"

" There are so many bumps and gullies, it's amazing you've stayed on your feet this long."

"Guess I was living a charmed life. Must be losing my touch." Damp earth darkened her chest and one cheek. She wiped and brushed at herself.

"Bobo, you should be ashamed," he scolded, then turned back to her. "He's harmless, really. He just believes that 'loud is good.' You probably think he eats people."

"I'm sure he's a wonderful dog."

"Wonderful, but rude." He extended his hand. "I should introduce you to his master, before you think I'm rude, too. Joe Strozza."

"Pepper Merlino. Strozza — you're Italian, too?"

"Isn't it obvious?" He accompanied the words with a little mugging and a few animated gestures with his hands. "Bobo, get down. My dog likes you. He's usually not very out-going. Airedales are one-guy dogs."

"He's branching out."

Bobo promptly buried his nose in her crotch.

"I'm so sorry!" exclaimed Joe, thoroughly embarrassed.

"No need for *you* to be sorry," said Pepper.

"Bobo, stop that!"

"Relax. Your dog did it. Not you."

Her careless words snagged them both into an awkward moment.

"What a luxury this park is!" said Joe, decisively changing the subject. "I'm from Chicago. Only in Seattle can you walk into a beautiful natural ravine in your own back yard."

"I agree, it's a treasure." She shook out her leg muscles to keep them from cramping. Her ankle didn't hurt too badly. "Usually I stay on my feet a little better." She cautiously tested the injured foot. "Doesn't feel like I hurt anything seriously. Lucky fall."

"If falls can be lucky—"

Bobo thrust his head between the two talking people, bumping them apart impatiently. Human beings could talk forever.

"Looks like my dear son wants to keep moving."

"Your son?" She smiled. "Ah, yes, I see the resemblance."

"I know. It's the nose. Well, nice to meet you. Hope our next meeting isn't quite so eventful."


## 2
## Mother and Daughter

Pepper left her muddy running shoes outside on the back porch and came in quietly, even though a glance at the kitchen clock showed her it was almost eight and everyone would be up. Walking through the kitchen and down the front hall, she could hear her mother upstairs, scolding Grandma about something. Pepper almost called out to announce her presence, then paused, motionless at the bottom of the stairs, listening.

"—no reason to keep hanging on to all that old junk," droned her mother. "Mama, you know he's never coming back. That basement is packed full of his garbage. How many more years are you going to save it? I say throw it out. All of it!"

Her grandmother mumbled something in reply.

"Mama, be sensible," said her mother in exasperation, "no one remembers anymore."

Grandma mumbled.

"Mama, no one has any such idea!" said her mother sharply. Then she stepped out of the room, stopping abruptly at the top of the stairs at the sight of Pepper standing there below. "And who do we have here? Somebody eavesdropping?"

"Mother!" said Pepper indignantly. "Of course not! I was just coming up to—"

"Leave your grandmother alone," said Rose Merlino, descending the staircase toward her. She was a powerful, big-boned woman still a year short of fifty who had removed all trace of gray from her helmet of black hair. Her olive skin had few wrinkles. She held herself well, still looked good in slacks and a blouse. She walked from the shoulders, which were broad and strong. Her features were clear-cut, striking, her makeup simple and skillfully applied. Her eyes were bright black, impenetrable. They were sad eyes, familiar with pain.

She turned her daughter around by the shoulders and aimed her back toward the kitchen. "Mama needs to rest. Keep me company while I make you some breakfast."

"Nothing for me, thanks."

Rose didn't seem to hear her. She circled around her daughter toward the sink. "I was just washing up the last of the breakfast dishes when she called. You know Grandma. When she wants you, she wants you right now." Damp strands of black hair were pasted into curls and question marks across her forehead. Her muscular arms splashed about in the sink. She wasn't looking at her daughter, but didn't miss a thing.

"You're limping."

"I twisted my ankle. It's nothing."

"God didn't design the human body for running every morning, and yet some people insist—"

"Mom, please, I know my own body."

"Sorry I said anything."

How typical! No sooner did Pepper get home than she and her mother were at each other's throats. Living at home to save money while she went through graduate school had been a terrible idea. She should never have let her mother talk her into it. Rose wasn't happy unless she was in control of every situation. She hadn't yet learned, after twenty-seven years, that it was time to relinquish control of her daughter.

"It smells like heaven in here," said Pepper, trying to change the subject without further irritating her mother.

"You're hungry," said Rose. "You can smell the sausage. I'll make you some scrambled eggs. We've already eaten."

"No thanks, Mom. So that's what I smell! Your spicy sausages."

"You know how Grandma likes them, nice and hot. You'll love them."

"Don't make anything for me," said Pepper. "I'll be gone before it's out of the pan. Which is why I wanted to say hi to Grandma before I leave."

'You'll just disturb her," said her mother.

"I won't disturb her," said Pepper defensively. "It's good for her to chatter away to someone who's genuinely interested. I like her stories. Let her enjoy herself, and soak up a little attention."

"Who knows what she may say? What crazy things might come out of that mouth?"

Pepper scowled at her mother, unable to understand what she could possibly be thinking. "Mom, she doesn't say crazy things."

"Well, don't keep her talking too long, that's all I've got to say," said Rose, sliding the rack of dishes into the dishwasher, closing the door, setting the dials.

"I can't," said Pepper. "I've got volunteer work with the Tree Stewards at nine. I should be back in time for dinner."

"And what is this you're wasting your time at now?"

"Mom, taking care of trees isn't wasting time."

"Taking care of trees?" said Rose, amused. "If you ask me, the trees did just fine before you came along."

No matter how much she tried not to let her mother get to her, she always could. "But the trees won't go on doing fine, Mom, not if we don't stop killing them. I want my daughter to have a chance to love trees just as much as I do."

"Your daughter?" Her mother gave a humorless bark to simulate laughter. "Did I miss something? What daughter?"

"Well, I do intend to have a child."

"You don't have any idea what being a mother means."

"And you do? The hateful way you bully Grandma!"

Before Rose realized what she was doing, she raised her hand and nearly slapped her daughter. Pepper stared at her mother in shock. Rose slowly lowered her hand. Neither was able to move. Though Rose appeared to be equally shocked by her own behavior, she didn't apologize. "I love your grandmother dearly," she whispered. "More dearly than you'll ever know. I've given more of my life to my mother than any child should ever have to give. More than you could ever dream of giving."

Rose and Pepper regarded each other.

"I promise I won't tire her out," said Pepper. She stared at her mother coldly. "If you ever hit me — ever — it will be the last time you see me."

Rose didn't budge from where she stood. Her mouth was open, lips working silently, staring helplessly at her daughter, trying to force words out, trying to tell Pepper how sorry she was, how much she loved her.

Pepper didn't wait to hear it. She turned and walked up the stairs toward Grandma's room.

# 3
# The Other Ravine

Unlike her smoldering relationship with her mother, Pepper adored her grandmother without reservation. Who cared if her old stories weren't exactly accurate? Grandma remembered a whole way of life far beyond Pepper's wildest guesses. She didn't want to take a chance on those memories being lost. Those stories had to be told or they would be forgotten.

The door of Grandma's bedroom was open a crack.

Pepper rapped lightly. No response. She swung the door open and quietly entered. Grandma was turned toward the window, lost in her own thoughts. Tears zigzagged down the wrinkles of her cheek.

"Are you okay, Grandma?"

No response.

Carmen Merlino looked ten years older than she was. She had been exhausted by life. She looked like she'd been wrestling since the day she was born and had finally been pinned to the mat. She might once have been pretty. Her eyes were watery brown, the color of weak coffee. She had lost some of her hair, and what was left was white and wispy as cobwebs, blowing about her face in the slight breeze from the cracked-open bedroom window.

Lately Carmen had been spending more and more time in bed. She was just in her seventies, too young to be bedridden, but she felt too weak to exert any more energy. She complained of perpetual tiredness. She had lost contact with her old friends and relatives, was completely unsocial and reclusive.

Pepper tiptoed closer to the bed. Though Grandma's room was kept thoroughly clean, a slight odor of sweat and old age seemed to have seeped into the walls. It was a smell that frightened Pepper.

"What do you want?" Carmen turned her head abruptly, flustered, clutching the flaps of her white bathrobe around her.

"Nothing, Grandma, nothing," said Pepper reassuringly, sitting on the edge of a nearby chair. "It's just me."

Carmen regarded her granddaughter warily, as though she might be an imposter. Then her features softened. She smiled weakly. "It's my princess—"

"Grandma, what's wrong?"

"Just remembering," she said. "Old people do that. Remembering someone who's gone. Someone I loved, someone I gave up so much for, someone who betrayed me. You never know when someone's going to change your life forever."

Pepper couldn't always understand what her grandmother was trying to say. "Change it how, Grandma?"

"By making you as evil as he is."

Rose stood in the doorway behind them. Neither of them had heard her arrive. "What are you saying, Mama?" she asked in a teasing voice that was slightly too aggressive. "Are you making up stories?"

"I don't make up stories." Grandma turned away from her daughter, sinking back into her pillows with resignation, clasping her granddaughter's hand.

"Don't pay any attention to her," said Rose, casually prying loose her mother's grip on Pepper. "She's been acting strange this morning."

Grandma smiled weakly, as though Rose were talking about someone else. "I was the one who worked all day. I brought home the paycheck. I kept food on the table. I loved him. He made me laugh. He was so handsome. But he was bad. He was so selfish. He took away my happiness for the rest of my life."

"He did what?" said Pepper. "Who do you mean, Grandma?" She turned to her mother. "Who is she talking about?"

Rose sadly regarded her mother, sunk crumpled into the covers, her old face twitching and shivering with emotion. "She's talking about her brother."

A light flickered in the depths of Carmen's tired eyes. "Gabriel—"

Rose wiped at her mother's wet face with a folded handkerchief. "Mama, stop crying. You know how I hate to see you crying."

"He wasn't worth it," said Grandma. "I don't forget. I know what he was really like. I'm wasting my tears, but — but I never wanted to—"

"Hush, Mama!" Rose turned back to her daughter. "She's been in a state all morning. She needs quiet and rest. You've already gotten her all worked up again."

"Mother, you're being too protective," said Pepper. "Sounds to me like she could use a little company. Grandma enjoys talking once in a while. Don't you, Grandma?"

Carmen smiled vaguely.

"And I enjoy listening. What's your objection, Mom?"

Rose had become too irritated to answer. She turned and stomped back downstairs to the kitchen.

Grandma didn't seem to notice.

"I don't want to upset you," said Pepper. "I just wanted you to tell me more of your stories. Have you really lived here in this house all your life, Grandma?"

"Long as I can remember."

"I wonder if I'll always live here, too. Or if I'll move away, and never see this house again."

"You'll come back. The Merlinos belong here. They always come back."

"I have so many happy memories here, Grandma, I really might come back," said Pepper, taking her grandmother's hand. "Besides, I'll always have to come back to see you."

Carmen shook her head sadly, as though she knew better.

"I love the way your window looks out over the ravine," said Pepper, gazing down through the trees below. "I love the ravine. Don't you?"

Her grandmother didn't respond. She just stared out the window, as though she were able to see through it straight back into the past.

"I'll bet you can tell me all kinds of stories about the ravine."

"Far too many stories," said Carmen. The thought seemed to disturb her. "When I was your age, I loved the ravines. Both ravines."

"Both?"

"There was another ravine, too," said Grandma. "A lovely place. The two ravines came together. The other one was called Cowen Ravine. Now it's called Cowen Park. Now there's a baseball field on top of it."

"Cowen Park was once a ravine?" Pepper was intrigued. "Tell me about this other ravine, Grandma."

"So long ago," she said. Her features darkened. The memory of the other ravine did not make her happy. Her brows lowered, troubled. "I think it was in — it was in—" She was becoming more upset. Carmen whimpered so softly it was almost inaudible.

"Grandma?" said Pepper. "Are you okay?"

Carmen stiffened slightly, caught up in a chain of memories. She had been snared by some kind of hook in the past. "Nineteen sixty—"

"I didn't mean to tire you out," said Pepper, trying to relax her. "We don't need to talk about it now. I want you to rest, so that you can get stronger. Then we can go for walks in the ravine again. Wouldn't you like that, Grandma?"

"Cowen Ravine—" said Carmen slowly, as though she hadn't heard a word Pepper was saying. "I remember Cowen Ravine. When Rose was just a child, I would take her there. We'd go for walks, long wonderful walks, from one ravine to the other. The trees then were so much bigger." The wrinkles on the old woman's face slowly crinkled, shifted. She was weakly smiling, remembering. "So much taller—"

"It must have been a beautiful place."

"Oh, yes, it was," said Carmen. "They destroyed it." Her eyes looked desolate. "I saw the tractors. I saw the dump trucks. It's all filled in now, the other ravine, all filled in."

"But who filled it in?" asked Pepper. "How could the Park Department allow something like that to happen?"

Grandma smiled bitterly. "The Park Department allowed it," she said, "because the Park Department did it."

"Oh, Grandma, that can't be true," said Pepper. "Why would the Park Department fill in one of its own ravines? Surely there were other places to build a baseball field?"

"It happened because of the freeway," she said.

"Freeway?" Pepper became afraid that she was pushing Grandma too far, that her mind was wandering from one story to another. "What about the freeway?"

"They were just building I-5," said Grandma. "They had debris to get rid of. They had dirt, trucks full of dirt. They needed somewhere to dump it all. So they dumped it in Cowen Ravine."

"Grandma, the city would never allow it."

"The city did allow it."

"There must have been some other reason."

"They buried the ravine and everything in it. They cut down the trees and buried them. They buried the lovely creek. They buried everything in tons of fill dirt."

"But, Grandma, I'm sure—"

"Buried!" Carmen was shouting. "You're too young to understand. You don't know what it was like. You think you can judge, but you can't!"

Her mother reappeared in the bedroom doorway, scowling at Pepper as though she had caught her torturing Grandma with hot matches. "I told you not to bother her."

"I didn't mean to. I'm sorry."

Grandma was getting more upset by the minute. She staggered up suddenly onto unsteady legs and lunged toward the window.

"Now, Mama, take it easy!"

Carmen pressed her face against the glass, staring down into the ravine. "It was so much harder in those days. You don't know what it was like. If you were a woman in a family of men, you didn't have a life. When your daughter is all you've got and you've got to feed her, you can't be choosy. You do what you have to do."

"Mama!" Rose wrapped her arms around the old woman. "That's enough of that."

"It was all for you," said Carmen. "They told me I was crazy, they treated me like dirt, but I did it for you. I love you, Rose, I love you too much."

"You shouldn't be wearing yourself out," said Rose. She tugged her mother away from the window, leading her back to her disordered bed, easing her down onto the crushed and flattened pillows. "You're all excited, and you know that's not good for you. I don't want you falling down the stairs." Rose turned to regard her daughter. Angrily she ran a

14

hand back through her turbulent mane of hair. "She's been stirred up enough. Isn't it time for you to leave?"

Pepper was horrified, mortified. "I'm so sorry, Mom!"

She was heading for the bedroom door when Carmen rose up weakly onto her elbow and called out to her in a hoarse whisper. "It's not your fault. You don't understand! No one can understand, not unless you're a mother and you've got a daughter and that's all you've got, no husband, no money, no choice—"

"Grandma, I'm sorry." Pepper bolted out of the room and down the stairs, grabbed her coat out of the front closet, and was out the door and gone, heading down into the trees of the ravine.


# 4
# Trail to Nowhere

Eleven-year-old Billy Beck had been left out of the war.

He stood abandoned at the eastern end of the park, wasting his Saturday far from anyone else in the game, guarding the Trail to Nowhere.

The trail was a neighborhood joke. One summer a dozen Volunteers for Outdoor Washington, all of them wearing bright yellow hard-hats, had built a banked thirty-foot-long gravel walkway. It stretched from the main trail, across a small wooden footbridge over the creek, into a perfectly-groomed gravel path with beam-reinforced sides which cut a graceful arc through the undergrowth and ended abruptly in a wild cul-de-sac of ferns and ivy and morning glory. Without explanation, the walkway simply abandoned the walker with nowhere to go. Meandering footpaths and wobbly plank walkways branched out to the right and left, like vague after-thoughts trying desperately to escape.

Billy had been assigned to guard the Trail to Nowhere, protecting it from the stalking Soldiers of the Undead. As if anyone in their right mind, dead or alive, would ever want to use that trail! The enemy would never take it in a million years. So there he was, stranded, forgotten by the other neighborhood boys taking part in the exciting beginning of the weekend-long War of the Stolen Sword of Three Powers.

Not a single other armored-and-weaponed member of the game was currently in sight. There was only Billy Beck, the skinny sixth-grader from Bryant Elementary School, the youngest and shortest kid in his class, standing unhappily at the end of the Trail to Nowhere, waiting for one of the older kids to remember him.

Two boys his own age wearing white athletic trunks and T-shirts with bold, red numbers jogged down the main trail, panting and scowling fiercely. He recognized them as they passed. They went to his school. Billy stood there feeling ridiculous in black boots and black cape, armed with his wooden sword. He thanked God for the aluminum-reinforced cardboard helmet tied around his head. Maybe they couldn't see his face. Maybe they didn't recognize him.

They laughed as they passed him, suggesting maybe they had.

Billy sighed and shrugged it off. He promised himself that he would never, ever again, under any circumstances, participate in the neighborhood Games of Adventure.

He turned his back on the main ravine trail, looking up at the high, wooden pedestrian bridge stretching across the end of the ravine. As he did so, he heard rustling in the leaves. He wasn't as alone as he'd thought.

He was rapidly being surrounded by what the rules of the game referred to as "reality." It came in the form of several dozen older kids and adults in sweatsuits and gloves and boots, combing the banks like hungry locusts, stripping them of blackberry briars and morning glory vines. He tried to ignore them, to remain at attention in the Divided Kingdom, to not notice their intrusive stomping and crunching, ripping and pulling. He listened, waited, on the alert, trying to be a good player in a game where no one remembered he was still playing.

One volunteer in particular was edging closer.

He hadn't noticed her working in the shadow of the nearby tree, not until she made a sniffling noise just beyond the abrupt end of the Trail to Nowhere. He caught a brief glimpse of her face on the other side of a large tree-root, her back to the stump, half-concealed by a sword fern's giant fronds.

Her cheeks were streaked wet.

*Trail to Nowhere*

*

Pepper wasn't concentrating on her work, which was one reason why it took her so long to notice the boy. Her departure from the house had been so disturbing. Her mother was mad at her as usual. Her beloved grandmother was upset with her, too, and she still didn't know what had caused the explosion.

Along with almost two dozen other committed members of the Ravenna Park chapter of Tree Stewards, armed with shovels and hand pruners, loppers and ten-gallon plastic buckets, she was clearing away an overgrowth of non-native invasive plants. In other words, she was weeding. They had almost finished clearing one side-ravine, and were working their way toward the other. Overhead, supported on a criss-crossing lattice of creosoted timbers, forty feet above them across both the side-ravines, stretched the old wooden bridges, so narrow only one person could walk across at a time. Pepper was cold, uncomfortable, dribbled on and splashed by leaves still damp from the last rain, one foot stuck in mud up to the ankle, the other still sore from her fall that morning, braced against a tuft of grass as she tugged out long, stubborn morning glory creepers by the roots.

In just a couple weeks, she'd be too busy for this, she reassured herself. She'd be starting classes again in her second year of graduate study. God only knew why she'd impulsively signed her name on a volunteer sheet. And now here she was, keeping her commitment, deep in mud.

All around her, other volunteers were ripping up vast reaches of vines and briars that annually choked the ravine, slugging their way through the swampy thickets undaunted by the September chill, undeterred by the approaching drizzle.

Uprooting a long vine of morning glory from its stranglehold on a big sword fern, she caught sight of the boy on the other side and flinched. "You startled me — I didn't see you! How long have you been there?"

"A long time," he said, with a sigh.

She noticed his unhappy expression. She regarded his costume. "You look like you've been left out of the war."

Billy was amazed at how completely she understood the situation. "They do it on purpose," he confided miserably. "I'm the youngest. They don't want me to play."

"Young people are always underestimated," she said in complete agreement.

What an unusual thing to say! Something in Billy decided not to let her escape from him back into her weeding. The War of the Stolen Sword of Three Powers could continue on without him. "Why are you crying?"

"Crying?" She wiped her cheeks with the back of her arm. "I'm not crying. I just got something in my eye." She sniffed. "Okay, so I'm crying. You caught me. I just got my grandmother all upset, and I don't know how I did it, and I feel terrible about it." She gave him a second look. "You live around here?"

He nodded.

"Know much about this park?"

He nodded again. "Every trail," he said.

She smiled. "I just heard there used to be another ravine near here."

"Another ravine?" repeated Billy. "There are these two little ravines down at this end—" He gestured toward the two high wooden bridges. "—but they hardly count. This one's blocked off by that cyclone fence. It goes nowhere, just like this trail. And the other ravine over there—" He gestured. "—is a lot bigger and goes back a lot farther, but it's real skinny and there are no paths. You can't go down in there without getting soaked and muddy, so nobody goes there. It sort of stinks. I've never been back there. It looks yucky."

"But other than that, no other ravine, huh? Ever hear of a second ravine over in Cowen Park?"

"Nope."

"You're too young, anyway. You weren't even born yet. Well, I just found out it existed. My Grandma became very upset when she talked about it. And I want to know why." She held out her hand, palm up, as though feeling the weather. "Looks like it's going to start raining any minute. Oh, boy, weeding in the rain. My idea of a good time."

A chilly blast hissed through the branches.

Billy pulled his cape closer around his bony shoulders. A few scattered raindrops splattered on overhead leaves.

"My name's Pepper Merlino. I live in that big house on the edge of the ravine."

"I know the house you mean," he said. "I'm Billy Beck. I live over by the basketball hoop."

She nodded. "That makes us practically neighbors." She extended her hand. Billy solemnly shook it. "Beck, did you say? Now, that's an interesting coincidence. The whole ravine was once owned by a man named Beck, back at the turn of the century. Do you know about him?"

Billy shook his head.

"Reverend William Beck, Presbyterian minister. I learned all about him writing my thesis on this park. He owned three hundred acres, including this ravine. You might be one of his descendants."

Billy stood straighter. "I might be."

"I've noticed you before in the park," she said. "I think I've seen you with a sketch book. Interested in drawing?"

"I draw all the time." She had struck a nerve, his favorite topic. "All I want to do sometimes is just draw."

She smiled at him. Her smile faded as she looked up. "Bad weather for drawing. Afraid we're both doomed to get soaked."

The unhappy young knight raised his homemade helmet to glance up at the darkening sky. Then something else caught his attention, making them both forget about the coming shower.

A section of wire-grid fencing had been cut open, link by link, along one side of the Revegetation Project. Standing on the other side of the fence stood the illegal trespasser, muddy boots ankle-deep in creek water, caught in the very act of violating restricted park grounds. In one hand the intruder gripped a bulging plastic bag filled with dripping watercress. In the other hand gleamed an enormous knife.

It was old Mrs Hayashi, who lived across the street.

# 5
## Escape from the Undead

Suddenly two bloodthirsty, undead creatures of the ruthless Death King leaped from their hiding-place behind a salmonberry thicket. At the sight of Billy, the merciless beings squealed with delight, charging toward him with hungry cries.

In terror, Billy found himself back in the game again, a spear-carrier in the wilds of the Divided Kingdom, an extra of no importance about to encounter a hideous fate, to be ripped apart, his soul sucked out of him. The creatures rushing toward him were pitiless, and Billy knew it. He sprang away from Pepper without so much as a goodbye. Lunging off the Trail to Nowhere, he bounded up the roots-and-dirt bank on his left.

He could hear sadistic squeals of anticipation getting closer behind him. Clawing hold of branches, using giant roots as foot braces, he clambered over the bank and hurtled down the other side, bounding across a long moss-covered cement trough channeling water into three silt-filled pools. He crashed through the bushes on the other side, through nets of ivy and morning glory, scratched his arms on blackberry thorns and prickly holly. On he scrambled under the looming spans of the wooden bridge, half-blinded by his cardboard helmet until he flung it off behind him, slashing out with his wooden sword, plowing into the bamboo.

The jungle of bamboo stalks closed over his head. Leafy caverns were hidden among the stalks, hollowed out by homeless people and high school boys. Billy crashed through them. He broke through one spider-web after another, batting at his face frantically to brush away clinging strands of web as well as any possible web-makers.

Skirting the twisted handlebars of a bike that had been thrown off the bridge, scrambling around the shattered shell of an old television, he darted under the wooden bridge, past the dangling rope on which he'd swooped and soared on lonely summer afternoons. He looked back. They were still coming. There was nowhere left to turn.

Nowhere but the part of the park where no one ever went.

"Halt, in the name of the Death King!"

21

He ran, leaving the bridge behind him, heading straight into the narrow, twisted, briar-defended gorge, into underbrush so deep his feet sometimes couldn't reach the bottom. Some leafy growths had rocks under them, some solid earth, some hid the shallow, chilly waters of the creek, some were just a thin green skin over the mud. No trails, no paths, just fallen trees and green thickets and soggy springs. He'd never dared to venture into that part of the ravine before. He'd never wanted to badly enough. There was no way to do it and stay dry.

His feet sloshed in deeper, through spongy, leaf-thickened mud. His pursuers gave angry howls of dismay as they sank up to their ankles. Now they were not only hungry for his soul. Now they were genuinely mad at him for making them get filthy.

Billy struggled onward. His shoes were sluggishly heavy, caked in ooze. He splashed through the shallow creek. Watersoaked logs blocked his way, crisscrossing the persistent, gleaming trickle. He slipped over one, climbed over the moss-covered bark of the next.

He waded frantically through the creek bed, stubbing his toes on the rocks, his old athletic shoes sopping wet, making his way toward a toppled maple trunk. Engulfed in brambles, half-buried in mud, the tree trunk offered a brief escape from the cold water. He tried to scramble up onto the log. The soft bark crumbled and snapped off. His foot slipped down into the fork of a lower branch.

It felt like someone had grabbed hold of it and wouldn't let go. He tried to tug free. To his amazement, he couldn't. The heel of his shoe was stuck. What a horrible smell, like sour milk and rotting eggs!

He tried to kick out with the other foot and lost his balance, knocking himself forward onto his hands and knees. One arm sank, fingers outspread, up to the elbow in slimy, decomposing plant matter. When he scrambled upright, his sopping legs were dark with muck and a thin line of blood ran down between the fingers of his right hand.

He knew he didn't have a chance. He was about to be caught by his two angry pursuers, tackled, pinned to the wet ground, made a thorough mess of, then splattered with white flour and officially retired from the game, slain in meaningless combat.

Struggle was useless. He turned to face the undead creatures who were about to pummel him.

With predatory screeches, his would-be executioners charged toward him gleefully. They were tromping through the wet undergrowth, fists clenched in anticipation, when a shout rang out from the deck of the three-story house overlooking the ravine. The chilling cry froze them in their tracks.

An old woman in a white bathrobe was yelling at Billy from the deck of the house Pepper said she lived in, shouting words he couldn't understand.

# 6
# What Happened

Billy and the other two in medieval costumes were making enough racket for a whole army, with plenty of noisy wails and far-fetched, vaguely Arthurian language. Boys! Pepper tried to ignore them, reaching down for another handful of invasive leaves. What was it about boys that made them need to be loud and smash things?

Suddenly they weren't the only ones yelling. She looked up to see her grandmother, clutching her white bathrobe around her, shouting from the deck of the house.

"Private property!"

Pepper gasped. "Grandma!"

For reasons she couldn't figure out, Grandma was yelling at Billy Beck who was down in the vine-choked, pathless part of the ravine, his foot apparently stuck in the mud.

Before Pepper could budge, the two boys chasing Billy scurried up the bank and out of sight, while Grandma disappeared from the deck. Utterly unnerved, Pepper watched the back of the house tensely. Her grandmother did not reappear. Pepper tried to sigh with relief. She tried to believe that her mother must have come to Grandma's aid, must have things under control. She tried to believe that Grandma had calmed down, had taken some aspirin, was back in bed where she belonged.

A moment later Carmen Merlino reappeared at one end of the wooden bridge forty feet above her. She was hurrying as rapidly as she could across the narrow length of the bridge. "Oh, my God—" Pepper peered up in horror from the ravine bottom.

Grandma didn't seem to see her, or anyone else. She saw only one thing. Gripping the green-painted wooden railing, she called shrilly down at Billy struggling to extricate his foot below her. "Private property! Get away!"

"Grandma!" cried Pepper. She flung down her uprooted vines.

"Mama!" cried Rose, appearing breathlessly at the end of the bridge, dishtowel still in her hands, wide-eyed, cheeks flushed from running. "Mama, what do you think you're doing?" Somehow her mother had managed to slip past her. "You've got no business running around dressed like that." She took a nervous step toward her mother, out onto the bridge. "You come back inside right now, do you hear me? Mama, you're too weak. You could get dizzy out here."

Carmen didn't hear a word. She didn't hear Bobo unleash a deafening volley of barking, as he and his master appeared on the trail below. She didn't hear Rose calling from the end of the bridge, or Pepper calling up from the ravine.

"Private property!" shouted Carmen, clutching the railing as she peered over the side of the bridge. "You, down there," she yelled at Billy, "you get away from our property, or I'll call your mother!"

"No, Mama, this land doesn't belong to us," said Rose, taking another step toward her on the bridge, trying to sound reassuring, reasonable. "Come on back inside, Mama. You're making a mistake."

Carmen scowled at her, then returned her full attention to the boy below her. "Away from there!"

Rose was literally wringing her hands. She was hesitant to upset her mother any further, anxious to calm her down, uncertain which choices to make, desperate to make the right one quickly. She took another cautious step, then another, getting closer and closer.

"Our land doesn't go this far, Mama," she tried to explain, her cheeks flushed, her eyes wide with fear. Her mother looked back at her like a wild-haired castaway on some unreachable island. "This doesn't belong to us. Please, Mama, come back."

From below, Pepper watched her mother take one step, another, struggling not to run, the wind flapping open her blue house sweater.

Carmen had no intention of coming back. She clung to the railing, refusing to look at her daughter. She was much more concerned with the boy under the bridge. "Go away!" she yelled down at him, beside herself with emotion. "Get away from there right now!"

"Grandma!" Pepper began scrambling on all fours up the bank toward the bridge, ignoring the pain in her ankle.

"You, there, little boy!" Rose called down at Billy, her face flushed. "Look how you're upsetting her! Go away!"

"I can't!" wailed Billy.

At that point, Joe Strozza came charging forward. After tying Bobo's leash quickly around a branch, Joe waded into the soggy mud-beds of wild grass toward the struggling kid. Behind him, Bobo loudly voiced his disapproval at being abandoned.

"Mama, please." Rose was walking faster now, as quickly as she could along the length of the bridge toward her mother. Something inexplicable was happening to Carmen. In what appeared to be a fit of agitation, the old woman was swaying back and forth as though she were wrestling with something, slamming up against the green railing.

"No — no, it's mine — you can't have it — go away!"

"Mama!" Rose was running now. Pepper appeared at the end of the bridge.

Joe reached the frantic boy. The kid's eyes were so fixed on the old woman shouting overhead that he didn't see Joe coming until he heard the last few sloshing steps. He gave a startled cry as Joe's arms closed around him. Joe scooped him up under the armpits.

"My foot's stuck!" Billy managed to explain.

Bracing his own foot against the vine matting over the fallen tree, Joe tightened his arms around the boy's chest and tugged. Along with the trapped foot came an explosion of fetid, decomposing matter. They stumbled backward, off-balance.

Joe gasped in pain. A speck of something had blown into his eye. He blinked, blinked again, nearly dropping the boy, who scrambled free. His left eye began watering. He wiped at his eye, trying to see.

Carmen Merlino cried out one final, terrible word before she clutched angrily at something which just eluded her grasp. She dropped suddenly, silently. Her body struck the rocks under the bridge, becoming abruptly still.

The cloud-choked sky bottomed out. Thick, black clouds cracked open. The rain came down in sheets.

# CHAPTER TWO

# That Night

## 1
## In the Rain

Joe managed to turn the boy's head away, so that Billy was spared the worst of it. Joe had a hard enough time himself. Suddenly, out of nowhere, his peaceful Saturday morning walk with Bobo had left him face-to-face with death. He recognized the icy feeling in the air when life has gone. It reminded him of Chicago. Hardening himself to its chill, keeping the boy back, he stumbled and splashed closer to where she'd fallen, just in case. The sight left no doubt in his mind that she was dead. He backed away, careful not to touch or disturb anything, guiding the boy to where Bobo was noisily protesting and straining against his leash, all three of them getting wetter by the minute.

"Easy, Bobo, we didn't bring our ear-plugs." He checked to see how the boy was doing. "Come on, up this way. We won't get quite so wet. My name's Joe. What's yours?"

"Billy Beck."

"I live right up there in that house." Joe pointed up at the last house on the ridge, nestled securely beside the short cement staircase leading down to the wooden bridge.

"I live one block over," said Billy, "just past the basketball hoop."

Joe nodded. He led the boy halfway up the bank to the partial shelter of an overhanging maple. Together they stood and watched. His grouchy neighbor, Mrs Skinner, had come out on her deck with her cellphone clamped to her head, speaking loudly as she called 9-1-1. Another neighbor appeared to have some medical knowledge, and had plenty to say until the wail of an ambulance cut him off. Two young medics in green managed to carry a stretcher down a steep, irregular footpath into the ravine under the bridge. Wet figures closed around the body.

Billy was all eyes, staring.

"Looks like you cut yourself." Joe raised the boy's hand. The soft pad of flesh beneath his right index finger had a tiny tear, brown-lined with mud, red-smeared, wet with rain. "Careful, try to keep it clean."

By that time, the police car had arrived. Joe untied his big Airedale, trying to distract Billy with unrestrainable Bobo. The boy hardly seemed to notice the dog at all. Joe was afraid the boy might be going into shock. Neighbors were crunching around them through the wet undergrowth, asking questions, appearing like dripping phantoms out of the increasing universal hiss of the downpour.

A police officer was asking for witnesses.

"Keep Bobo quiet, would you?" Joe passed the leash to the boy. "Hold on tight. I've got to go tell this policeman what I saw."

At a distance Joe could hear Pepper crying. What a heartbreaking sound! She wasn't the only one. She was joined by the woman who'd been trying to save the old lady. Together they followed the stretcher up the path to the street.

Joe waited his turn, told the police officer what he'd seen, and then stood nearby while Billy answered questions. Afterward, when the police had finished, when the ambulance had departed and the rain had eased to a drizzle, Joe walked over to him. The kid was drenched, yet hardly seemed to notice he was wet.

"You okay, Billy?"

The boy nodded.

Joe squatted down beside him, looking him directly in the eye. "Sorry you had to see that. You're going to have to be strong and cope with what you saw. You can do it. Talking about it will help. I'm there if you need me."

Billy looked as though he needed someone very much, as though he wanted to clutch this kind stranger impulsively, to bury his face against him, to cling to him until he had to pry his arms loose. He didn't. He

28

stood frozen, trying to stand up straight, staring back through the scaffolding of the bridge toward the terrible, weed-strangled log.

"Thanks."

"I promised the policeman I'd walk you home," said Joe, taking his hand. "Come on. I'll explain to your mother."

"I don't have a mother," said Billy.


# 2
# Father and Son

The well-kept Tudor-style house with its surrounding manicured hedge was scrubbed and wholesome and freshly-painted, the perfect size for a single parent and his son.

Paul Beck opened the door and filled most of the doorframe. He was a tall, big-shouldered man just edging past his mid-thirties, with a round, wide-open face, boyish cheeks, a thatch of straw-brown hair as unruly as his son's, just less of it, clipped shorter. His blue eyes looked slightly tired, like he'd been rubbing them with his fists to stay awake. He had a sideways lean to his stance, the tilt of a man who was starting to wear down from trying to do too much. His long-sleeved pin-striped shirt was rolled up at the sleeves over tense forearms. A navy-blue necktie hung around his throat in a relaxed, casual noose.

Sopping wet, Joe tried to look as respectable as he could, hoping Bobo wouldn't start barking behind him where he had tied the dog beneath the neighborhood basketball hoop. "Mr Beck, I live at the end of the next street. My name is Joe Strozza."

"Glad to meet you," said Billy's father guardedly. "Paul Beck." He offered his hand in a mechanical handshake. His eyes and attention were elsewhere, quickly taking in his son's miserable face and damp, muddy condition. "Billy, what in the world happened to you?"

Billy fumbled for words, not knowing where to start.

Joe came to his rescue. "An accident in the park."

"Accident?"

"A woman fell off the old bridge about an hour ago. Billy saw it."

Paul Beck groaned. He lowered his big hand onto his son's shoulder, giving him a squeeze of sympathy as he listened to Joe in stunned silence, learning the details, his eyes constantly turning back to his son. Midway through Joe's story he awkwardly interrupted him.

"Sorry to be so rude!" said Paul. "You're soaking wet, and I keep you standing outside on the porch. Please come in." Joe wiped his shoes on the doormat. Paul stopped his son from following Joe through the door. "Whoa! Take off those boots, pardner. I can smell them from here. What have you been wading in?"

Leaving his muddy boots outside, Billy rose to his feet, pale and unhappy, standing in his wet stockings in the entrance hall. Paul impulsively bent down and gave Billy a bone-crushing hug. "Hey, pal, don't worry, we'll get it all worked out." Paul turned to Joe. "I can't thank you enough for getting him home."

"Glad to help," said Joe. "Really, I just live a block from here."

"You feel like eating something, Billy?"

The boy shook his head. He looked exhausted. He also looked slightly sick to his stomach.

"Well then, go up to the bathroom, take off those muddy clothes, and take a hot shower," said Paul. "I'll be right up after I say goodbye to our neighbor here." He ruffled the boy's hair as Billy headed for the stairs. Not until then did he notice the bloodstains on Billy's fingers.

He reached out and caught the boy's shoulder. "Hey, what happened to your hand?"

Billy stared at the tiny cut, his eyes watering. "Nothing."

"That's not nothing, Billy. Do a really good job washing that out, okay? I'll put something on it when you get out of the shower."

Billy continued up the stairs. "Thanks, Joe," he said, without turning around.

"He's got a lot to think about," said Joe. He heard a door close upstairs. "How terrible it must be for him!"

"Kids are resilient. He'll deal with it." Paul grinned confidently, trying to convince himself. "He's a tough little cookie. A lot tougher than I give him credit for. Tell me, this old woman — what was she upset about?"

"For some reason," mused Joe, "she seemed to think the park was her property, and that Billy was trespassing."

"That's a new one." Paul massaged the sandy stubble of his chin, producing no answers. "What harm could she possibly have imagined Billy was doing to the park? And to get so worked up about it! Do you think she was trying to kill herself?"

"I think she fell," said Joe. "She didn't want to die. That's what made it horrible."

"You mean she slipped?"

"I didn't see her actually slip," said Joe awkwardly, with a shudder. "It was more like she lost her balance. Something knocked her sideways."

"Knocked her? Was anyone else with her?"

"A woman ran out on the bridge. Kept calling her 'Mama.' She never got to her in time. I've seen her before. She's a checker down at the QFC in the Village. This morning I met her daughter — she's a jogger, she was there when it happened, kept screaming, 'Grandma.' As for the one who fell and died, never seen her before."

"And somehow Billy got into the middle of it."

"She shouted something when she fell." Joe turned back toward the front door. "Some word I didn't recognize. Sounded like 'happy.' Except more like 'get me.' Or maybe 'help me.' Don't suppose it matters. Better be going so you can check on Billy. Let me know if there's anything I can do."

"You've done more than enough." Paul opened the front door for Joe. "Thanks for being there for my son," he said, closing and locking the door as Joe walked away across the street, toward the basketball hoop where Bobo was already starting to bark.


# 3
# That Night at Joe's

At first he just wandered through the rain, pacing the streets, criss-crossing nervously through the park, letting Bobo drag him wherever the dog wanted to go. Joe was still shaking with emotion, utterly preoccupied with what he'd just witnessed.

The old woman was dead. Soon Joe Strozza would die, too. Summer was over. How many summers did he have left?

Ahead of him his house appeared, a snug, flower-surrounded craftsman cottage he rented from a landlord in Los Angeles. There was his cheerful, yellow bungalow, peacefully waiting for him at the end of the street. The sight made him sigh with relief. Bobo gave a sharp bark to announce their arrival. Refuge! Escape from the craziness of the world.

He walked up the short driveway, slid aside the plywood dog-barrier that spanned the open garage entrance, and nudged Bobo ahead of him into the garage-turned-workshop that led into the basement-turned-studio. He flipped on the lights, turned on the heat, glanced at the sketches he'd been working on last night. He shrugged off his wet jacket, hung it up in the corner to dry next to his shelves of art books. Then he trudged upstairs, glanced in the refrigerator, tasted this, sipped that, peeled off his wet shirt. Bobo could finally contain himself no longer, and bounded up into the kitchen after him through the open basement door.

"Bobo, what do you think you're doing in the kitchen?"

The big Airedale's answer was always the same. He swiftly thrust his muzzle at Joe's crotch. Joe knowingly dodged, stepped sideways into the bathroom, flipped on the light, and glanced in the mirror.

The sight brought him up short. He backed up, leaned up to the glass. That speck of bothersome rotten wood had cut him. A thin line of blood crossed the white corner of his left eye.

He panicked. The far edge of the eye looked like it was bleeding. A tiny red line. Perhaps a vein had burst.

Or perhaps it was his worst nightmare come true.

Joe was HIV-positive. He had come to Seattle to die. He had fled from Chicago two years ago, Chicago and all the ghosts, his dead lover, his dead friends, taking only Bobo with him. He'd come to Washington because it was a right-to-insurance state. He'd intended to paint the ever-changing Seattle sky until he could no longer lift a paintbrush.

He hadn't expected to bother with living. And then he hadn't died. He'd been struggling to survive financially ever since, a talented but old-school artist without computer skills who had left behind all his clients and connections. He was currently making ends barely meet by painting cartoon characters and cloudy skyscapes on the bedroom walls of rich children, by painting the interiors of restaurants and furniture show-rooms and jazz clubs.

Perhaps the time had finally come. Perhaps he was about to get worse. Perhaps that little red line was the beginning of a lesion, of a breakout of cancer, of *Kaposi's sarcoma*. He broke into a terrible, stinky sweat, the kind of sweat produced by fear. He blamed it on the fatal accident he'd just seen. He took off the rest of his clothes, stuffed them in the hamper, and turned on the shower full-blast. He let the water beat down on him.

No sign of anything anywhere else on his body.

He tried to relax watching a video that night, tried to get lost in the visual extravagance of *Baron Munchausen*, but his heart wasn't in it. He was still in shock from witnessing the death in the park. He made too much pasta, put too many ingredients in the sauce, ate too much of it anyway. When he took out his contact lenses, he consciously avoided glancing in the mirror. His left eye felt tender. He got quickly into bed.

He pulled the electric blanket up over his shoulders. He couldn't get warm enough. He couldn't forget that unhappy old woman, so upset about something, wrestling with something, fighting desperately and losing.

"I'm in shock," he said to himself. "I'm making too much of it. I need to sleep. I need to let the shockwaves go through me. It isn't every day you see someone die right in front of you. Not even in Chicago! I need to let my system cool down. I've got to close my eyes and stop thinking about that old woman."

He was finally able to sleep, but it was more like a troubled doze and provided little rest. No sooner did he lose consciousness than he found himself in the grips of an unnervingly realistic dream—

*

He could feel his body being moved, jiggled. He could feel hands touching him, sliding under his limbs, gripping him, lifting him. He was no longer lying on a mattress. He was being pulled, shoved, towed along over the ground.

He was stretched on his back, being dragged through leafy undergrowth, over rocks. He could hear shuffling feet. Footsteps on either side of him. Tired, heavy cracklings through the weeds.

"Just a little farther," whispered a woman's voice harshly. "Over this way."

Joe blinked open his eyes. He was looking up into the night sky. He was being hauled by the arms and legs over the ground, being jostled through shadows, wet leaves, crackling twigs, broken tree limbs. With difficulty he raised his head to see where he was. He was in the darkest part of the ravine, at some very late hour. And something was wrong with him. He was numb.

Two shadowy figures accompanied him. Both were women, the older in front, the younger behind him. He couldn't see much of the older and less of the younger. They didn't talk much. They grunted and groaned and whispered. He could hear their heavy breathing. The older woman's eyes were huge and white. She was obviously scared out of her mind. The younger one whimpered behind him. Both of them struggled with him, hauling him along impersonally as though he were dead. He tried to let them know that he was very much alive, but he couldn't quite raise his arm, or manage to bend his leg, or force his lips to speak a word.

No one else was anywhere in sight.

"What do we do with him?" asked the young one behind him, panting.

"I know a place we can bury him," said the older woman.

Joe tried to scream. Nothing came out.

# 4
## That Night at the Becks'

When Billy opened the door of the steam-filled upstairs bathroom, his father was anxiously waiting in the hall, sitting on the top stair, trying not to look worried. He was crushing and mashing a dish towel in his hands.

"That was quite a shower," said Paul, smiling. "I was afraid you'd gone down the drain."

A flicker of an answering smile from Billy, as he switched off the bathroom light.

"Did you clean up that cut?" asked his father. "Let me see your hand."

Billy extended the injured palm for inspection. "I washed it with soap."

"It looks swollen." He clasped Billy's hand gently in both of his own, and examined it more closely. "Looks like you've got a nasty splinter in that cut."

"A splinter?" said Billy uneasily.

"A tiny black one."

"Must be from that rotten log where I caught my foot."

His father released his hand. "Go get me a needle."

"No, don't, Dad," said Billy uncomfortably.

"Come on, I'll take it out. It won't hurt."

"Won't it come out on its own?"

"Sooner or later, after getting infected," said Paul. "If there's a sliver in there, the best thing to do is get it out as soon as possible." He smiled confidently, squeezed his arm around Billy's shoulders reassuringly. "And pardner, I'm the man for the job. That splinter is as good as out!"

He certainly tried. No matter where he poked the needle, he couldn't seem to reach the splinter.

"I've almost got it," said Paul, scowling down intently. "No, not quite, almost, almost—"

He didn't give up easily, but he finally did. "I think my eyes are just tired. Let it work it's way closer to the surface. I'll give it a try later on tonight."

35

For the rest of the day Billy was uninterested in just about everything. He didn't know what he was doing. He didn't care.

His father was busy with the usual catching-up on Saturday, doing the laundry, washing a sink full of dishes, vacuuming, buying groceries, but he continued to watch his son anxiously. He made a few overtures, a few openings but without insisting, giving him time, giving him space. Billy sat in front of the television and stared at the screen, forgetting to stop watching during the commercials. Then he went upstairs, lay on his bed and stared at the ceiling.

His familiar, reassuring mobile of the solar system dangled overhead from the light fixture. The ceiling and walls were covered with posters of *Bladerunner* and *Alien*, *King Kong* and *Jurassic Park*, Spiderman and the Fantastic Four. The bookshelves were packed with paperback fantasy epics. Taped to the wall above his desk were some of his best sketches. It was all invisible to him. All he saw was the bridge.

He skipped lunch. He stayed indoors the rest of that Saturday and avoided his father. He managed to survive on quick, nervous raids on the refrigerator. He hid quietly in his room, hoping his father would forget he was there.

He looked up from his bed. His father was standing in the doorway. He was hard to fool. Dad loved him so much he noticed almost everything.

"How's it going, pardner?"

"Okay."

"You feel like talking about it?"

"No."

Paul Beck wasn't used to people refusing him. He was the western division vice-president at DataMaster, his rapidly-growing computer company. His work was highly-valued and very highly paid. He was used to calling the shots.

He nodded patiently. "Take it easy, then." He ruffled Billy's hair affectionately. "Don't stay up too late."

He left the room. Downstairs the television set turned on, a sports announcer droned excitedly. Billy relaxed. An hour later, when he went downstairs, his father was staring at the television screen intently, muttering a passionate running commentary play-by-play. Billy crossed the living room unnoticed, snatched up the book he'd forgotten, and darted back up to his bedroom, closing the door behind him.

He flopped on his bed. Nothing could take his mind off what he'd seen at the bridge.

He reached up and squashed down his baseball cap lower over his thick, wheat-blond hair. He couldn't stop brooding, remembering. That shouting old woman! His father hadn't been there to see her, to hear her. He would never understand.

Billy was used to no one understanding him. His mother had always been thinking about something else. She had seemed like she was listening and nodded her head, but she wasn't. His father really tried, especially after his mother left, but Dad couldn't exactly figure out why he did things. Like why Billy loved drawing the things he saw in nature.

The only adult who had ever encouraged him in drawing had been a teacher at Bryant Elementary School last year. She had taken him down into the ravine on biology projects and ecology projects and art projects, too, among them his favorite, the "square foot of art," where he drew whatever appeared inside his cut-out cardboard square. He still had those drawings.

His father hadn't encouraged him. He wanted his son to be like other kids, to throw a ball with him in the backyard, to help him fix the car, to play computer games with him, to watch the NBA playoffs with him. He had looked forward to his son participating in neighborhood soccer and Little League baseball. Instead Billy had become a boy who didn't play catch, a sensitive loner who would rather draw the rocks in Ravenna Creek.

Dinnertime came and went. Billy didn't get hungry, didn't change his mind. Paul didn't press him to come downstairs and talk. He let Billy keep to himself. The boy stayed in his bedroom and did homework till it was dark. Paul was starting to nod in his armchair when he saw Billy standing beside him. He'd obviously come downstairs to say good-night. He hugged his father.

"Good night, son," said Paul. He reached out and caught him by the arm. "Let's see how that hand is looking." He carefully peeled back the Band-Aid and examined it. "Not too bad." He taped it smoothly back into place. "We'll give it another look tomorrow morning. Maybe then I can get that splinter out."

"Oh, great," said Billy, with a tired smile. "More torture."

"I can hardly wait," said Paul. "I love you."

The bedroom door closed. The light snapped off.

Just before falling asleep, Billy's hand started throbbing.

*

Ka-thump, ka-thump.

Billy was panting, gasping for breath, running as fast as he could (which wasn't very fast at all) over the rain-slick, echoing trestles of the high wooden bridge. He didn't know exactly what he was afraid of, but he knew the situation had suddenly become very dangerous. He was desperately trying to get far away from there. And not succeeding.

Ka-thump, ka-thump.

Thud-thud, thud-thud, thud-thud.

The green railings on either side squeezed in toward his shoulders. He was a fast runner, but his feet would hardly move. It felt like he was running in Jell-O. He could feel the trestles under him rattling and shaking. Not just from his own feet. Someone was coming after him. The boards of the bridge were slippery. The rain made it so dark it was hard to see what was happening.

Ka-thump.

Thud-thud. Thud-thud.

He could feel the wooden bridge vibrating beneath him, the heavy footfalls pounding after him. He couldn't see who it was. He opened his mouth to scream when something icy struck him on the side of the cheek. Then something struck him square in the chest. He was never sure what it was. He slipped, lost his balance. His elbow clattered, his foot banged. He flapped his arms for balance, but it was too late.

38

With a silent scream, he tumbled over the green wooden railing — down — down — toward the shallow, trickling creek which cut through the gleaming rocks below.

*

Billy woke with a gasp.

He lay stiff in his bed, his hand throbbing, his heart pounding. He was about to roll over and try to go back to sleep when something made him afraid to move. Something warned him that he wasn't alone.

A dark figure filled the doorway.

His mouth was open to scream when the figure stepped into the light from the corner streetlamp and became his father in undershirt and boxer shorts, wide-eyed with alarm.

"Billy! What's wrong?"

His father hurried forward. He sat on the side of his son's bed, touched Billy's sweaty forehead. "Do you realize you were shouting in your sleep?"

"I was?"

"You woke me up," said Paul. "You didn't even hear yourself, did you?" He lovingly stroked the back of his son's head. "I know how awful it must be for you. What you saw today would upset anyone, Billy, no matter how old they were. So don't think you have to be tough about it. Anything you want to tell me?"

"No, Dad," said Billy, his voice quavering.

"You're sure?" said Paul, taking the boy's hand, rising up off the bed to stand beside him. "Think you can go back to sleep?"

Billy let go of his father's hand reluctantly. "Yes, Dad."

# 5
## That Night at the Merlinos'

In spite of the offers of several relatives, Pepper and her mother spent the night alone. The house was no longer the same. It was bigger, emptier, touched by death. They avoided turning on the television or radio.

39

They avoided Grandma's room. The kitchen was the heart of the house, and that was where they came uneasily together.

They endured a strangely flavorless dinner at the same table, mumbled a few obligatory phrases to each other to get through the meal. Neither of them ate much, or remembered what they had eaten.

Stranded together in the kitchen, Rose tried to rescue herself by pushing back her chair and rising to her feet. When in doubt, Rose began cleaning. The kitchen was her domain. It was seldom less than spotless. An arsenal of gleaming pots and pans lined the stovetop, stretched above five shelves crowded with little vials and shakers of herbs and spices. Polished canisters lined the drainboard. A rack of well-tended, razor-sharp knives waited to chop and slash and dice.

What few dishes she had used for dinner were almost washed when she dropped a soapy plate. It shattered. Rose swore, something she rarely did. Then she broke down into body-wrenching sobs, sinking to her knees on the linoleum floor to pick up the jagged pieces.

"Let it go, Mom," said Pepper, hauling her to her feet, embracing her. "You'll cut yourself. I'll get it." She had never seen her mother so upset. Pepper held her in her arms. Mother and daughter avoided looking each other in the eye.

"Why did she do it?" Pepper repeated quietly, miserably. "Why? I don't understand, Mom. What came over her?"

"God only knows" said Rose, pulling away. "I heard her shouting, but I couldn't understand what she was saying. I didn't even know she was out of bed, and she was already outside." The words tumbled out of her. Rose paced while she talked. "I was just getting ready to go out on the deck and see what was upsetting her when I saw her pass by the kitchen window. By the time I searched both sides of the house, she was halfway across the bridge. She got there before I could stop her. It all happened so fast."

Rose finished clearing the table. She wiped down the drainboard. She began cleaning the stove top, trying to ignore the sudden, horrible change in her life. She had already made the necessary calls, the relatives, the funeral home, the lawyer. With the coming of night, there was nowhere else for Rose and Pepper to turn except straight into each other's eyes, straight at the loss which was hurting them both so much.

Rose couldn't keep the bitterness inside any longer. "I knew asking all those questions would upset her."

Pepper slowly looked up from staring at the formica table-top. "I don't believe I heard that. What are you trying to say?"

Rose looked back at her daughter defiantly, undaunted by Pepper's scowl. "I'm saying you should never have made her remember so much. This is the result."

Her mother's accusation stung Pepper. "My talking to her this morning had nothing to do with Grandma falling."

"It didn't?" said Rose. She couldn't let it go. Her grief needed direction. "Then what do you think upset her?"

"It was that boy down below," said Pepper defensively. "It was just kids, and Grandma got confused and misunderstood—"

"It was you," said Rose. "It was you meddling in what you don't understand. You stirred up Mama's memories. You asked questions you shouldn't have asked. Some memories should be left alone. The pain goes away if you don't touch them. But if you keep touching the bad memories, if you keep poking and jabbing at them, they start to fester—"

"What memories, Mom?"

"Memories better left where they are." Rose had said all she was going to say. "You don't need to know everything! Leave that to God." She smiled bitterly. "I love you, Pepper. I want you to be happy. Why should I make you unhappy?"

"Mother, nothing you say is going to change my love for you. What is it you won't you tell me?"

"Sometimes love knows when to be silent," said Rose. "Love always has secrets. If you'd ever been in love, you'd know that."

In sheer exasperation, Pepper turned around without another word, went directly upstairs to her room, and closed the door. She stayed in her room the rest of the night. She was just down the hall from her mother's room, close enough to hear the crying, even though Rose tried to muffle her grief in her pillow.

The unnatural hush of Grandma's room seemed to roar through the other rooms. The tossing and turning, the moans and coughing, the creaking of the bed, the weary groans of old age, the sounds Pepper had become used to hearing, were all thunderously loud in their absence.

# CHAPTER THREE

# September Fears

## 1
## Neighbor

With Sunday morning came the first calls and visits. Word spread quickly among the uncles, aunts and cousins. The telephone was constantly ringing. The invasion had begun. Over the next few days, curious relatives from the far reaches of the family tree, unseen for decades, began appearing in every room, conjured up out of the past and suddenly very interested in reclusive Auntie Rose and her daughter with the funny name, kissing, condoling, asking questions, peeking in closets, prowling for mementos, looking for dust.

Pepper was in the kitchen helping her mother serve coffee and cookies to Aunt Lorraine and Aunt Addie when the doorbell rang. Pepper hurried to open the door, expecting to find more relatives. She did not expect to see their nosy neighbor, Wanda Skinner.

Pepper's heart sank. Mrs Skinner was wearing a burgundy sweatband around her limp blond curls, and had poured herself into a blue-and-burgundy running suit. She was carrying a two-foot slab of peach cobbler in one hand, and in her other hand a blue ceramic dutch oven filled with vegetarian barley casserole.

"I can't tell you how sorry I am, Miss Merlino!"

Pepper smiled tightly. Trapped!

Clever, aggressive Wanda Skinner, neighborhood telephone activist, political doorbell-ringer, self-appointed judge of all human activity and professional in-depth complainer, stood facing her on the front doormat. The woman could complain about any topic for hours at a stretch. All she needed was an audience.

"I brought you a little something," she said, pushing past her. Shoulders rounded, neck stretched forward, nose thrust out with stubborn persistence, she bustled down the entrance hallway of the Merlino house as though she had been there numerous times before.

She unloaded her offerings in the kitchen, where she introduced herself, made a few general comments, and promptly put both aunties to work cutting and serving. She accompanied huge portions of food with generous doses of her inexhaustible, wide-ranging critical assessments of life, talking the whole time, bitterly listing in detail all the ills besieging the world. She concluded her monologue by saying, "Now, I want you to stop calling me Mrs Skinner. My friends call me Wanda."

Pepper's heart fluttered in alarm. The woman wanted to be friends! "Wanda, then." Awkward pause. She continued with difficulty. "You can call me Pepper."

"What a charming name!"

"It's short for Perpetua. Family name. A couple of my aunts are named the same thing. And here is my mother."

Rose Merlino was suddenly standing there, as motionless and expressionless as an effigy on a tomb.

"Mother, this is our neighbor, Mrs Skinner. She just brought us all this food."

Rose coolly regarded her neighbor and the cluttered drainboard. "How kind," she said. "Ah, yes! I know where you live. That greenish-brown Frank Lloyd Wrightish house with the overhanging porch."

"Why, yes," said Mrs Skinner, "that's the one."

"Right directly across the ravine from us," said Rose. "I believe I've seen you out on your deck."

"Ah, yes," said Mrs Skinner.

"With your binoculars. You must have quite a nice view of our house." Rose turned away from her and walked over to talk with the aunties.

Mrs Skinner stammered out fragments of a half-hearted reply as she backed toward the door.

*

Carmen Merlino's death was reported in a small article in the Local News section of Monday's *Seattle Times.* "Elderly Woman Falls." Tuesday morning a four-paragraph follow-up appeared at the bottom of page 3 of the *Post-Intelligencer.* "Death in Ravenna Park." A few general facts, names, times, official conclusions. No explanations. No answers. Various theories attempted to explain what exactly had upset her. It began to look like no one would ever know.

Through the next few difficult days, Pepper watched her mother anxiously. Rose Merlino seemed to be in a daze. She refused to take more than the standard three-day leave from her cashiering job at QFC, insisted on behaving like nothing was wrong, the indestructible workhorse, bagging groceries with energy to spare. She acted like she was planning a charity luncheon, not busily arranging for the intering of her mother.

Only Pepper knew about the breakdowns. Only Pepper heard her sobbing through the long nights.

## 2
## Funeral Rites

It poured the morning of the funeral.

Half a dozen cars slowly boated through the rain to park by the graveside in Calvary Cemetery.

"Where were they when she needed them?" said Rose, looking out the window of the limosine.

Pepper took her mother's hand.

"Look at them all!" muttered Rose. "Now that she doesn't need relatives, they're here like flies."

The funeral director helped Rose out of the car. As she emerged, her black raincoat slid open revealing a stylishly cut black dress. She wrapped herself up quickly again in her raincoat. Her features were haggard, swollen with crying, blotchy from tears no one ever saw her shed.

Pepper's face showed nothing. She had long ago learned how to erase all emotion from her features. She conducted herself flawlessly, keeping herself perfectly under control throughout the service and burial, polite, graceful, appropriate, her feelings locked deeply inside her.

Head bowed, looking out at the world through a mourning veil of black lace, she listened to the murmuring voices of her relatives all around her at the graveside, the numerous progeny of the seven brothers and sisters of Grandma's father, Salvatore Merlino.

"Really, whatever else you say about her, Carmen was an incredible mother—"

"Rose always talks about her like she was some kind of saint."

"She was! Poor thing, she was under her father's thumb. That man, if he'd had his way, he'd have cheated his own daughter."

"A woman didn't have many choices in those days. Auntie Carmen was brave — and stubborn, too."

"You should have seen the way her father treated her. Like a fallen woman!"

"Like mother, like daughter. No one ever knew who Rose's father was. No one ever found out who Pepper's father was, either."

"Oh, is that so? I heard no one wanted to talk about it."

"That's not what I heard."

"One thing for sure. Merlino women don't make very good choices when it comes to men."

"No wonder Pepper hasn't gotten married yet. With a family history like that, who could blame her?"

An anxious rustle. Somebody jabbed somebody else with an elbow. They had noticed she was listening.

"Pepper honey, Nina's getting married, did you hear? Nice boy. The last week in October—"

"Now, we'll see you at the wedding, won't we, Pepper?"

"I don't think so, Uncle Mike," said Pepper warily. "You know my mother never goes to weddings."

"Oh, that Rose! Well then, you come without her. You're a part of this family, too!"

"Do come, Pepper. See you at the wedding—"

Only twice did Pepper's formal mask crack to reveal the turbulent feelings underneath.

She happened to glance up from the rose-covered coffin and noticed the boy whose presence in the ravine had triggered Grandma's death. He stood quietly on the outskirts of the crowd surrounding the grave. Billy appeared to have come by himself, to have walked up the 55th Street hill in the rain. He avoided looking at her. He kept his gaze fixed unwaveringly on the coffin. The sight of him caused her eyes to fill with tears.

She was equally disturbed shortly after, near the end of the graveside service, when several sharp, ringing barks caused her to look up. Across the wet, green lawn of tombstones, at the other end of the cemetery, she could see a man standing under a tree with a large dog.

# 3
# Spirits

With the conclusion of the burial, the brief flurry of social activity in the Merlino house ground to a halt. The last old aunties paid their house calls. The last cousins telephoned. The last sympathy cards arrived in the mail. The last visitors from out of town were about to say goodbye. For a few days there had been voices, coats in the front closet, women in the kitchen. Now the house was changing into a hollow, lonely shell, a house that had stopped, a house with the ambiance of a funeral parlor.

Pepper dreaded coming home. She stayed as long as she could now at the Center for Urban Horticulture. Her fieldwork analysis and most of her studying were there at the Union Bay Campus, in the far north-eastern corner of the University of Washington, on the other side of the soccer fields. Reluctantly leaving behind her desk in the graduate student room in the basement of Isaacson Hall, she headed home in a short-cut that zigzagged through University Village. Weaving through the shops, she wondered briefly if her Mom were working that afternoon as she passed the mall-spanning length of Quality Food Center. Rose had begun taking on extra cashiering shifts. She had been avoiding the house, too. Rose had nowhere else to go.

The wind had worked itself into a foul mood that afternoon, hissing through the leaves and tugging at everything that moved. Pepper cut across the end of the ravine and started up the path toward the bridges. A cloud-heavy sky pressed down on a blowing gray world.

The front door was unlocked. Pepper heard water running and the clinking of silverware in the kitchen. She found her mother standing at the sink, absent-mindedly washing dishes. Rose looked up with a start.

"I didn't hear you come in."

"You shouldn't leave the front door unlocked," said Pepper. "It might not have been me."

"I did lock it," said Rose. She scowled, perplexed. "Well, I guess I didn't, but I thought I did."

"Uncle Carl and Aunt Lena are gone?" asked Pepper, peeking under the lid of the covered pan on the stove.

"A few hours ago," said her mother, turning off the water. "They said to say goodbye to you. They seemed pretty sure they would see you at Nina's wedding. I told them I doubted you'd be there, but they didn't believe me." She paused long enough for Pepper to confirm or deny. When she didn't, Rose continued. "It's going to be right before Halloween. Odd date for a wedding. Your cousin Gloria left this morning."

"Good," said Pepper.

"It's about time," said Rose. "They were only in the way. There's nothing they can do to help us — or Mama. They would have been better off staying home."

"You're being a little cold-hearted," said Pepper. "I know they're nosy and insensitive, but they mean well. After all, they came to pay their respects to the dead. Aunt Fran flew up from San Diego."

"You're too young," said Rose. "You'll understand some day. You'll see what thorns relatives can be."

"I understand, all right," said Pepper.

"You think you do," said Rose. "Death is fascinating. It's like a chunk of meat that gets the sharks all excited. The relatives go into a feeding frenzy."

Pepper stared at her, genuinely shocked. "Mom, stop it! Why are you being so nasty?"

"I'm sorry, sweetheart." Rose realized that she really *was* being nasty. "I'm just grouchy. I miss Mama so much it feels like it's never going to stop hurting."

"I miss her, too, Mom," said Pepper gently. "It hurts like crazy. But you can't let the sadness just take over. Sooner or later you've got to put a little energy into keeping a good attitude. It's like a tomb in here. Why don't you at least play some music?"

"I don't mind the quiet," said her mother, drying her hands, not turning around to face her. "Turn on some music, if you like. It's all the same to me. I won't hear it."

She took her mother by the shoulders, and turned her around to face her. "Some music might lift your spirits," she suggested in a gentler voice.

"My spirits don't need lifting," said her mother, shrugging free of her daughter's hold. Her voice had developed an edge of irritation. "Hearing music isn't going to make me smile. I don't have anything to smile about."

"Mom, I know you loved Grandma, but we've got to start pulling our lives together again. Once in a while I'd like to see a smile on that pretty face of yours." She gave her mother a peck on the cheek. "It isn't going to make matters any better to keep mourning over her."

"You only loved her at the end. She was the most incredible person I ever knew. She had more heart, more guts, more spirit. She gave up everything for me. She was the best mother ever. And now she isn't here anymore. You don't understand yet. But you will."

"Oh, Mother—"

Rose Merlino turned to face her. The sight caused Pepper a chill of sadness. Her face had aged terribly. It was wet with tears. "You'll understand when I'm gone. I feel like part of my heart has been ripped out."

A sudden rap on the front window.

Rose gasped, spun around to face it. "What was that?"

"Really, Mom!" Pepper sighed with relief. "It was just that tree branch. There's a wind out there."

Rose visibly relaxed. "Silly of me. I'm a little nervous lately, that's all."

"Nervous?" said Pepper. She put her arm around her mother's shoulders. "Why nervous?"

"I don't know what it is, exactly," said Rose. "I feel slightly afraid without her. Oh, I know it doesn't make sense. Mama could hardly help herself, much less anyone else. But I've got no one to turn to anymore, no one but God. You'll understand when I'm gone. Just knowing she was there—"

Rose looked out the window and continued to stare, peering back through the years at faded memories. "That branch—"

"The one right here by the window?" Pepper pointed at the thick branch that dipped down in front of the glass before stretching out to its full length over the ravine edge.

"You should have seen how Uncle Gabriel used to drive Mama crazy on that branch. He'd climb out there and swing on it. I remember seeing him — I must have been only seven or eight. I was so scared I started crying. That just made him laugh. His feet would kick out over the edge. Mama would scream at her brother and beg him to come down. Oh, how he liked to torment her! When he finally dropped back into the yard, I remember Mama ran up and started pounding him with her fists. He just laughed. Something about Uncle Gabriel, he could get away with anything."

Together they stood in the darkening living room, looking out the picture window at the creaking branch.

"I'm afraid now that she's gone," said Rose, not looking at Pepper, staring out through the glass. "I feel uneasy." She took a deep breath, slowly released it, and turned her back on the window. "That branch is dead. It should be cut off."

# 4
# Watcher

Joe found himself half-uncovered after a long, sleepless night of shifting and turning. He swung his legs over the side of the bed and sat there with a groan, scratching his short, bristly salt-and-pepper hair. Streetlamp light made it brighter outside than in the darkness of his bedroom. Bold beacons of light poured in through the windows, spilling bright bars across the floor.

A shadow moved outside. Joe froze, staring across the room toward the glass. Something was on the other side of the fluttering curtain, something about the size of a human head and shoulders. He stared at the rustling, shivering curtains. Someone was out there, staring into his house.

Joe took a cautious, quiet step across the bedroom floor, then another, approached the window, and rested one hand on the windowsill. He reached the other hand toward the curtain, to draw it aside, to see who was staring into the room.

Before he could touch the curtain, a hand lunged through the open window and seized him in an icy grip—

\*

Joe woke with a cry.

He was still in bed. His entire body was tense with terror. He turned toward the window in panic, but the curtain hung motionless, the window closed. Wiping the sweat from his forehead, he lay back on the pillow, waiting for his heart to stop pounding.

Another one of those terrible dreams! He was becoming seriously concerned. Why were they persisting? If they had been nightmares about an old woman falling off a bridge, he would have understood. That would have made sense. But for some reason, ever since the accident, he had been tormented by alarming dreams about an ominous man standing in the yard watching him.

He closed his eyes, tried to make himself relax. He had to get some rest. He had to! Joe had almost fallen asleep again when something upset Bobo in the downstairs studio. His sharp, echoing barks reverberated through the house, ringing down the street.

"Bobo, stop it," he muttered. "Please, be a good dog."

Another volley of barking. Bobo had no interest in being good. The dog had a statement to make, a loud statement. Something wasn't right. Something had to be done about it. Bobo was just warming up, and the dog knew from experience how to get the best acoustics possible out of the resonant basement.

"Please, Bobo, shut up," mumbled Joe. A spider was probably making its way across the basement floor, and Bobo had decided to inform the entire neighborhood. Joe shifted his head in the pillows to muffle the dog's bark.

For a moment, he almost sank wearily back into that dream-world of sleeplessness. Then suddenly he found himself anxious and alert, listening, not daring to breathe. This time it wasn't a dream. He knew, beyond any doubt, that he wasn't alone.

"Who's there?" he whispered.

Not a shadow budged in his bedroom. Not a sound from the depths of his house. He knew that the front door of his small craftman's cottage was securely locked, because he always checked it before he turned off the lights. Other than his loud-mouthed dog, the house was silent.

Without turning the lights on, he pulled free of the sheets and quietly approached the bedroom window. No shadow outside. He drew aside one corner of the curtain.

At first he didn't see anyone. Then he detected a slight shifting behind one of the trees. A glimpse of an arm, a shoulder, a head.

It was him. He was there again, exactly like the man in his dreams, staring at the house. As Joe watched, the dark figure retreated into the branches. Who was he? What was he doing lurking in Joe's back yard? Joe had first noticed him last week, just a glimpse through the window as he was returning from a late-night visit to the refrigerator. Joe had written it off to living near a park. Then he thought he saw him again

Monday night. But he wasn't really sure. It could have just been nerves. But this was the second time this week.

He took another look, squinting at the trees in the corner of the yard. The porch light feebly caught the edge of a gleaming black jacket, collar up. Black eyes stared at Joe's house, straight into Joe's bedroom window, straight into Joe's eyes—

Another volley of loud barks from Bobo downstairs snapped him out of the spell. Perhaps the figure in the yard was only the lookout. Perhaps someone else was downstairs right now. He turned away from the window.

Pulling on his sweatpants, he fumbled in the bedstand for the flashlight and a pair of glasses, then approached the bedroom door. He listened. Someone was behind the house. He could hear shuffling feet on the boards of the back stairs.

Joe crept quietly down the hall, pausing just out of sight but close enough to see into the kitchen. A neighbor's garage light cast an orange sheen across the dark refrigerator. Tomatoes lined the windowsill. Silent wind-chimes hung from the eaves. Through the window in the back door he could see the shifting shadow of someone outside.

The doorknob on the back door turned. Slowly and quietly, it turned back and forth, one way, the other way. The click of the doorknob turning echoed through the empty kitchen.

Joe gripped the flashlight, prepared to use it as a weapon if necessary, and crossed the floor. Sliding open the cutlery drawer, he took out the biggest knife he could find. Then he pulled aside the curtains.

No one was on the porch.

Someone had to be out there. He'd heard the footsteps. He'd seen the doorknob turn. Joe flung open the back door in exasperation, and stepped bravely outside onto the porch, angry enough to deal with anyone who dared to show his face.

No one anywhere in sight.

Closing the kitchen door quietly behind him, he started down the back stairs into the stinging coldness of the night. He circled around the side of the house. He stood in the house's shadow looking into the back yard. Wind rustled through the leaves of the chestnut tree. A shadow shifted in the corner, behind the Japanese maple.

Joe strode halfway across the lawn and stopped, confounded. The only thing in the corner of the yard was shadows. Then what had moved?

The back yard was empty.

He retreated around to the front of the house and inside through the converted garage. His giant brown Airedale was bounding about the studio in agitation. Bobo gave a few house-shaking barks.

"Bobo, stop it!"

Heart hammering, Joe came back upstairs and managed to walk through the kitchen, all the way to the bathroom. Then the anger drained out of him. So did the adrenalin. His confidence evaporated. He started trembling so badly he had to lean against the bathroom sink.

He stared in the mirror, studying the red line across the edge of his left eye. Then he returned to the bedroom and climbed under the covers with a knot of dread in his stomach, the knife within easy reach.


# 5
# Dreams and Not Dreams

Billy didn't remember exactly when his eyes closed. He had fallen into a lazy Thursday afternoon doze after school, lying on the floor in front of the fifty-inch television screen, alone in the warm, quiet house for the two hours before his Dad got home. He'd done his homework, finished the library book he'd checked out, re-read all his newest comics. He'd finally tried to become interested in a talky old black-and-white movie. Now he was opening his eyes, stiff and groggy and confused, stretched out on the carpet.

That he was sleepy was no surprise. Ever since last Saturday morning, his nights had become occasions of dread. Nights of peacefully falling asleep, his arms wrapped lovingly around his pillow, were things of the past. These days he turned off the bed-light anxiously, after a quick scan around the room, and then dived under the covers. He dragged himself out of bed in the morning unrested, exhausted.

His nightmare that first night had not been an isolated incident. More nightmares had followed. That terrible bridge where he had seen the old woman plunge to her death had become a permanent part of his dream landscape. Again and again he awakened in terror while slowly walking across the old wooden bridge, or tumbling over the railing, or fleeing across the trestles in slow motion, with the echoing hollow thud of pursuing footfalls growing louder and louder in his ears.

Strangely enough, he never dreamed of the woman who fell. Old Mrs Merlino, shouting at him in her white bathrobe, did not return at night. Someone else did. Someone he began to detect loitering in the darkness. The shadow of a man, lurking, threatening, a man in a black leather jacket, the collar up and partly hiding his face. One night the man was at the end of his street, standing under the streetlamp. One night the man was down in the ravine, looking up at him. One night the man was in the back yard, staring straight at his window.

That Thursday afternoon, waiting for his Dad to get home from the other side of the lake, Billy opened his eyes, lying on the floor in the hush of the house. His school books, library book, comics surrounded him. The characters in the old black-and-white movie were still talking, talking, talking. The steady drone of falling rain had lulled him into a doze.

What had woken him from his nap? He looked around him. A television commercial blared at him. Scrambling up from the carpet, he clicked off the set.

Two sharp knocks. He stepped out of the living room into the kitchen, and that explained everything. Someone was knocking at the back door. That could only be one person. His father was home. Dad was standing outside on the back porch, waiting for him to unlock the door.

No one else but his father would use the back door. He'd come home from work early. They'd have a real meal together, not frozen dinners. They'd have the whole evening to spend together. Long enough for his Dad to relax and smile. Billy darted happily through the kitchen, skidded on the linoleum tiles, and unlocked the door, swinging it open wide to surprise him.

It wasn't his father. The man standing there was younger than his father, with black eyes, black hair, a stubbly jaw, a black leather jacket. He grinned at Billy.

With a scream, Billy slammed the door and locked it.

Another volley of knocking.

Billy's legs were shaking so badly he couldn't walk. His knees gave out from under him, and he dropped to the floor. He managed to drag himself under the kitchen table, cowering there out of sight of the windows, huddling like a prisoner among the shiny chrome legs of the kitchen chairs.

Knocking on the back door.

Pounding, harder and harder.

With a crack, the door swung clattering open—

\*

Billy woke with a gasp of terror. He lay on the carpet. It hadn't happened. He was imagining things. Another one of those nightmares.

He managed to get up onto wobbly legs. He took a deep breath, and walked slowly into the kitchen. The back door was safely closed. He crossed the linoleum floor and checked the doorknob. It was locked. He drew aside the curtain and peeked out. The back porch was deserted.

He wasn't fooled. He wasn't imagining things. It was him — trying to get into the house.

# 6
## Underground Creek

After a brisk walk on a windy night down 25th Avenue, Pepper set off across the vast, crowded parking lot of University Village toward the pumpkin-yellow lights of busy, prosperous Quality Food Center. Though the neighborhood meeting was upstairs, Pepper took a quick detour into the supermarket to say hello to her mother who was working that night.

Crossing through the bakery, past the espresso bar, beyond the bay of shopping carts, she spotted her mother cashiering at the Eight-Items-or-Less check-out, wearing her QFC apron embellished with QFC service buttons. Winding away from her counter trailed a line of a dozen people with shopping-baskets, waiting impatiently.

"Just going to the meeting upstairs," said Pepper, "and thought I'd say hi, Mom."

Rose turned quickly at the sound of her daughter's voice, beaming. She gave Pepper a quick hug, a peck on the cheek. "Hi, Pep." Then she turned to the customer, handing him back two paper clippings. "I'm sorry, sir, these coupons are for Safeway."

"Talk to you later at home," said Pepper, giving her mother's hand a squeeze. "Hi, Molly! Hi, Barb! How's it going, Kristy?" called Pepper to other cashiers who were smiling and waving down the front line, women she knew from working with them every summer since high school, saving up her wages to put herself through college. Pepper darted back out the side door, hurrying on her way.

Up the back stairs on the second floor above the supermarket was a large, low-ceilinged meeting room. Neighbors had been urged to gather there at seven o'clock for an emergency meeting of the Ravenna Creek Daylighting Project. As Pepper came through the propped-open double doors, over a hundred local residents were rustling into chairs and social clusters. Half a dozen yard-long graphs and cross-sections were taped along each wall, along with blown-up aerial photos of Ravenna Springs.

Pepper began walking slowly down the length of the wall, studying the charts.

Ravenna Creek had once flowed from Green Lake in north Seattle through the ravine of Ravenna Park all the way to Lake Washington. It was a beautiful natural resource. But now that living creek came to an abrupt halt at the end of the ravine, where it was diverted roaring down an underground pipe which carried the water to the Metro sewage plant.

Over eight hundred people had formed an alliance to bring the creek back up into the daylight. They had convinced the City of Seattle to spend five years and a quarter million dollars on a feasibility study. Their goal was to prevent a million gallons of water daily from being dumped into the sewerline and transported to the treatment plant. The water didn't need treatment. It was a living creek. It was being piped-away and buried. The municipal authorities were balking at the cost of bringing Ravenna Creek back to the surface.

The meeting began dully enough. The moderator gave lengthy explanations of various obstructions, objections, miscalculations. King County favored the less-expensive channeling of Ravenna Creek into a storm drain. The audience of environmentalists and home-owners, anxious for the more attractive, more costly daylighting of the creek, were slowly buried in dull facts, worn down through sheer ponderous details.

Finally Wanda Skinner could no longer restrain herself. She rose impulsively to her feet. "When are you going to let somebody else speak?" she interrupted with spunky impatience. It was the crack in the dam. There was thunderous applause. Public outcry had broken through.

One by one, neighbors rose up on all sides and spoke out emotionally in support of a natural public creek. Wanda Skinner waited till last. Her outspokenness was already well-known. When she rose to her feet, there was a scattering of applause. Her voice boomed out passionately across the meeting room.

"I'll tell you what I'd like to know," she said. "If Seattle can build two stadiums simultaneously at a cost approaching a billion dollars, why can't Seattle afford a measly couple million to save a real, live creek?"

An uproar of applause.

Encouraged, Wanda continued. "Nature is dying, my friends. We've almost succeeded in destroying it. In our own lifetimes, we're watching the salmon become extinct. We've got to take care of what's left. We've got to restore what we've lost. Look around you. That despair you see in the eyes of most people — it's because they've lost nature. Take away nature and what do you have? Shopping malls and mud-slides!"

Clapping, whistles, cheers.

Pepper had been standing at one end of the meeting room, impressed by her aggressive neighbor and applauding her outspoken comments, when she noticed a man coming toward her from the other side. A bulky, teal-green parka hung open on a paint-speckled gray T-shirt. Pepper promptly recognized the Italian neighbor she'd met in the ravine on the morning of Grandma's death.

"Hello," he said. "I just wanted to say again how sorry I am about my dog's behavior."

"Forget it," she whispered. "Joe, isn't it?" They shook hands.

"And you're Pepper. Was that your grandmother who—?"

Pepper nodded, emotions tightly checked. "A wonderful woman. I loved her so much! It was such a shock. That was kind of you to help that poor boy."

"You mean Billy. He's a great kid."

"He's a neighbor, too," said Pepper. She spoke softly enough not to disturb the people on either side listening to Mrs Skinner. "Funny how you can live for years down the street from people and never talk."

Joe risked a question. "Have you discovered what caused your grandmother to do it?"

Pepper shook her head sadly, hesitated, then guided him into the hallway outside the double-doors of the meeting room. "No one knows. I had a conversation with her shortly before it happened. She was telling me about another ravine that used to cut through Cowen Park. I've looked it up in the library. What she told me, it's all real."

"A second ravine?"

"They filled it up in 1960. It's buried now under a baseball field. Just talking about it upset her. Then the trouble over Billy, whatever that was. Not even my mother can figure it out — and she knew Grandma better than anyone."

"I saw your mother," said Joe awkwardly, "that day."

"Yes," said Pepper. "I'm living with her right now, in the same house where I grew up. The park has always been my back yard."

"I walk through the ravine every day," said Joe. "It keeps me sane."

"We should take a walk together sometime," said Pepper.

"I'd love to." said Joe. "I don't suppose you're free after the meeting? It's a little late for tree-watching, but I could invite you over to my place for a late latté and some homemade biscotti from my aunt in Chicago."

"Homemade biscotti!" said Pepper, thoroughly tempted.

"My aunt makes the best." Joe put the tips of his fingers to his lips, and blew them away in a gesture of ecstasy.

Pepper grinned, then gave him a long, frankly assessing look. "Sure it's not too late?"

"Not for me," said Joe. "I'm a regular night owl."


# 7
## Espresso and Biscotti

"Delicious!" said Pepper, popping the last bite of biscotti into her mouth. "Almost as good as my Grandma's."

"How about one more?" said Joe, starting to rise.

"No, no, three's my limit!"

Pepper sat happily in the candle-lit shadows, cradling a mug in both hands, not in the least sleepy, due in part to Joe's powerful latté. They were sitting together at one end of a solid oak dining table, which had been hastily swept clear of envelopes, brochures, unpaid bills, sketch-book, phone book, and glossy open volume of French Impressionists. Biscotti crumbs were all that remained on the cookie plate between them.

They had walked home together up 25th Avenue, beneath the bright streetlamps. On the edge of the park, he'd led her to a house she'd frequently noticed before, perched above the ravine beside the stairs leading down to the bridge.

"Well, if you get the urge for another one, say so." His smile was contagious.

"You seem happy enough," she had to remark.

"I didn't realize it showed."

"Good news?"

Joe regarded her assessingly. "Just got some results from my doctor."

"Looks like the diagnosis was good."

"My own little miracle story," said Joe. "Somehow, after eleven years my T-cell count is still stabilized."

His candor caught her off-guard. He was so casual about it. She wasn't sure how to respond, and decided to treat the subject casually in return, to be as up front as he was. "You're HIV-positive?"

He nodded. "My time was up, a long time ago. The doctors don't know why, but my count stays the same."

"Glad to hear it," she said. "It gives you such a nice smile."

He sensed her awkwardness. "For reasons unknown to medical science, I'm not getting worse. And this—" He pointed toward the little red line across the inside corner of his left eye. "—this isn't a lesion, I'm happy to tell you. It's just a tiny broken blood vessel."

"It must have given you quite a scare," she said.

"It feels like a suspended death sentence." He smiled at her. "The doctor says I've got nothing to worry about."

"Wonderful!" said Pepper. "Stopped worrying?"

"Not exactly. At least I'm worrying about different things now. Enough about me. Tell me more about your grandmother, if you don't mind me asking."

"Not at all," said Pepper. "I love talking about Grandma. A genuinely good woman. She had a very hard life, but she was tough enough to survive and be an honest person, too. I always thought she was beautiful. That white hair of hers, when it wasn't all rolled up and pinned, used to reach almost to her waist. She was in her seventies, but looked a lot older. Mom and I took care of her."

"Was she in good health?"

"She'd been getting a little weaker, not much. She kept to herself most of the time. Her bedroom was upstairs. Mom tried to move her downstairs when Grandma started having dizzy spells, and she threw a fuss. So she lived at the top of the house, at the top of the stairs, and left her room only two or three times a day.

"That's quite a house," said Joe. "It's got old-fashioned style. Did your family build it?"

Pepper nodded. "My great-grandfather built the house. Salvatore Merlino. The first Merlino to come to this country, back in 1918."

"Where from in Italy?"

"A little village outside Naples."

"Ah, Neapolitan!"

"They used to call him Sal. He made his home in Seattle with his wife. Her name was Teresa. She died young. They had two kids, Grandma and her younger brother, my Great-uncle Gabriel."

"Small family for Catholics."

"They were poor. The house took all their money. Grandma supported her brother and her father when he got old. She ran the house and worked, too. She cleaned out Pullman cars down at the King Street Station for years — until she got pregnant. Without a husband. Shocked every relative on the family tree. Then she shocked them again by refusing to get rid of it."

"Since when did Catholics approve of abortion?"

"Catholicism had nothing to do with it. Italians don't approve of soiling the family honor. Grandma stood her ground, had the baby, and never told the name of the guy who got her that way."

Joe sighed. "She sounds like a strong woman."

"You see why I loved her," said Pepper. "She was my hero. A feminist before her time. No one ever figured out who the father was," said Pepper. "You know Mom's theory?" Pepper chuckled to herself. "There was supposed to be this good-looking oil-man who checked the meter at the house every month. Mom's convinced she's the daughter of the oil-man. Grandma never told."

"Incredible!" said Joe. "Don't you love family gossip!"

"Grandma wasn't the only colorful character in the family, believe me. Her brother, Uncle Gabriel, was the family favorite. He sounds like a smart, good-looking loser. He got into the drug scene early."

"You mean back when the beatniks were just turning into hippies?"

"Exactly. When Grandma's father demanded that Uncle Gabriel change his ways, they had a terrible fight. Uncle Gabriel stormed out of the house and never came back. Some people said he got himself killed dealing drugs. Some people said he died of an overdose. No one ever knew for sure."

"Sad. Must have been pretty hard on the old man, losing his son."

"Grandma said he never recovered from the fight. Sal Merlino died in 1959. To everyone's amazement, he left the house to Gabriel instead of Grandma."

"You've got to be kidding!"

"It was outrageous. Grandma had taken care of the family, cooked and cleaned for the two men, worked six days a week down at the railroad terminal and supported her daughter, too. Luckily Uncle Gabriel never returned, so Grandma got the house she deserved, where she raised my Mom, where my Mom raised me. Three generations of Merlino women have grown up in that house."

"Did your father live there with you?"

"I never knew who my father was," said Pepper. "Mom used to joke about it. Said Merlino women were like black widows. They mated with males and then ate them."

"I think she means the praying mantis. Like in those wonderful documentary films where you watch them eating off the male's head."

They both laughed. "Instead of a Dad, I had my wonderful Grandma. I can still hardly believe she's gone. My poor mother! Seeing Grandma fall from the bridge—" Pepper sighed. "Mom will never be the same."

"Seeing something like that leaves its mark," said Joe. "On some people, the mark is forever. I just hope that poor boy isn't one of them."

# 8
# Child's Cry

Paul Beck was deep in dreamless sleep, the house hushed, the neighborhood still, the refrigerator purring, the heater downstairs grumbling contentedly, when he heard the scream from Billy's bedroom.

He jerked up into a sitting position.

Ordinarily the sound of his child's cry would have brought him leaping from bed, lunging down the hall to Billy's door. That, in fact, was exactly what he had been doing night after night.

Paul shook his head wearily in defeat. "I can't take it anymore," he muttered into his pillow. "I've got a kid with a serious problem."

He had tried to convince himself that the nightmares would stop. That they were just a natural phase, a release mechanism. How many kids Billy's age actually see something like that? But the release phase wasn't coming to an end. Billy wasn't healing. He was just getting worse. He needed the help of a professional. Paul wanted a decent night's sleep, or he was going to need professional help himself.

He flung back the covers, sat on the side of the bed, then rose reluctantly to his feet. He shuffled barefoot down the hall to the door at the far end, which he swung open into Billy's room.

Streetlamp light filtered through the curtains. He could detect the outline of a trembling lump underneath the covers of Billy's bed. He crossed the room, sat on the edge of the mattress, and gently peeled down the blanket to reveal his son's wide eyes, his tear-streaked face.

Billy's rowdy thatch of hair was matted and crushed. His lips trembled with all the things he would never dare put into words. "Sorry, Dad."

"No need to be sorry," said Paul. He put his hand on his son's shoulder. "Hey, pal, they're just dreams. Doesn't mean they aren't scary. But they go away."

The boy stared at him. He didn't try to argue or explain. There wasn't anything he hadn't already said.

"Billy, try to think it through one more time," said Paul, stroking his forehead lovingly, brushing back a sweat-damp lock of hair. "There has to be something else, pardner. Try to remember. When this whole thing happened, were you in any way teasing that poor old woman?"

"I swear we weren't, Dad."

"Now, think," said Paul, betraying a slight urgency in his voice. "Try to remember and be honest with me. I won't get mad. You'll feel better if you tell me everything. Nobody gets upset over nothing. They say she was very upset."

"She was freaking out," murmured Billy in agreement, remembering the awful sight with a shudder. "But I didn't do anything, Dad, I swear." He was nearly whimpering with frustration. "I told you what happened. It had nothing to do with her. My foot got stuck between the branches of this old rotten log."

"A log down in the wild part of the ravine, where you had no business being."

"But, Dad," he protested, "I had to get away from these demons of the undead who were going to suck out my soul."

"Stop it!" Paul's patience snapped. He recovered quickly. He spoke in a softer, controlled voice. "Don't start in on that again, Billy. Not at this hour of the morning."

"Dad, it's just a game."

"Just a game, but you don't talk about it like a game. Don't you see, pal? That's the problem. You talk about this game like it's real. You have such an over-active imagination. I don't want you playing that Dungeons-and-Dragons stuff anymore."

"But Dad, it's not Dungeons-and—"

"Billy, don't!" Paul tried to keep his voice calm and steady, to be sensible and forgiving, to do everything he had to do to save the shocked and frightened mind of his son. "You seem to have a very difficult time telling the difference between reality and the crazy things you dream up in your imagination. That can get you in big trouble. You've got to know what's real. And what's not."

"I know what's not real, Dad, but—"

"Dreams are not," his father interrupted him. "Games in the park about knights and demons are not."

"I know, Dad, but—"

"And the man you think is looking in your window is very definitely not."

Billy's mouth closed. He didn't try to say anything. He just looked at his father. His eyes said it all.

Paul combed his fingers back through his rumpled hair in frustration. The boy was beyond his reach. Paul had no choice. Tomorrow he would make an appointment with Dr Griffin.

# 9
# Credibility

Joe eased himself down the ravine bank, from boulder to boulder beneath the trees, to peer under the wooden stays of the old bridge, determined to find the source of the burning smell. He saw the back of a boy's head topped by a backward baseball cap. The boy was far down on the lowest crossbeam. Beside him rose a tiny line of smoke. A twig snapped under Joe's foot. The boy jumped to his feet and spun around.

"Oh, it's you," he said in relief. "You scared me."

"Hi," said Joe. "I haven't seen you around for a while. Not since that day." He sniffed. "Should you be smoking?"

"You sound like my Dad." Billy took a long, earnest puff. "Next year I'll be in middle school," he said, blowing out a cloud of smoke, "and everyone in middle school smokes. Well, almost everybody. Everybody except for the straight-A kids. They don't smoke. They don't do anything."

Joe smiled. Long ago he had been a straight-A kid. "Been smoking long?"

"Yeah."

"How long?"

"This is my second time."

"That's not too long. Wouldn't be very hard to stop."

"Who wants to stop? My friends would all think I was a dork. They think I'm weird enough, as it is. Besides, I like it. It keeps me cool. I'm too nervous lately."

"What are you nervous about?"

"You don't want to know. You wouldn't believe me, anyway."

"How do you know I wouldn't believe you?"

"You're an adult." He pronouced the term as though it were an incurable mental illness. "Adults never believe kids about anything. That's what being an adult means."

"I'm an adult, and I believe you. You look smart enough to know what's real and what's not."

"Hah!" Joe's words caused an outburst. "That's what you think. My Dad doesn't think so, and he knows me better than you do. He says that's my problem. I can't tell the difference between reality and made-up stuff. He thinks I don't know what's real. When I try to tell him why I've been so scared, he doesn't listen. He says I have no credibility."

"But why have you been so scared?"

"I don't want to talk about it any more."

Joe almost tried to persuade him, glanced at the boy's eyes, and decided to drop the subject. He noticed something behind the boy, a drawing pad propped across the beam he was sitting on, a torn-open box of charcoal drawing pencils. "May I look?"

Billy became very self-conscious. "Sure, go ahead."

Joe picked it up. The spiralbound sketchbook was brimming with picture after picture. Sketches of the ravine. "You're very good."

The boy's eyes brightened for a moment, and then narrowed. "How would you know?" he challenged boldly.

"I'm a professional artist, that's how I know," said Joe. "I do illustrations in books. And frescoes on walls. And landscapes in oils. At least, I used to, back in Chicago."

"Oils?" repeated Billy enviously. "They don't let us use oils in school. I like colored pencils."

"You can do a lot with colored pencils," agreed Joe. He admired a sketch of the bridge. Another. Another. "You have a very nice sense of composition. A natural instinct for how to show space."

"Do I?" Billy listened, entranced, enraptured. He was being praised as an artist.

"Yes, this one's especially good. Taking it from an angle is very dramatic. And this one — good perspective. Very nice."

"Thanks," said Billy. It was the only word he could force out of his throat.

"You like drawing the bridge, I see."

"It's my favorite thing to draw now," said Billy. "I draw it every day, ever since—"

A call from directly above interrupted him. "Billy!"

The boy semed to snap awake from a trance of happiness. "Jeez, that's my Dad!" Billy forced the cigarette into Joe's hand, grabbed his sketchpad and pencils, scrambled to his feet. "Do I smell like cigarettes?"

Joe sniffed at him. "Nope. You're fine."

"See ya." He scrambled up the footpath toward the bridge.

Footsteps rattled across the trestles overhead and Paul Beck loomed over the railing, scowling down at Joe. "Hello again," he said, with a cautious air of suspicion. "You're the one who brought Billy home that day." He noticed the boy making his way up the dirt trail toward him. "Billy, head on home. I want to have a word with our neighbor."

The boy obeyed, with an anxious glance over his shoulder.

Billy's father strode back off the bridge, and began scuffling and sliding down the rock-strewn bank, swatting aside wet fern fronds, ducking under the wooden support-beams of the bridge.

"You were talking with my son just now," he said, as though he'd caught Joe committing a crime.

"He let me look through his sketches," said Joe. "He's got a good eye, a natural sense of composition. I'm an artist. With some training, a talent like that could really blossom."

"Sorry my kid was bothering you."

"But he wasn't—"

Billy's father noticed the cigarette in Joe's fingers. "I'd appreciate it if you wouldn't smoke around my son. You obviously don't have kids, or you wouldn't be setting such a bad example."

Joe swallowed back his irritation at the man's aggressive tone. "I hope Billy is doing all right."

"Billy is not doing all right," said his father. "He's very disturbed. I've got him in therapy, but the shrink doesn't know what to make of him. He's never been the same since he saw that old woman fall."

"I'm sorry to hear that," said Joe. "I've had a little more experience with death. And it was still very upsetting, even for me. It must have been much worse for him."

"That's just it," said Paul. "It was too much for him. He's having a hard time getting back to scratch. I don't want him upset any more." He sighed, expelling a long, weary stream of air. "I'll be frank with you. I don't want him reminded of what happened. I want him to forget the whole terrible incident as soon as possible. I don't want him talking about it with you."

The time had come to face him.

"Sometimes forgetting isn't the answer," said Joe. "What's forgotten and buried can fester and get worse. Sometimes what's needed is understanding."

"Understanding!" A ripple of anger in his voice. "Easy for you to say. I don't think you realize quite how upset he's been."

"What's he afraid of?" asked Joe.

"Nothing in the real world," said Paul affirmatively. "Look, Billy doesn't know, but I've called the police. They've checked out possible prowlers. No footprints in the yard. No nothing. The entire thing's in his mind. The doctor says we may have to start medication. Quite frankly, I can't take much more. I appreciate your interest in Billy, but I'd like you to stay away for a while. Even though you mean well, you could be a bad influence on him. I hope you understand."

He turned his back on Joe and climbed up the bank again toward the bridge above and the street.

Joe was still standing there with the cigarette smoking between his fingers, fuming over the rudeness of Billy's father, when he saw, in the distance, Pepper Merlino turning up the footpath through the trees that led toward her house.

# 10
## Glacial Rock

The doorbell rang.

Pepper ignored it. She had just come home from the first day of classes. It was a bright, crisp afternoon, and she'd enjoyed her half-mile walk from the Center for Urban Horticulture, up 25th Avenue and through the ravine. She was now in the kitchen with her mother, jacket still on, backpack on the table, reading the front page of the newspaper.

The doorbell rang again.

"Can you get it, Pep?" said her mother, continuing to stir as she carefully poured a stream of flour-and-milk into a pan of hot gravy that refused to thicken.

Pepper left the paper spread open across the kitchen table, crossed through the dining room and hallway, and opened the front door. To her surprise, it was Joe Strozza, her neighbor.

"Well, hello there," she said.

"Who is it, Pep?" called Rose from the kitchen, her knife rattling efficiently over the chopping-board.

"It's for me, Mom." She turned back to him. "What a surprise."

"I hope I'm not disturbing you," said Joe. "I saw you walk by just now while I was in the park. I was hoping to talk to you. Is this a convenient time?"

"Now is fine." She stepped out onto the porch with him, closing the door behind her. "Let's talk outside, though. That makes it harder for my mother to eavesdrop."

He smiled. "Thanks, I — I just needed to talk with somebody who could understand. Someone who was there. Ever since it happened, I've been a wreck. I mean, I know it was so much worse for you, but — well, I was hoping you wouldn't mind letting me talk to you."

"Of course," said Pepper. "I don't mind at all. Obviously I've been pretty shook up about it myself. I'm glad you decided to stop by." A moment of awkwardness passed between them. "What exactly did you want to talk about?"

He looked around, ill at ease. "Can we take a walk or something?"

"How about down in the ravine?" she suggested. "Didn't you say you liked walking down there?"

"It's my favorite place," said Joe. "I'm planning a series of paintings based on different places in the ravine."

"You are?" She looked at him again in a different light. "What a great thing to do! Perfect, let's take the main trail." She opened the front door just wide enough to call inside, "I'll be right back, Mom," closing it quickly to avoid any of her mother's questions.

They left the Merlino house behind, walking together to the end of the street and down the short flight of cement stairs to the footpath angling down the root-bound bank to the ravine bottom.

They stopped beneath the high, green arched girders of the 20th Avenue bridge. Amid fallen tree trunks, in the middle of Ravenna Creek, was lodged a massive glacial boulder, covered with moss and lichen, surrounded by a zigzagging wooden plank bridge a foot above the rippling water. Joe and Pepper scrambled up onto the rock and sat there together, trees above them and around them, the creek gurgling and shimmering on either side.

"So, why did you want to talk to me?" she prompted.

"I just needed someone to—" He fumbled, started over. "I need to talk about — I don't know how to say it — ever since the day your grandmother fell, I've been a mental wreck. I feel like I changed that day. I mean, changed in my mind, somehow. It's like a depression I can't seem to shake. But it's not a depression. It's more like a dread."

"I'm missing something," said Pepper. "What does this have to do with my grandmother?"

"Wish I knew," said Joe. "Somehow they're connected. All I know is it started right after she died. I keep feeling like something very bad is going to happen."

"Something bad always does," said Pepper. "There's no getting away from it. That's just life."

"Something worse than usual. Something unnatural. It's like an oppression — it just keeps hanging over me, making me afraid to look over my shoulder. Every night—" He faltered. How could he tell her about the nightmares? He'd feel like a child. He felt silly enough as it was, without confessing to being afraid of his dreams.

"How strange!" said Pepper. "How unfortunate for you. I wish I could help."

They were both confounded. For a while they sat together in silence, groping for explanations, coming up with no answers.

"I love this old rock," said Pepper finally. "It's one of my favorite places in the ravine."

"Sketched it often. One of my places, too."

"They say it comes from two hundred miles north of here in British Columbia. Picked up by the Vashon ice sheet five thousand years ago, dragged along and dumped here. Glacier probably didn't even notice."

"I bet the glacier noticed," said Joe with quiet confidence.

A black-winged flurry of crows swooped from branch to branch overhead, cawing in irritation.

"Look at them!" said Pepper. "You'd think they were trying to tell us something."

"They sound exasperated," said Joe, glancing up uneasily. "Like we're too thick-headed to understand."

The ravine echoed with a racket of inexplicable protest.

"Maybe they're trying to explain about your nightmares," said Pepper. "Maybe they know the answer."

"Whatever they've got to say, I get the feeling it's not good news."

# 11
## "Who's There?"

Pepper closed the front door behind her and walked down the hall back into the kitchen. She had only been gone an hour, yet her thoughts were in complete upheaval, tumbled into confusion by the odd, unexpected happiness she felt inside her after talking with her new friend.

She noticed that her mother had gathered up the newspaper Pepper left out, folded it neatly, and set the table.

"Look who's back," said her mother. She glanced over her shoulder at her daughter from the stove, tending to several pots and pans on the range. "What's so funny?"

"Nothing's funny," said Pepper, disconcerted.

Rose turned around to confirm her intuition. "Then why are you smiling?"

"I didn't realize I was smiling." She stopped smiling.

"So, where have you been?" persisted her mother.

"Just down in the ravine."

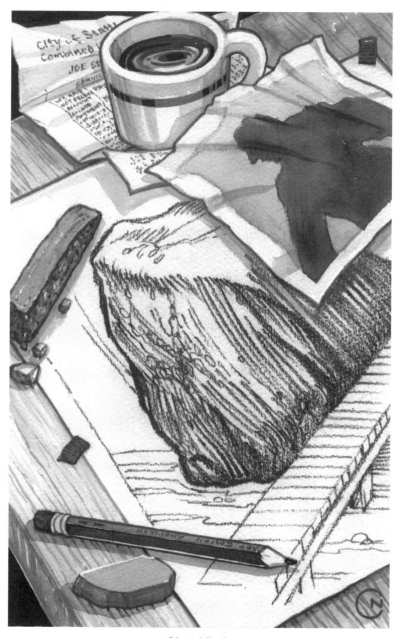

*Glacial Rock*

"By yourself?"

"With a neighbor of ours."

"Neighbor? That's a new one. Who is this neighbor? Is that who knocked at the door?"

"Yes, Mrs Sherlock," said Pepper, indulging her mother's curiosity. "His name is Joe Strozza. A nice Italian boy."

"A sudden interest in boys? Something's fishy here."

"You know perfectly well I've always been interested in men. I'm just not anxious to rush into anything."

"You, interested in men? You're smarter than that."

"Mom, just because you've had bad experiences doesn't make them all monsters."

"I'm not talking about all of them. Most of them."

"Mom—"

"I'm just looking straight ahead, and saying what I see. I see a lot more than you think. Someday you'll understand. You don't know your own heart. You think you're so smart, but you're a stranger to everyone, including yourself. When you fall in love, you'll be the last one to know."

"Mom, what happened today wasn't love. It was a walk in the park."

"Believe me, whatever he is, he's a man."

"He's a neighbor."

"He's a man. Men have traits in common. As a species."

"Mommy dearest," said Pepper, nearly laughing with exasperation, "he's old enough to be my father, and besides, I think he's gay."

"What difference does that make?" said Rose. "Old or young, straight or gay, don't fool yourself. A man's a man. Men act the way they do. They can't help it."

*

That night Pepper heard footsteps in the hallway.

She knew whose footsteps they had to be. Her mother often got out of bed once or twice during the night for brief visits to the bathroom or kitchen, with familiar patterns and lengths of duration. Pepper had noticed that ever since Grandma died, her mother was sleeping worse than usual, getting up more often. Rose was troubled, preoccupied, restless. Losing her mother had taken its toll.

Without rustling the covers, Pepper listened, ignoring all the other well-known sounds that came from three floors of a eighty-year-old house. The familiar creaks and floorboard groans were practically childhood friends. Every one of those sounds Pepper knew by heart. It wasn't those noises, or her mother's footsteps in the dark, that caught her attention. What brought Pepper up onto her elbow, listening intently, was the sound of the kitchen door downstairs opening and footsteps outside on the back porch. She waited for the door to close.

It never closed.

Pepper folded back her comforter and climbed out of bed. Since Grandma's death, the house had been so much quieter at night. Shuffling into her slippers, she carefully stepped around her Forestry textbook spread open on the throw-rug by the bed. She padded down the carpeted staircase barefoot, then quick-footed across the cold wooden floor to the kitchen.

The only illumination came from the light over the back porch, sending a weak ripple of brightness across the dark linoleum. The back door was open — wide open — letting in the cold night air. She could see her mother standing outside on the porch, arms folded across her chest, shivering in her bathrobe, peering into the darkness, her black hair the usual disorderly tumble, seeming not to feel the first drops of rain.

"Mom—"

Rose turned around abruptly, startled. "Who's there?"

"Mom, it's me," said Pepper. "Who were you expecting?"

"Don't get smart with me."

Pepper sighed. "Who else could it be, Mom?"

"It didn't look like you."

"I know, I know. It never looks like me anymore. Please, not another lecture about my hair. So, tell me, what are you doing up at this hour?"

With a gentle, reassuring smile, Pepper reached out a hand toward her mother. This was a new, breakable Mom, not the undefeatable powerhouse she had always known, not the unpredictable tyrant who had shaped her childhood with the iron fist of love. She could sense a new fragility, a vulnerability, which had opened up in her mother since Grandma died. "Come on, Mom, let's go to bed."

Ignoring her daughter's hand, Rose stepped back inside the house and closed the door, but she didn't follow Pepper. Instead, she remained with her face pressed against the glass of the back door window, eyebrows scowling as she peered into the darkness of the back yard.

"You didn't hear it, did you?" she whispered.

"Hear what?"

Rose paused, almost didn't go on. "It woke me up. Sounded like someone was knocking on the back door."

Pepper shivered uncomfortably. "Knocking, at this hour? It couldn't have been, Mom."

"I heard someone knocking down here."

She didn't like the look on her mother's face. "It was probably just rats making too much noise," said Pepper, "or else a raccoon. Who would come visiting in the middle of the night?"

But Rose wasn't listening to her daughter's sensible explanations. She was staring at the back door, as though she expected at any moment to hear another rap. "I heard knocking."

Pepper had seen that look in her mother's eyes. Mom had made up her mind. No use trying to convince her otherwise.

"Well, I didn't hear anything." Pepper put an arm around her, surprised to discover how cold her mother was from standing on the porch. "Come on, doesn't a warm bed sound good right now?" With the gentlest pressure, drawing her mother closer to her as though to share her warmth, Pepper guided her toward the hallway and the staircase.

"I know what I heard," said Rose, leaning on her daughter as she left the kitchen. "Somebody wanted in."

Pepper glanced back one last time. A gleam of reflected porch light flickered on the shiny edge of the doorknob. For a moment, the doorknob seemed to be turning.

# CHAPTER FOUR

# October Nightmares

## 1
## Pictures without Stories

Billy stood hesitantly in the office doorway. This was his third session, and they still made him nervous. He had been dreading it all day.

Dr Jane Griffin placed on her desktop what looked like an enormous deck of cards. "Hi, Billy. You can hang up your jacket behind the door. Come over here and sit down with me." She smiled. Dr Griffin smiled a lot. She had a big nose and big teeth and a huge smile. She was always pushing up her glasses on her nose when she needed to think.

He felt utterly uncomfortable in his itchy slacks and an itchy sweater. His father made him wear his best clothes, which he hated as much as he hated that small, dark room with green walls. He glanced at his watch, knowing that his father was sitting down in the car, parked in a no-parking zone, tired from work, hungry for dinner, waiting for him.

"You look very tired today, Billy," she said gently. "You look like you're losing weight. Are you still having the dreams?"

Billy nodded again. He didn't like talking about it.

"Well, what we're going to do today can be a fun game." She smiled. "These cards all have pictures on them. The pictures show a scene. Something is happening. Your job is to tell me what's going on in the picture. There's no right or wrong answer. You just tell me the story that you see there. Okay?"

He nodded. "Okay."

"Good. Let's try one." She held the card up in front of him. A man and a woman were embracing each other, while another man stood nearby watching them, frowning. "Tell me what's happening here, Billy?"

The boy studied the picture. "That man by himself is very upset. Because that's his wife. He's going to start crying because she doesn't love him anymore."

"Why did she stop loving him?"

"Because he worked too much. He worked all the time and came home late and tired and grouchy. So that's why she likes this other man. He's fun and they go places. They're going to run away together."

Billy folded his arms across his chest, scowling at the floor.

"Good. Exactly the right idea." Dr Griffin turned over another card. "How about this one?" A wolf silhouetted on a mountaintop, howling, while a man holding a rifle stared at it. "What's happening here?"

Billy scrutinized the picture, as though searching for secret meanings. "That's a big dog. It's barking. This man is the owner. This is the leash he's holding. He should have the dog on the leash."

Dr Griffin smiled. "Good." Another card turned over. "How about this one?"

It consisted of a simple black square frame around the silhouette of a male figure. She wasn't expecting Billy to leap to his feet in terror. "It's him!"

"Who, Billy?"

He was backing away from the table. He almost knocked over his chair, so great was his hurry to get to the door. "The one who keeps following me!"

"Now, Billy, stay calm. Come back here." She rose from her chair and came toward him, putting her arm around his shoulders, steering him over to the leather recliner, easing him down. "It's just a picture. You're perfectly safe here in the office with me."

"I see him outside in the ravine."

"Who, Billy?"

"And outside on the back porch."

"Who is he? Relax. Lie back."

He felt like crying, but refused to let himself. "I don't know who he is. I dream about him. He's always watching me."

That was all he wanted to say. He didn't want to talk about it. The man would be waiting for him in his dreams when he got home. And possibly — possibly in the back yard, outside his bedroom window.

"Would you like me to help you deal with him, Billy?"

"Yes, please," he said.

"Then close your eyes," she said softly, soothingly. "Go back to the last time you saw this Nightmare Man of yours. Let's see what we can find out. No need to be afraid. The answers are there. Will you help me find them?"

"Yes," he said.

"Good, Billy," said Dr Griffin. "Now, I want you to remember the last time you saw him watching you."

He was still for a moment, and then his body abruptly tensed. "I was in my bedroom."

"When was it, Billy?"

"It was last night." He frowned unhappily, scared. "I was in bed. I thought I was alone, but — but I could see someone else's shadow. Some-one was on the other side of my window curtains."

"Now, try to tell me, Billy," said Dr Griffin, leaning closer to him, murmuring next to his ear. "In your mind — on the other side of the curtains — can you reach out? Can you draw the curtains aside? Pull them aside. Reach out, go ahead, pull them away right now — and tell me who you see in the window."

Billy reached toward the window. Then his body suddenly stiffened in fear. His eyes snapped open. He sat up with a jolt and screamed.

A man's shadow crossed outside the window curtains of Dr Griffin's office.

"What is it, Billy?" cried Dr Griffin, taking him by the shoulders. She never saw the shadow. She never knew what had terrified him. "Who do you see?"

His lower lip trembled, but he didn't speak.

"Tell me, Billy."

He didn't. He couldn't. The more he told her, the more she'd make him come back for these appointments. Better to say nothing. Better not to look out the window. Better to pretend to be cured, to pretend that the nightmares were over.

"Billy, your father is worried about a man you talk with in the park. Is this the same man you see outside your window?"

"No."

"Are you sure, Billy?" said Dr Griffin. "Try very hard to remember. Nightmare Man and the man in the park — are they the same man?"

# 2
## "Stay Away from Him"

Nights had never made him nervous before. Now Billy hated them. It wasn't so bad while his father was downstairs watching television. Then his bedroom was a shelter, a hiding-place. It was a wonderful room.

But it could be a scary room after Dad went to sleep, when his bedroom door closed and the crack of light under the door went out and the house became hushed and the little noises began.

He pulled the covers up over his ears, afraid to fall asleep, afraid to remain awake.

*

Billy's eyes snapped open in the middle of the night.

He was stretched out on his bed, head sunken in pillows, his blankets tangled low enough on his body to be just out of reach. At first he couldn't figure out what had awakened him. Then he heard it again, someone knocking downstairs. He waited for his father to answer the door.

The knocking repeated.

Billy scrambled out of bed, but was afraid to go any further. What should he do? He quickly padded down the hall to his father's bedroom. "Dad!" he whispered outside the door. No answer. "Dad?" He tried the bedroom doorknob. Locked. Why would his father lock the door? Again the knocking below. He would have to answer it himself. Reluctantly he crept downstairs. Just as he reached the bottom of the staircase, he saw someone's shadow pass by the window.

Someone was out there. Someone was going around the house to the back door. The thought made his stomach knot in dread. Someone wanted in very badly. Billy tried not to let himself get frightened. He walked quietly down the hall, tense with apprehension, approached the kitchen slowly, cautiously stepped around the corner for the briefest glimpse.

The kitchen was empty, icy cold. The back door was wide open. He froze in his tracks, looking wildly around him in all directions, unable to believe what he was seeing. Open? How could the door be open? Whoever he had seen circling around the house had managed to open the back door. Someone was inside the house with him now.

A soft footstep behind him.

*

The boy woke with a cry.

To his amazement, he was no longer in bed. He was standing in the middle of the night-darkened kitchen, hugging himself shivering, barefoot, in his underwear.

A tall, broad-shouldered figure was standing across the unlit kitchen, facing him. He was inside the house! Billy wanted to scream, to run, but he was too scared to budge. The shadowy intruder took a step toward him, and became his father.

"Dad!" he exclaimed.

His father regarded him in concern. "Billy what are you doing down here? It's the middle of the night."

Billy stared at his father with eyes that were filling with tears. "I don't know," he confessed.

"Were you walking in your sleep?"

"I must have been."

"Did you have another nightmare?"

Billy nodded.

His father sank down at the kitchen table, groaning as he propped both elbows on the cold formica tabletop and cradled his forehead in both hands. "Do you want to tell me about it?"

Billy didn't, but he knew his father was waiting for an explanation. "I dreamed someone broke into the house."

"Who do you think is trying to break in?"

Billy didn't want to talk about it. Things would only get worse if Dad started worrying. "It's a man, that's all I know. He comes from the park."

Before he could say another word, his father interrupted him. "A man in the park? Billy, let me ask you something. That man who brought you home the day of the accident. You see him in the park. Have you talked to him much?"

Billy nodded.

"Does he ever say or do anything that scares you?"

Now Billy was getting nervous, but he tried not to show it. He shook his head. "No."

The answer didn't matter. "I don't like to see a grown man hanging around boys in a park," said Paul, watching his son for any betrayal of what he was feeling. "From now on, Billy, I don't want you talking to him anymore. Do you understand? I mean it. Just stay away from him, and don't answer him if he talks to you. Okay? Promise me, Billy. Stay away from him."

# 3
# Basement

Crackling maple leaves, caught in a blast of wind, tried to squeeze through the front door with her. Not quickly enough. Pepper slammed the door shut behind her.

"Mom?"

No reply. The motionless hush of an empty house. She remembered her mother mentioning an extra shift at QFC that afternoon, covering for someone's vacation. The extra dollars helped. They had just lost Grandma's monthly social security check. Pepper knew it wasn't easy for Mom to own and maintain that large house, to put food on the table and pay the bills. Yet Rose insisted on helping pay her tuition, too.

Pepper slung off her backpack, shrugged out of her jacket, and reached in the refrigerator. Outside the wind hissed through the shrubs and vine maples surrounding the house. She was enjoying a quick swallow straight from the orange juice carton, a liberty her mother abhorred, when a repeated creaking outside caught her attention.

At first she couldn't figure out what was causing the sound. Then the wind blew again and she realized it was the dead bough outside the picture window. It didn't use to creak. Every blast of wind through the ravine caused the branch to bend toward the window and groan.

Another sound, from behind her.

Startled, Pepper spun around. "Mom?" It came from downstairs. Who on earth could be down in the basement? "Are you down there?" Pepper crossed the kitchen, swung open the basement door. No lights were on downstairs. She flipped the light switch. "Mom?"

That her mother could possibly be down there in the dark was not to be considered. Could she have fallen downstairs? The thought chilled Pepper. She quickly descended the wooden stairs. At the bottom she promptly switched on the basement lights. No sign of her mother.

The basement consisted of partially-finished wall board, exposed two-by-fours, brown insulation paper. It had become the hodge-podge place where things disappeared in the Merlino house when their usefulness upstairs came to an end. Chipped or wobbly furniture, mismatched chairs, faded drapes, the old coffee table, piles of magazines, books no one read anymore, boxes of unknowable, forgotten things. She seemed to remember hearing that long ago, during the last years Uncle Gabriel lived in the house, he had made the basement his private domain.

Something rustled in the corner. It sounded suspiciously like a rat. The closet door swung open.

Pepper froze, ready to bolt for the stairs, staring at the closet, waiting for something to come out. Just a swinging door, for no reason. Could a rat possibly have knocked it open? Resolving to not be afraid, Pepper strode forward and decisively closed it.

Nothing happened.

She shrugged, smiled. For some reason, being alone in the house was making her nervous. She actually looked forward to her mother's return from QFC. She decided to make lunch, to have sandwiches ready when her mother got home. Maybe some soup to go with it.

She turned to go back upstairs and had reached the third step when the closet door swung open.

Pepper stared at it. What was going on here? She was stubbornly preparing to go back downstairs and close it again when something made her hesitate. Something made her back up a step, uneasy, confused, then turn around and hurry up the rest of the stairs, closing the basement door with a slam.

# 4
# One Bag

"All in one bag, please."

Rose was at the end of a long shift, smiling automatically, making polite small talk without thinking, noticing that the line to her check-out counter never got any shorter, no matter how quickly and efficiently she passed each item over the price-scanner. Every aisle of the giant supermarket was clogged with shopping-carts, crying children, house-wives consulting their lists, old women trying to make up their minds, students lugging cases of beer.

"Meat Department, line one," announced the voice over the QFC intercom.

"Order out on nine," said the next cashier into her microphone.

"I asked for one bag," repeated the customer in front of her, his cheeks flushed with rage.

"Excuse me," she said, afraid she had missed something. "Will there be anything else?"

"I asked for one bag." He was a skinny student in a black T-shirt and frayed denim jacket, with wire-rimmed glasses, a dotted complexion and a ponytail. He was glowering at the two bags on the counter. "What does it take to get you people to care about the environment? Can't you stop wasting bags? Look at these, both half full! How many bags do you waste a day? Is it too much to ask for people to pick up their bags from the bottom?"

Customers waiting in other lines were turning to stare. Rose's brain was dead from long hours of cashiering. She couldn't think of any answers. She had never questioned the rules. The rules required easily-carried bags. Elderly people couldn't carry heavy, full ones. This customer wasn't out of his twenties yet. He couldn't understand a bad back or arthritis.

He was getting madder by the minute. She mumbled an apology and began re-packing his groceries into a single bag.

"No wonder our forests are being wiped off the face of the earth. You're wasting precious paper! If you'd just stop and think about the damage you're doing—"

She could see the assistant manager peering in her direction from the customer service stand.

Tears stung her eyes. Rose was used to dealing with customers of all kinds, but she was emotionally drained, weary with fatigue. She tried to smile courteously. She tried to nod politely in agreement.

"Don't you feel any responsibility toward this planet?" scolded the student, snatching up his bag of groceries off the counter. "What does it take to wake you up?"

*

Joe usually didn't shop at the QFC in University Village. He did most of his shopping at less expensive supermarkets. That night was an exception. He had put in a long day painting fantasy castles on the walls of a little girl's bedroom in Bellevue. Bobo didn't have anything to eat and it was the quickest, easiest place on the way home to pick up a couple cans of dog food and a bag of dog biscuits.

A loud, angry voice at the front of the store caught his attention. A customer was upset. He recognized the woman cashiering at the check-out stand. It was her! The same woman he had seen trying to coax old Mrs Merlino off the bridge. That had to be Pepper's mother. The cashier didn't notice Joe. She was too busy trying to calm down the scrawny young man at her counter.

Something about the woman made Joe uneasy. He watched her cashiering, but he stayed in his own line and left QFC without saying a word.

# 5
# Spiderweb

October rains had left the ravine a muddy mess.

The maple leaves scarcely had time to turn gold and red and brown before they were stripped from the branches in a savage, whirling dance, flung to the ground, and transformed into crushed and soggy mulch underfoot. Joe tried to step clear of the worst of it as he guided Bobo out of the upper picnic grounds, tugging his dog away from someone's discarded half-eaten sandwich, one of those under-the-table treasures that Bobo loved to gobble. Patiently, firmly, he steered his eager pet down one of the steep, dipping trails toward the creek below.

They had almost passed by when he noticed someone crouching on the edge of the creek. It was Billy, intently drawing. A sharp bark from Bobo caused the boy's sketching pencil to swerve.

The kid looked up sharply. "Oh. Hi."

"Sorry to interrupt you," said Joe. "Always a pleasure to find an artist working in the park." He edged closer, restraining Bobo, so that his big-footed pet didn't get in the way. "So what are you drawing today?"

Billy half-smiled. He liked being called an artist. "The bridge again." He almost didn't continue, then rashly pressed onward. "Except this time, looking at it from over here, through this spiderweb on the edge of the creek."

Joe had to look twice before he could actually see the web. "Ah, yes, there it is. A very good choice. That's a real beauty. It's the spider-mating season. Bobo, down. Can I look?"

The boy held his work up, so Joe could see it more easily. "I, uh — thanks for last time."

"Thanks for what?" asked Joe.

"For not ratting on me about that cigarette. I heard how my Dad talked to you." He looked over his own drawing, one eye squinted, critically assessing. "So, what do you think?"

"It's really good!" said Joe. He meant it. "You're talented."

"I've drawn places all over this park," the boy blurted out.

"I'll bet you have," said Joe. "I bet you know almost as much about this park as I do."

Billy smiled. "I bet I know more."

"More?" said Joe. "I know a lot."

"I know every trail in this park by heart," he claimed with complete confidence. "Including secret ones."

"You know secret trails?" said Joe. "We should definitely get to be friends then, and trade secrets."

"We can't be friends," the boy confessed sadly.

"Why not?"

"Because my Dad doesn't want me talking to you."

"Oh," said Joe. He considered that. "Do you know why you're not supposed to talk to me?"

Billy nodded. "It's because my Dad's afraid you might do bad things to me."

Joe weighed that. "How about you? What do you think?"

Billy regarded him. "I like you." He glanced at his wristwatch, jumped nervously to his feet, closing his sketchbook. "Gotta go. Dinner. My Dad doesn't like it when I'm late to dinner."

"Don't be late, then," said Joe. "Maybe I'll see you out here drawing sometime."

Billy didn't respond until he was halfway up the footpath. "See you tomorrow."

# 6
## Taste in the Mouth

Joe had stayed up all night sketching. It was better than trying to sleep and suffering through those dreams and waking up in a sweat. Now, with the first light of day touching the curtains, he realized he was exhausted.

He stepped back from his drawing table and assessed the night's effort. It was another rendering of the pedestrian trestle bridge over the wild end of the ravine, this time seen from below, distorted and titanic, peering up through a strangling jungle of blackberry vines. Not bad. But it needed something. Maybe a spiderweb in the foreground.

Another yawn stretched open his stubbly face. He'd get another look at the bridge that afternoon when he took Bobo for his walk.

He went upstairs and sat down at the newspaper-covered dining room table. Joe had finances on his mind. He wasn't getting enough jobs. No one knew him in Seattle yet. He couldn't fall behind any farther on the rent — he was one month behind, already. There was only one solution. He had to find a renter to share the house.

Yesterday afternoon he had placed a house-to-share notice in the Student Housing Office on campus. He was now carefully wording ads to place in *The Weekly, The Stranger, The Seattle Gay News*. Somewhere out there was the right roommate who would help Joe get back on sound financial footing. He made a couple half-hearted attempts to put together the right combination of abbreviations and coded comments to lure a good tenant. He put down his pen. Words didn't always come easily to Joe. His brain was too tired to describe the advantages of paying five hundred dollars a month to share his house.

He got up from the table in a bound and grabbed his jacket out of the front closet. Time to take Bobo on his walk. Time to rake up maple leaves on the walkway. Time to sweep the front stairs. But not even the fresh air of a brisk October morning could revive him.

"Face it, I'm dead," he muttered. "I'm a walking corpse. Until I get some sleep, I'm going to be useless."

Back inside the house, he dropped his jacket on the sofa, kicked off his shoes, stretched out on his green settee in the living room and closed his eyes for just a minute—

*

He was crumpled on the ground.

It was dark and cold. He was outside in the night. Someone was pushing him, shoving him. Hands, rough, hauling hands, desperate hands. He was doubled over on the ground, helpless. His body was being forced down into someplace damp and rotting, into a stench-filled, crumbling hole. Thorns tore at him in the wet darkness. Vines crackled around him. The hands kept pushing him in deeper, pushing him down.

He tried to scream. Nothing came out.

A sobbing woman stood over him with a shovel. She rammed it down into the ground. Swish! Slash! The darkness rang with chilly metallic slicing sounds. Shovelfuls of wet earth were landing on top of him. He opened his mouth to scream. A load of mud splattered into his face, down his throat—

*

Joe woke with a shout.

The late afternoon sun was going down. He had slept the day away. He looked at his watch. Five o'clock! How could the day be gone already? He could hear Bobo pacing in the studio, anxious for his dinner.

Something in his mouth tasted funny. He moved his tongue around, smacked his lips, swallowed. What was that taste? Then he realized with a shudder what it was.

It was dirt. The taste of dirt in his mouth.

The phone jangled. He picked it up. "Hello."

Static.

Joe slammed down the receiver. He was shivering. It was scarcely back in its cradle when it rang again with a jolt.

He snatched it up. "What do you want?" he cried.

"Sorry to interrupt you," said Pepper. "I just wanted to ask what you were doing Saturday morning? Is this a bad time?"

# 7
# The Planting

Saturday morning came very early.

Pepper was standing on Joe's porch at ten minutes to nine, ringing his doorbell, already back from her morning run, dressed in her thermals and sweats, boots and gloves, her cheeks flushed from the chilly air, a thermos of hot coffee tucked under one arm, a bakery bag of croissants in her other hand. Repeated ringings finally succeeded in rousing him. Sleepy-eyed and unshaved, he squinted out the window of the front door as he opened it.

"You're early," he said, pulling his bathrobe closed, fumbling with the tie-cord.

"Look at you!" she said. "I thought you volunteered to help."

"Are you sure your watch is right?"

Pepper pointed up at the clock on his wall. "Your clock says the same thing mine does."

"I was hoping mine was wrong. Excuse me, while I pull myself together."

He disappeared into the bathroom, emerging shortly after smelling of toothpaste and suited up in an old sweatsuit. He tugged on a well-used pair of boots, gulped down a hot cup of Pepper's coffee, and followed it with two bites of croissant.

"Lead the way," he said bravely.

They hurried across the old wooden bridge, down the footpath into the ravine bottom and then back up the other side toward the picnicgrounds. The morning was cool and crisp.

"The Tree Stewards were given a grant," explained Pepper, striding along briskly. "That's how we can afford this planting. It's a four-hour volunteer work-party to fill in the gap in the tree line along the north bank. You look like you know how to steer a wheelbarrow and handle a shovel. We've got two trucks full of trees to plant."

"Two trucks full?" Joe tried not to think about the last time he had worked with a shovel and wheelbarrel. "Why not?" he said. "I've always wanted to plant a tree."

They arrived at the designated picnic shelter right on time. They managed to remain together for about the first twenty minutes, as other volunteers converged in twos and threes at the parking lot.

Suddenly Pepper was in one truck, Joe was in the other, and the two trucks were circling around the park toward the maintenance area, where potted alders, cedars, firs and vine maples were lined up in orderly rows, their roots contained in tight, black plastic buckets, waiting to be carted away to their destinations and planted.

Pepper joined in loading one truck with trees. Joe helped load the other. Pepper ended up working in the nearer planting zone, on the other side of the frothing, foot-high falls of Ravenna Creek. Joe got assigned to the other planting zone, the treeless thickets farther up the north bank, reached by a soggy trail composed of slippery planks.

Before he knew it, Joe found himself ankle-deep in mud, trying not to notice the stink of decomposing vegetation, arms aching, legs aching, slicing his shovel downward again and again into roots and stalks and rocks.

He dug five holes altogether that morning. The digging provoked unpleasant memories. He kept recalling his vivid afternoon nightmare, the digging in the wet, weedy ground, the sound of the shovel burying him, the taste of dirt in his mouth.

He worked hard, without taking a rest. He carried potted cedars and alders from the trucks up along the slippery planks to the tree gap they were re-planting. He transported buckets of wood-chips and mulch down the muddy banks to newly-planted cedar saplings. He helped secure and plant two vine maples.

Pausing a moment to catch his breath, he looked up to find Pepper smiling at him. "You win the Muddiest Volunteer award," she said. "If we take a group picture, you have to stand in front."

He wiped a fleck of mud off his eyebrow with the back of his hand. She burst into delighted laughter.

"You just smeared mud across your entire face," she said. "I'd give anything for a camera. No, wait, don't move. I'll wipe it off for you. Stand still."

She stepped forward to wipe off his face. Her foot wasn't securely placed, and slid out from under her.

He caught her in his arms, but lost his own balance. They went down together in a soggy splat. Both thoroughly muddied, they burst into shocked laughter, continuing to laugh as they struggled, slipping and sliding, to their feet, both of them mucky and soaked. Their peals of delight rang through the solemn trees of the ravine.

*

By that evening he could hardly move. He felt like he'd been hit by a truck. Every joint was locked in place. Every muscle ached. He had been digging holes in the mud for almost three hours. What had he expected?

His body wasn't the only thing that was out of shape. So was his heart. He was nervous and excited at the same time. He was genuinely enjoying the company of Pepper Merlino. He had actually made a friend.

He was rinsing out his muddy work clothes in the wash basin downstairs when something caused Joe to glance up at a shelf of Todd's old books that he hadn't been able to throw away. Now he skimmed over the titles. One caught his attention. He pulled it down. *After Death Experiences*. Todd had developed an obsession with things like white lights and bardos near the end. Joe took the old paperback with him when he went upstairs, set it by his armchair, and later that night started reading. He remembered it. He'd read parts of it before, during the last terrible months of Todd's life.

Memories of Todd resulted in the usual fears. He found himself tossing and turning in bed. What was this thing called death that he was moving toward? He tried to get it out of his mind, but death was all he could think about. Death controlled everything. Life-loving Todd was only an urn of black ashes now. How he longed to talk to Todd again, to hold him in his arms! But Todd wasn't there anymore to hold. He had crossed over.

# 8
# The Calling

Daylight Savings Time came to an end. The clocks rolled back, giving Pepper a last few mornings bright enough for early jogging before winter darkness made the park too dangerous. Every morning now her ravine runs took her through a dim, black-and-white world of leafy grays of every shade.

That morning she was alone. The only sounds were the crunch of her footfalls, the steady puff of her breath. A squirrel rattled through the ferns. A couple of crows commented bitterly on her passing. She came to the end of her run at the three silt pools, walked to the little falls and back to cool down. She had started up the footpath between the two bridges when she saw a man down in the wild end of the ravine.

At first all she saw was his back. Someone in shirtsleeves and suspenders had waded into the boggy undergrowth, had splashed through the shallow creek out to the very place where Billy had caught his foot. Now he was simply standing there, staring down at the log like a psycho in some kind of trance.

She had almost escaped to the top of the ravine when a rock slipped out from under her foot. It tumbled noisily down the bank. The man looked up suddenly. It was Joe.

*

He'd been on the back porch taking out the trash, in the blur that preceded his first cup of coffee, grumpy from lack of sleep. He only intended to be outside long enough to empty the trash cans. The cry from the ravine made him freeze, startled him out of his sleepy reverie. People were perpetually calling their dogs there. This wasn't one of those calls.

Joe listened and heard it again. No doubt what that was. It was a man shouting in fear.

He dropped the recycling bin and started to run. The cry seemed to come from below the bridge, from the branch of the ravine that twisted by the back of his house. From the place where Billy's foot got stuck.

He dashed recklessly down the path between the bridges, down through the trees toward the three silt pools. Past the cement water trough green with moss, he lunged into the unpredictable wetland thick with bamboo.

The cry again. A muffled shout of unmistakable terror.

With both shoes quickly soaked, he went sloshing, splashing, trampling forward. He passed under the wooden stays of the old bridge into the side-ravine, pathless and overgrown. He splattered up the shallow tributary of Ravenna Creek. He clambered over a fallen tree.

And there it was. Ahead of him, tipped over onto the rocky bed of the creek — the dead maple trunk, mantled in a thick net of morning glory. He drew closer and saw the place where the boy's foot had broken away a swathe of rotten bark.

That old vine-strangled log! The sound seemed to come from near there—

He paused. For a moment he thought he heard footsteps. He was tense, ready to defend himself, ready to strike out at any threat. No one in sight.

The crunch of a footstep, much closer.

The crackle and snap of a rock bounding toward him. He turned to face whoever it was.

*

"Joe, are you okay?"

"Huh?" He snapped out of it. "Oh, it's you. Sure, I'm fine."

"You don't look fine." He looked completely disoriented, his glance darting nervously in all directions, pant legs muddy, fingers knotting into nervous fists at his sides. She stopped several feet away, on a last tentative foothold of dry land, regarding him. "You don't think it's a little chilly for no jacket?"

He shivered, and seemed to realize for the first time that he had no coat. He scratched the short bristle of his hair. "Guess you're right. Colder than I thought."

"Can you tell me what anyone in his right mind is doing down here staring at weeds at this hour of the morning?" She didn't give him time to answer. Pepper couldn't help noticing the pallor of his face. "Hey, what's wrong?"

"I thought I heard something."

"Something bad?"

"You didn't hear it, then?" said Joe. He seemed to be in a fog, confused, embarrassed. "Somebody shouting. I heard it from my back porch. Sounded like somebody seriously needed help. It seemed like it was coming from down here."

"I didn't hear anything," admitted Pepper. "I was just heading home from my run."

"Some guy was shouting like he was really in trouble."

They waited together, turning around to look in all directions, listening, until they were both shivering in the morning chill.

"Must have been kids," said Joe. "Just seems a little early in the day for pranks. Well, nice running into you." He looked to the side of her face, avoiding her eyes in embarrassment. "You must think I'm a pretty strange character."

"You *are* a pretty strange character," she said. "No doubt about it. That's why I like you."

They laughed together.

"Wait a second!" she said, stopping him mid-laugh. He was closer now, and she startled him with a finger poking him in the chest. "That's it! You're the answer."

"I don't know what you're talking about."

"Listen, I have a really big favor to ask you. I know we don't really know each other that well, but — well, to put it to you bluntly, would you be my date to my cousin's wedding?"

"Your what?"

"My escort. It's the Sunday before Halloween. Yes! You're the obvious choice. We'll have a ball."

"Whoa. A wedding? I don't think so—"

"I'm dead serious. Look, I've got to show up. Bad enough my mother isn't going."

"Not going to your cousin's wedding?" repeated Joe. "I thought all Italian mothers loved weddings."

"Not my mother," said Pepper. "She acts like marriage is a form of suicide. But I can't show up at an Italian wedding alone — it's out of the question. I need a date-for-hire, and you're the guy. We go for the church service, we stay long enough to have one drink at the reception, one bite of the wedding cake, and we're out of there."

"Well, I suppose — I guess I don't mind—" Joe fumbled awkwardly. Then he smiled decisively, reached out and shook her hand. "That means yes, I'd love to."


# 9
## "Ave Maria"

He knew it would be a big Italian wedding, and he was ready for that. He had only one suit, but it was a nice Italian one with a vest. He looked like a dashing, prosperous young Mafioso. Pepper looked ravishing, her body hugged in a stylish, low-cut sky-blue dress.

They drove in his black van (which he washed for the occasion) to Our Lady of the Lake, a big, modern Catholic church in the neighboring district of Wedgwood. The parking lot was packed. He managed to squeeze into a spot over against the cyclone fence. Dodging a few drops of rain, Joe accompanied her into the church like a lovesick admirer, her arm tucked into his, his head tilted sensitively toward her, escorting her from relative to relative, poised, confident, always the gentleman.

As an Italian, he knew exactly what was expected of him, the appropriate courtesies, appropriate humor, and he laid them on at the right time. Many a mother beamed at him approvingly as he followed Pepper into a pew near the back of the church to wait for the service to begin. He was prepared for it all, and he would have passed the test with flying colors.

He just didn't know someone would sing "Ave Maria."

As her cousin prepared, on the arm of her father, to walk regally in her long white gown down the center aisle toward the altar, Pepper turned to Joe and noticed tears streaming silently down his cheeks. "Joe, what's wrong?" she whispered urgently. He couldn't speak.

She helped him out of the pew and, as the wedding procession began, the two of them hurried down the side aisle, out of the church into the bright, cold light of the October morning.

"Are you okay, Joe?"

He nodded. She walked him to the van, got him inside. She sat down beside him on the bench seat and quietly waited. In a moment, he sniffed, hastily wiped his cheeks with the back of his sleeve, and laughed at himself. "That song! It has such an effect on me."

"So I noticed."

"Associations." His smile, a brave attempt, faded. "It reminds me of someone. But you don't need to know all this."

"What are friends for?"

"I guess I need to talk about it." He clenched his hands together into a knot of fingers. "The last time I heard 'Ave Maria' I was in Chicago, down on my knees in Holy Name Cathedral—"

\*

His lover of seven years, Todd Downey, had died in 1991 while the horrified world was looking the other way, watching the bombing of Baghdad in the Gulf War.

By that time, Todd's long dying had left Joe in financial disaster. He was late on mortgage payments, in debt up to his ears, his credit cards maxed, his savings exhausted.

Todd had been an early subject of AZT-testing. He'd been mega-dosed. Then came the fainting spells, the dropping T-cell count, the loss of vision, the loss of forty pounds. During the last two weeks of Todd's diminishing life, he had been so hurt and angry and scared at what was happening to him that he had refused to speak another word to anyone, not even to Joe.

His last sight of Todd had been of him lying in the hospital room drenched with sweat, hyperventilating, morphine dripping into his arm. After fighting for so long to keep him alive, Joe couldn't stand there watching Todd lose the fight. Unable to talk, unable to break down and cry, Joe ran out of the hospital, threw himself into his van, and began driving around the streets of Chicago like a madman.

He ended up in Holy Name Cathedral.

The floral shop where Todd once worked had been two doors away from Joe's studio. Both florist and studio were directly across the street from the cathedral. It was there, outside the cathedral, where they had first met, on that intersection where it all began. Something had steered Joe back there, convinced him that Holy Name Cathedral was where he needed to be.

He dropped into a pew. Making the sign of the cross for the first time in a decade, he was trying to remember the words to a few prayers when the organ filled the cathedral with resonating warm-up chords. A woman singer was rehearsing for an upcoming wedding.

She stood at the podium in blue jeans and a sweatshirt and sang Schubert's 'Ave Maria,' one of Todd's favorite pieces. Joe broke down crying. He knew at that moment that Todd was dead.

"She was just warming up her voice in an empty church," said Joe. "She didn't realize she was giving a command performance. One last love song for Todd and me."

\*

Pepper and Joe sat in the van outside the church for some time after he'd finished, alone together in the middle of the crowded parking lot. The sound of rain beating on the windshield made them feel isolated and private. The windows of the van were steamed.

"Let's face it, I should be gone by now. But for some reason, my system won't close down. Who knows why? Who knows for how long?"

He sighed, gave a funny, half-hearted smile. "I can remember the words of the caregiver who came to the house in Chicago every week to check on Todd. She took me aside one day just as she was saying goodbye. She was a tough old girl. I guess you'd have to be, to do what she did.

"'You realize Todd is dying,' she said. 'There's nothing you can do about that. But what about you, Joe? Who's going to take care of you? That's your job now. Start doing it.'

"So that's what I'm doing. Taking care of myself. One day at a time. Some days are better than others. This is one of the others." He wiped the back of his knuckles across his wet cheeks. "Thanks for listening."

"And no one since Todd?"

"I'm afraid I lost interest. Didn't feel there was enough time left to start up anything meaningful. How about you? The guys must be lined up at your door."

"The line is pretty short."

"Hard to believe," said Joe.

She smiled back at him. "I've had my share of boyfriends. A lover or two. I'm the one who always screws it up. I end up feeling caged in. As soon as Mr Right starts telling me what to do, he turns into Mr Wrong and I'm out of there. Some guys think they can own you."

"Sounds like you've been meeting the wrong guys."

"It's a family tradition. Merlino women always choose the wrong men. My Grandma was miserable. My mother was miserable. I'm not real eager to be miserable too. That's why I like being with you. I don't feel like you're busy tying ropes around me while we talk. I feel I can trust you."

"I'm glad." He took her hand and squeezed it. "I really needed a friend like you. Someone who could understand me. I was downright lonely here in Seattle until you came along."

"And you unleashed your dog on me."

They laughed together, comfortably.

"I feel so close to you," she said. "I needed a friend, too."

"I'm beginning to like Seattle more and more."

Neither of them intended to end up in each other's arms.

While all the other wedding guests poured out of the church and hurried through the rain toward the brightly-lit doorway downstairs, Joe and Pepper remained out in the van, clinging to each other as though if they didn't hang on tightly enough, they might lose everything that mattered.

Pepper eased away first, glancing toward the door of the crowded reception hall, spotting aunts and uncles and cousins. "We should probably go in. I think they're all downstairs now. Are you up for this?"

"I'm ready when you are," said Joe. He got out of the van and came around to open her door, smiling in the rain. "We've got an appearance to make."

He offered her his arm. Together they set off running through the downpour toward the church.

# CHAPTER FIVE

# Halloween Night

## 1
## Check-Out

Friday nights were always busy at QFC. That Friday night happened to be Halloween, which made everything a little worse.

Intermixed with all the other people waiting in line at the check-out counters, amid the perms and buzzcuts, knitted sweaters, business suits, denim jackets, designer overcoats, hardhats and backpacks, were now a haggard witch in black, a bloody-chinned vampire in a sweeping cape, and Darth Vader. They had all converged there just at twilight to buy a last forgotten item before indulging in their unspeakable rites.

Joe was standing in the middle of the crowd. He had been trying to deny a tickle in his throat all day. He kept clearing his throat, again, again. Now the actual coughing had started. He had it. The annual fall flu had thoroughly infected the city. Joe had to be more careful than most. For Joe, getting sick was a little more dangerous.

"Order out on four," said the intercom voice.

"Price check on six!" called a cashier down the row.

The line toward the cash register inched forward. Joe stood there patiently, waiting to buy a bottle of Vitamin C tablets, a bottle of zinc tablets, a carton of orange juice, a bottle of apple juice, a bunch of grapes, and a can of chicken soup. All around him rasped the coughs, sneezes, sniffles and throat-clearings of the flu's current legion of devotees.

Then he noticed, cashiering at the head of the next line, Pepper's mother. Her jet black hair was slightly mussed. She looked vaguely uncomfortable, as though she were wearing somebody else's uniform. For some reason, Pepper never invited him into the house, seemed to make a point of keeping him away from her, never wanted to introduce him.

Joe stepped out of place, carrying his fruits and medicines to the end of the next line. He watched her dealing with each of her customers, always polite, always guarded. When his turn at the counter arrived, Pepper's mother spoke without looking at him.

"Hello, there," she said automatically. "What kind of bag for you today?" She didn't appear to recognize him.

"Paper with handles." Joe cleared his throat, leaned forward. "Excuse me," he said awkwardly, "I'd like to introduce myself. I'm a friend of your daughter's. I'm your neighbor, Joe Strozza."

She stopped moving his grapes out of the basket to the scale on the counter. She stared at him, assessing him. "Oh, yes. My daughter's mentioned you." She extended her hand to him warily across the check-out counter, allowing him to shake it. "Rose Merlino."

He shook it, cleared his throat again, sniffed his runny nose. "Sorry. I'm catching something. I just wanted to tell you how sorry I am—"

She cut him off. "Oh, yes, we're all sorry. Of course, you're sorry." She almost sounded sarcastic. "But sorry won't do anyone any good, will it? Sorry doesn't get us anywhere. So let's not be sorry."

She moved Joe's medicines quickly over the price-scanner.

He coughed, sniffed. "I didn't mean to offend—"

"You don't offend," she said, with an insincere smile, quickly and mechanically bagging his purchases. "Not at all. You're very charming. And much too sick to be out of bed. Which is where you ought to be. Now, how would you like to pay?"

She took his two crisp bills without another glance at him, counting back his change, handing him his receipt, thanking him. Joe didn't leave the head of the check-out line. He coughed.

When she saw him still standing there, she turned and faced him. "Let me give you some advice, since you seem to be interested in my daughter. First, she's too young for you."

"I'm not interested in Pepper. She and I—"

"Second," she said, overriding his objection, "that girl has got such a hard head, she's gonna make some man in this world truly miserable. If I were you, I'd be running in the other direction. Now, would you like some help getting your groceries out to the car?"

"No, no, there are so few—"

"Then have a good day." She turned away from him abruptly to face the woman behind him, pulling forward her loaded shopping-cart.

## 2
## What Mrs Hayashi Saw

Pepper was striding down the sidewalk, backpack straps cutting into her shoulder-blades, eyes tired from studying long hours in Bloedel Library, looking ahead toward the trees at the end of the street on the edge of the ravine. That was why she didn't see the old woman standing in the shadow of the two dark maples. She flinched when she noticed her. Old Mrs Hayashi, alone in her front yard, scarcely moved. Her thin lips formed a subtle smile. She wore her pale blue housecoat and matching slippers. Instead of a knife and a dripping bag of watercress, as Pepper had seen her last, this time she cradled a teacup in her hands.

"Hello," said Pepper. Mrs Hayashi had lived in the neighborhood almost as long as the Merlinos. Her deceased husband had been a gardener for most of the houses on the street.

The old woman didn't echo Pepper's greeting. Instead she said carefully, "Your grandmother, the one who died, she had a brother?"

Pepper was taken aback. "Uncle Gabriel," she faltered. Her jeans and blouse were wrinkled from a day crunched over books in the library. She was anxious to get home and change into something more comfortable, but first she needed to assure herself that her neighbor was fine. Mrs Hayashi seemed a little lost, preoccupied. "He disappeared without a clue. Never came back. Pretty safe to assume he's dead."

Mrs Hayashi nodded, unconvinced.

Pepper couldn't decipher what the old woman was thinking. She hadn't expected her to reply, much less to say anything as startling as, "I saw him, the brother, in the early morning, very early, down under the bridge."

Pepper was thoroughly puzzled. "Under the bridge — you saw who? Are you talking about Gabriel Merlino?"

Her frail neighbor nodded. "Yes, him. Very interested in something."

"You don't say?" Pepper was very interested, too. What could possibly draw a great-uncle who was supposed to be dead down under the bridge early in the morning? Her imagination was running in circles. "What was he doing?"

"Looking at the big tree," said Mrs Hayashi, "the one that fell down."

Pepper smiled. "A lot of big trees have fallen in this park. Can you show me? Can we see it from here?"

Instead of answering, Mrs Hayashi turned and proceeded through the front door, leading Pepper inside, past a small shrine, up the staircase, and down a narrow, shadowy hall lined with teacups in cabinets with leaded glass doors, into a dark room fragrant with incense. She set down her teacup, put on her wire-rimmed glasses, scowled out through the glass of the window, then pointed. "That one."

"I see," said Pepper. "Now I understand. That wasn't Uncle Gabriel. That was our neighbor, Joe."

"No, it was the brother."

"You're mistaken, I'm afraid."

Shadows lengthened across the floor.

"Your grandmother's brother ran away," said Mrs Hayashi quietly, staring out the window. "But he came back."

"I don't think so," said Pepper.

"He came back," said the old woman firmly, stubbornly. "I saw him."

That got Pepper's attention. "What exactly are you saying?"

"Many years ago. When I was getting watercress. He was down in the ravine, all shabby and dirty, looking up at the house."

"Looking up at his own house?" repeated Pepper incredulously. Why would her great-uncle be shabby and dirty, if he had a whole house to inherit? That didn't make any sense. "It must have been someone else. Perhaps you're mixed up."

104

"Mixed up!" said Mrs Hayashi, with a mild snort of exasperation. "I am not so old and foolish. I know what I'm telling you. The old woman's brother. He came back."

"Well, you must be talking about Grandma's brother, but he's the one who didn't come back," said Pepper. "So even in those days you were after the watercress?" She could tell the conversation had come to a brick wall. Time to change the subject. "I shudder to think how many years you've been creeping down into the ravine and taking a chance on breaking your leg." Pepper paused, considering. "That old tree you mentioned, the one that's fallen across the creek down there. That's where the boy got his foot stuck. Is there any watercress there?"

"Never go there."

"Why not?"

"Once I tried to get watercress there. Your grandmother, she yelled at me. Oh, what a temper! She told me to stay away. Never come there, never! So I stay away."

"She did, did she?" Suddenly Pepper had much more to think about. Why had her Grandma been so anxious to keep people away from the wild end of the ravine?

# 3
## "I Met Your Boyfriend Today"

Rose worked till nine, then closed off her check-out line, counted her till, and turned it in at the front desk. Five minutes later she had her coat on and was quickstepping through the bakery and out the door, across the vast, wet blackness of the University Village parking lot.

She walked north up 25th Avenue toward the park and her house, sucking in the cold night air as though it were a refreshing drink, trying to relax, to not get a headache. A demanding day had been topped by the unpleasant appearance of her daughter's new male interest.

Rose unlocked the front door with a thrust of the key. At last, an escape from all those people, all their needs, all their demands. She strode into the kitchen, broke a banana off the bunch in the fruitbowl, quickly and neatly skinned it, and flung the peeling down into the garbage under the sink. She had just popped one end of the banana into her mouth when she was startled by a face looking in through the kitchen window.

With a cry, Rose dropped the remains of the banana and strode across the kitchen up to the window glass.

No one was there.

She sighed, and put her hand over her heart, as though to slow it down again. The surge of courage drained out of her, leaving her nervous, strained. She picked up the banana, threw it away. Then Rose pulled open the dish towel drawer, reached back behind the towels for the small flask of vodka hidden there, and took a long swallow. She hid the bottle again, rinsed her mouth with tap water and settled into gloomy brooding, sitting in her armchair by the window, looking down into the leafy darkness of the ravine.

No longer would she be called upstairs by her mother's million needs. She had finished taking care of her mother forever. Not that she was through worrying. Now, instead of her mother, she would be worrying about her daughter, Pepper, who was much too smart for her own good.

She heard the front door close. "Is that you?"

"It's me."

She waited for the footsteps to make their way through the house and become her daughter standing in the doorway. "Hi, sweetheart. How'd your day go?"

"Fine." Pepper entered the kitchen, red-cheeked, windblown, shrugging out of the straps of her book-heavy backpack.

"I met your boyfriend today."

Pepper froze, scowling in puzzlement. "My what? Who are you talking about?"

Rose was mildly amused by the look of alarm in her daughter's eyes. "You know who I mean. Your new love interest."

Pepper's face darkened "I don't know what you're talking about, Mother. I'm not in love with anyone."

"You're in love with our attractive Italian neighbor. Joe What's His Name."

"Love?" Pepper was shocked by the very idea. She sighed in exasperation. "You've been watching too many soap operas. He's hardly my type."

"Not your what?" repeated her mother. "And what is your type? As far as I can see, you're attracted to no one."

"Mother, what a thing to say!"

"Why not just admit you're totally unromantic?"

"That's so unfair! Well, you ought to know about romance. You picked my father."

"I know too well. And I know you're a Merlino woman. We have a terrible history of choosing the wrong men."

"What are you trying to say, Mother?"

"I'm just saying what I'm saying," said Rose, shrugging her shoulders. "No need to get snappy."

"Just don't start in on men again."

"You'll learn what men are worth in your own good time. All I said was that I met your new boyfriend. He came through my line." She smiled, and watched her daughter's face. "He wasn't doing well. He looked sick to me."

# 4
## Jack O'Lantern Light

The flu struck him down before nightfall.

His throat thickened with phlegm. Body-rattling coughs shook through him. He started swallowing handfuls of Vitamin C tablets, but he was already sinking into the worst of it. Joe managed to pop out his contact lenses, get under the covers, turn up his electric blankct. He quickly became a sweating, shivering mess.

Falling asleep only made things worse.

*

He was somewhere down in the ravine. It was too dark to see exactly where. It was night. He shouldn't have been there, would never have dared to go there that late. He had to get out of there immediately. But at least no one else was anywhere in sight. He was alone with the icy hiss of the wind through the bare, brittle twigs.

He heard crackling.

Something was crawling through the underbrush. It sounded heavy, at least the size of a big dog. He heard gasps for air, panting breath. Whatever was making the noise, the dragging crawl was getting louder, slowly making its way toward him. He was afraid to budge, afraid to cause the slightest sound. He strained his ears, trying to hear which direction it was coming from—

A hand thrust out of the mud and gripped his ankle.

\*

Joe woke with a gasp. It was dark in his bedroom, with only the window-curtains lit by the nearby streetlamp. It was sometime in the middle of the night. He was drenched in sweat, his blankets in knotted turmoil. He was very, very sick. He was utterly alone.

Breathing was almost impossible through his stuffy nose and throat. The difficult task of sucking air into his lungs began to absorb more and more of his attention. He began wheezing. His skin turned cold all over. Being sick made Joe scared. His body might not be strong enough to fight it off. He always expected it to be the last time.

The walls of his bedroom were shuddering. Was something wrong with the streetlamp? Was something wrong with his eyes? Had he accidentally overdosed on cough medicine? Had he mixed unmixable flu remedies?

He rose shakily from his bed and walked toward the pulsing light that was rippling through the curtains. He drew aside a corner of the curtain and looked. A big carved Halloween pumpkin squatted on the neighbor's back porch, hollowed-out eyes flickering. It grinned toothily at him, making the walls shiver with jack o'lantern light. So that's what it was. He returned to his bed, burrowed back into the warm covers, and turned toward the shuddering curtained window.

Someone was looking in.

The curtain blew away long enough for Joe to glimpse the man outside in the shadows, a disturbing young man with night-black hair and black, defiant eyes — eyes that were filled with tears of rage.

Joe cried out.

The curtain blew across the window.

When he looked again, no one was there. He sank back onto his damp pillow, weak, exhausted.

*

He had almost fallen asleep when he was startled by knocking on the front door.

Joe looked up, trying to focus his eyes, to see across the bedroom. What time could it be? The clock seemed too far away. The lamp was out of reach. His throat was so thick with phlegm he could hardly breathe. Who would come knocking at this hour? Joe struggled to sit up in bed. Was he so sick he was hallucinating?

More knocking.

But it wasn't coming from the front door. Now it came from the kitchen. He rose up onto unsteady legs. Clutching his bathrobe around him, trying not to shiver, Joe shuffled down the hallway. The moment his feet touched the cold linoleum floor he stopped, looking across the kitchen at the back door.

The doorknob turned.

Joe stared speechlessly.

The door swung open. He hadn't locked it! A figure stepped into the room, with a bulging bag. The moment the figure saw him, it gasped.

"Oh, you scared me!"

"I scared *you?* What are you doing in my house?"

"Trick or treat!"

"Pepper!"

She set down the shopping bag on the kitchen drainboard. "Hope I didn't startle you too badly."

Joe felt weak in the knees. "I can't hear you. My heart's pounding too loudly."

"Sorry. Mom told me how sick you were." Pepper closed the door behind her to keep out the cold. "I was afraid you might not have food."

He leaned against the doorframe. "How nice of you," was all he could manage to say. He was staring at her, as though uncertain whether she were real, clutching his bathrobe around him to keep warm. Then he added, "What time is it?"

"A little after nine. Have I come too late?"

"Only nine?" The long night seemed to be endless. "I feel like I've spent a week in this bed."

"Would you like me to heat up some soup? I brought some of my mother's minestrone."

"It sounds awesome. But not right now. It's so kind of you to bring me a care package. But one thing I don't understand. Since your mother saw me buying groceries, what convinced her I didn't have enough food?"

She smiled. "Italians always think you don't have enough food, silly. Coming here was my idea. I brought you food tonight because I couldn't get you out of my mind."

"Thanks." The word felt stupidly inadequate, but it was all he could think of to say.

She noticed he was shivering, his arms folded across his chest as though hoarding his body warmth. "You should be in bed. Come on, let's get you back where you belong." She escorted him down the hall, steering him by the elbow to his bedroom. When she drew back the covers and saw the bed soaked in sweat, she stopped him from getting into it. "Wait, you can't sleep in this. Where are some other sheets? I'll change your bed for you, nice and fast."

He pointed across the room. "Second shelf, on the left."

She deftly stripped the drenched sheets from the bed, and replaced them with dry ones. Before he could catch a chill, she tucked him quickly under the covers, then paused in the midst of changing his pillowslip, while punching his crumpled pillow back into life.

"Wait. Your eye — it still isn't better?"

"Not much."

"Stay still. Let me take a look." Pepper tipped his head to catch the light. She peered at the bloody corner of his eye. "What exactly did you do to it?"

"I'm not sure," said Joe. "I think some dust blew into my eye down in the ravine."

"Dust, huh? Not much dust in a wetland."

"You know what I think it was? When I pulled that kid out of the mud—" He didn't go on. She knew what day. "I think something got into my eye then. The two of us tromping and stomping around probably disturbed things that have been down in the ground who knows how long. Dirt and spores and bits of who-knows-what."

"It's the who-knows-what that gets you." She tucked the fresh pillow under his head, and snapped off his bedside lamp. "Gets you every time."

# 5
# What's True

It was all in the hands of God.

With a groan, Rose hauled herself up from her knees in front of the bedroom crucifix. She blew out her two prayer candles. She'd been praying more since Mama died. Her nerves were out of control. Prayers anchored her, calmed her, assured her that she was trying her best to be a good woman. That was all she could do, pray and try her best.

She crossed the hall into her mother's room, and looked out the window. He was still there, watching! Rose glared at the trick-or-treater standing on the bridge. She couldn't see much of him. He just stood there staring at her house. Probably one of those awful high school boys. They'd be sorry if they tried anything, Halloween or not. They would find her waiting and not in a forgiving mood.

The ravine was darkening. Halloween night — and nasty pranksters were prowling on every side. Parks drew them like magnets.

She turned away from the window, back toward the empty bed in the guest room. Her mother was no longer there, but the bed still didn't

111

feel empty. It felt like Carmen Merlino had just slipped away down the hall for a moment. How often near the end she had found her mother at the window, peering down through the trees at anyone who happened to linger on the bridge, anyone who dared to venture a step into the trackless tangle below.

"Don't let them bother you, Mama." She had said it over and over again, guiding her bewildered, upset mother back to the rumpled blankets she was trying to escape.

"Nosey pests," her mother would grumble. "Can't mind their own business. They'll regret it. You get into trouble when you don't mind your own business."

"Calm down, Mama. Don't let them worry you. They're just people in the park."

"It's not me I'm worried about," said the old woman. She had gripped her daughter's hand. "I'll be gone soon. I'm worried about you, Rosie."

"Mama, you don't have to—" She heard the door close downstairs. Suddenly her mother's fingers no longer gripped her hand. The bed was empty. The conversation was over. She was acting like a grief-stricken old lunatic talking to herself. "Pepper, is that you?"

"It's me, Mom." Pepper appeared at the top of the stairs, still bundled in her jacket.

"Where have you been at this hour?"

"I took some food over to Joe's since you said he was so sick. And he was! But I think your incredible minestrone will cure him. What were you doing up here?" She took another look into her mother's eyes, saw the pain. "Were you thinking about Grandma?"

"I never stop thinking about her." Rose turned away. Pepper reached out to hug her mother. Rose avoided her daughter's arms. "I was thinking I'd better get started going through all her papers."

"I'll help, if you want."

"Help?" It was the last thing Rose wanted, to have her daughter snooping through those old papers. "You can help if you want to, Pep, but I don't advise it. Much too boring. There are boxes and boxes. You know how Grandma hated to throw anything out."

Pepper hesitated. "Mom, why did you and Grandma always stop talking whenever I was around?"

Rose turned to face her in surprise. "What an odd thing to say! That's not true at all."

"It is true. Come on, Mom, I'm not mad about it. I just want to know. You two were always so full of secrets."

Rose embraced her daughter, squeezing her too tightly, holding on too long.

"Pepper, I'll tell you what's true," she said. "What's absolutely true is that I love you more than anything in the world." Her words should have reassured Pepper, but instead they only made her more anxious. Somehow they were desperate words. "All the room inside my heart right now is taken up by one person — Pepper Merlino. Now that Mama's gone, there's just you. You are my reason for being here. You are my world."

"Oh, Mom, come on, really." Pepper pulled free of her mother's arms. "That's the problem right there in a nutshell. You know that kind of talk isn't healthy."

Her mother stiffened. "Since when is a mother's love not healthy?"

"It's not the love part that's a problem," said Pepper, her feistiness aroused by her mother's tone. "It's building your life on another human being. That's a problem. You need more than me. It was bad enough while you were taking care of Grandma. You need a life of your own now. You can't just lock yourself up in this house, and expect me to be your social life."

Rose had allowed herself to be open about her feelings, to be vulnerable, to show her daughter how much she felt for her. The reprimand caused her temper to flare. "I don't expect anything!"

"You've got to get out of here once in a while," persisted Pepper. "Get away. You act like this house has swallowed you alive. You need to make friends."

Rose knew all about what life had to offer. She didn't need condescending tips from her daughter. "I have all the friends I need! Ask anyone at QFC. I'm one of the most popular checkers."

"Those are customers, Mom, not friends."

"I don't need *friends*." She pronounced the word with disdain. "I've got family, if I need anyone."

"Great!" encouraged Pepper. "Then go see your cousins. Go see your aunts. Give them a call once in a while."

"Why should I?" barked Rose contemptuously. "Why would I want relatives meddling in my business?"

"Well then," said Pepper, not giving up, "maybe you should try to meet someone. You know what a lot of people do, Mom? Have you ever thought about placing a Personals ad—"

"You, of all people," said her mother, a quivering edge to her voice, "giving me dating advice. Your love affairs are tragedies."

"Mother!" Pepper was stung.

"Well," said Rose defiantly, "look at you now! You're falling in love with a gay man—"

Pepper sputtered in indignation. "Mom, that's absolutely preposterous! I'm not falling in love with anyone."

"I've heard that before," said Rose, with a confident smile. "Must you always be the last one to figure it out?"

"Listen, Mom, I'll tell you the truth," said Pepper, taking a deep breath, scowling. "Yes, I admit he's an attractive man, but he's gay — I knew that from the get-go. I like being with him because we have fun together. He loves the ravine. He's honest. He makes me laugh. I'm not falling in love with anyone."

"You're not?" Rose smiled. "You should listen to yourself. Sounds to me like you've got it bad."

Pepper's face tightened. Did conversations with her Mom always have to turn into fights? "Forget I said anything. Don't date. Do what you like. Seal yourself up in this tomb. It's your life. But don't expect me to share the prison with you."

Rose's cheeks flushed. "Don't you dare call this house a prison. You're free to go anytime you like."

"Fine, I'll go. The sooner, the better." Pepper nearly stomped away, then impulsively turned. "But first I want to ask you something."

114

Rose blinked, re-evaluating her cautiously, as though Pepper had politely suggested slitting her throat. "Not now. I'm too angry."

Pepper politely ignored her refusal. "There's a boy who lives near here— "

"I'm not interested," said her mother bluntly.

"You know the boy I mean." Pepper was as stubborn as Rose. "He was in the park the day Grandma fell."

Rose concealed her feelings. "So were a lot of unfortunate people."

"Why do you think Grandma was so concerned about that poor boy?" asked Pepper boldly.

Rose's eyes flared with alarm. "I don't know what you're talking about." She didn't like being cornered. She practically bristled. "Take my advice," she said, in an even, steady voice. "Stay out of this."

"What is it you're not telling me?"

"I'm telling you to stay out of that ravine."

Pepper was becoming irritated. "You have no right to tell me to stay away from anywhere. Don't be ridiculous. I'll go down into that ravine any time I feel like it."

"I am not being ridiculous," said her mother. "Use your common sense. Why poke your nose into other people's business?"

"That ravine is my business," said Pepper, "and I intend to push my nose into it, as far as my nose will go."

"Be smart enough to take my advice," said Rose. "It's dangerous down under the bridge." Anger crackled in her voice, making it slightly too loud. "Sometimes homeless people sleep down there. Sometimes nasty high school boys do things down there. I see what they do. They're like animals." Pepper stormed downstairs. Rose tried not to call after her daughter. She couldn't stop herself. "People get hurt down there."

The closet door clattered. The front door slammed.

Rose stood as though she'd been turned to stone, but her body was trembling. She looked out Grandma's window. The trick-or-treater was gone. Or was he? She looked again, peering closely through the glass. Something was moving down in the ravine. Someone was creeping through the bamboo, slowly coming closer to the house.

Rose closed her eyes and prayed silently. She was determined not to give in to fear. As she was starting down the stairs from the second floor, she thought she heard the basement door close.

She listened. She was imagining things. Rose was completely alone in the house. It was time to go light her prayer candles. She would kneel in front of the crucifix on her bedroom wall. She would pray — pray for forgiveness, pray for understanding, pray for her daughter's love.

There, kneeling before the crucifix, was the only safe place in the house.

# 6
# Bamboo

Could old Mrs Hayashi be right? Had Uncle Gabriel returned?

What if he was lurking in the park at that very moment, keeping hidden for some reason of his own, intending some terrible revenge?

Maybe Joe had good reason to be afraid.

All she could think about were the clues. They were starting to fit together. She could glimpse a pattern vaguely, but not enough to understand.

Again and again her thoughts and suspicions returned to her mother. She knew her well enough to see through her. Mom was troubled by something. What did she know that she didn't want anyone else to know? Was Uncle Gabriel really back? Secretly in touch with her?

Pepper grabbed her overcoat out of the front closet. She made the decision so fast she hardly knew what she was doing. She slammed the front door. Before she went to bed that night, she would know a few more facts.

She went around to the back of the house, unlocked the garage door, and reached into the darkness until her hand closed around the light-string. A moment's blaze through the back window, and the garage was dark again. Pepper came out with a shovel, a flashlight, boots and gloves.

She pulled on the boots and gloves, started toward the footpath down the bank, and paused. Was she insane? After all, she would surely be violating Park Department codes, she'd be trespassing, commiting vandalism in the park after hours. Gripping the flashlight and shovel in her gloved hands, she walked to the end of the street, and on through the bushes and trees, toward the footpath leading down the bank. She was going to find out if there was something under that log.

The ravine was silent. Scarcely a rustle. Not a soul in sight.

Slowly Pepper made her way through the dark hush of the trees, shielding the flashlight beam, listening to each crunch of her feet. When she came to the cement trough of creek water, she headed upstream into the bamboo. The beam of light poked and darted. The bamboo stalks reached up over her head. They rustled and whispered in the night breeze.

She could see the light in her bedroom window looming over her. Pepper approached closer through the undergrowth, dodging the glistening spiderwebs. She looked up toward the outward thrust of the deck, jutting over the leafy depths. The deck was deserted. No sign of her mother, or anyone else.

Pepper crept closer, through the support beams under the bridge, past the dangling rope attached by neighborhood boys. She stepped carefully, relying more on her flashlight, placing her feet one by one on solid ground, so that she didn't sink too deeply into the leaf-thickened ooze. She thought she could see someone moving inside the house. She could see the overgrown maple trunk up ahead, fallen across the creek, where Billy's foot got stuck. Another couple steps, and she was there.

Aiming the beam at the log, she used rocks to brace the flashlight in place. Using both hands, she tugged at the log. The vines gripped it. She tried to drag the log sideways, but mud and rocks and its own sheer weight held it fast. Gripping the shovel, stepping into the damp ground lit by the flashlight's circle of light, she poked into the thick matting of leaves draped over it. A solid tangle of vines.

Pepper was so intent on what might be buried under the log that she failed to hear the crunching and crackling slowly approaching through the dead, brittle grass. When she consciously realized that the sound was not part of the wind through the bamboo, it was too late.

She reared up in time to glimpse someone stride toward her out of the bamboo stalks and kick aside the flashlight, which leaped and clattered into the darkness.

Pepper raised the shovel in self-defense. It was knocked out of her hands. She didn't linger long enough to glimpse his face. She had already bolted away, splashing through the underbrush, desperately heading back toward the wooden supports of the old bridge. Once she got that far, all she had to do was beat her way through the bamboo down to the main ravine trail. Something whirred past her in the darkness. A crackling, splintering crash. She realized her attacker was wielding some kind of weapon. Branches beside her exploded into snapping, broken fragments. Footsteps thudded behind her, with a heavy, huffing breath.

Pepper scrambled over the slippery, wet rocks in the creek bed, beat away the bamboo stalks leaning over her. She got lost in the bamboo, turned around, and for one terrible moment didn't know which direction she was running.

Not until her pursuer crashed through the bamboo and was almost upon her did Pepper realize that he was swinging a baseball bat. She held up one arm instinctually to ward off the blow, stumbling backward against a tree. The bat connected with a branch above her, which struck the side of her head.

The impact stunned her. She staggered.

Her head thundered with pain. The figure of a man loomed before her against the night sky. Tall bamboo stalks lashed in the wind behind him. A ripple of reflected streetlamp light edged the collar of a black leather jacket, as he swung the bat up again.

She tumbled backward, away from him, tripping over a twisted root underfoot, knocked off her feet.

*

No one heard old Mrs Hayashi shriek as she watched from her front window. She had been shocked enough when she first discovered Pepper's flashlight beam jiggling over the ivy-strangled rocks down below in the

*Bamboo*

ravine. And then to see her attacked — struck down brutally out of nowhere before her very eyes.

Mrs Hayashi called 9-1-1. She was scarcely coherent with fear. Then she pulled on her boots, tugged on her overcoat and left the house with a wail. She rushed to the end of the street, then proceeded recklessly slipping and scrambling down the footpath toward the shape lying face down in the wet rocks under the bridge.

Her attacker was nowhere in sight.

Mrs Hayashi was down there with Pepper when the entire neighborhood was awakened by the ambulance siren.

CHAPTER SIX

# November Secrets

## 1
## Not Real

"You are not to go over there," said Paul Beck, lowering the open Sunday newspaper and looking squarely at his son across the breakfast table, "and that's all there is to it, Billy. You don't know her well enough to be bothering them. It's none of your business. They've got enough to deal with — and so do you. Believe me, I know best."

He wasn't so sure he knew best. How he wished he did! In his T-shirt and sweats, Paul was trying to relax that Sunday morning and not doing a good job. He grabbed the newspaper and opened it to hide his face. He didn't want Billy to see how worried he was by what had happened to Pepper Merlino.

The ambulance siren wailing through the neighborhood that Friday night had awakened them. Mrs Skinner had stopped by Saturday afternoon as a concerned neighbor going from house to house to make sure everyone had seen the article in the newspaper. She told them all about it on the porch.

"The way I see it, that could have been any of us," said Wanda. "She was in the wrong place at the wrong time. We all need to be on the alert."

"The thing I don't understand," said Paul, "is what she was doing down in the ravine so late at night."

Mrs Skinner leaned closer, lowering her voice, but not so low that Billy couldn't hear. "They think he lured her down there. Or dragged her." She shuddered at the thought. "No one knows why he did it — or why he stopped." She showed them the article in *The Seattle Post-Intelligencer* that referred to the incident as "a particularly brutal Halloween prank." The twenty-seven-year-old UW graduate student was in good condition, hospitalized overnight to make sure she didn't have a minor concussion. A neighbor reported seeing a homeless man prowling about the ravine that night.

Paul waited until Wanda was far enough away, knocking on his next-door neighbor's door. "Billy," he asked in a casual voice, "do you see many homeless people down in the ravine?"

"No more than usual."

"Do you ever talk to them?" He spread strawberry jam on his toast. "Do they ever talk to you?"

"No," said Billy, spooning up the last of his Frosted Flakes. His Dad's questions were starting to scare him.

"Billy, I don't want you going down in the ravine for a while."

The boy stared at him in wide-eyed horror. "But, Dad—!"

"You heard me," said Paul sternly, lowering the newspaper with a trembling crackle. "It's not safe."

"But—" Billy rose from his chair, like a prisoner desperately pleading his case. "Dad, you've got to believe me. It's not a homeless man. It's the man in my nightmares. I know it's him!"

"Billy, the man in your nightmares doesn't exist," said Paul with forced patience. "There's no one lurking in the back yard. There's no one looking in the window. He may seem real in your dreams, but he's not real anywhere else. Trust me, mister, you're dealing with enough without scaring yourself by going to see this woman."

"But she's really nice, Dad, and he tried to hurt her."

"Right. Listen, I want you to stay away from the Merlino house. And out of the ravine!" He said the words with finality. The conversation was over. The misery in his son's face weakened him. "I care about you deeply, Billy. I want you to get better. What happened to her has nothing to do with your dreams." Paul tried to be calm and reasonable. He finished a last swallow of coffee. "Your Nightmare Man can't hurt you because he exists only in your imagination."

"But I see him—"

"You think you see him," said Paul sharply. "That's not the same thing. That's why I get upset, Billy. You can't seem to tell the difference between real and not real."

"I can tell the difference," said Billy with conviction. "Somebody really hit Pepper. That's real." He turned away and retreated sadly up the stairs to his room, his skinny shoulders slumped forward in defeat.

Paul let the newspaper slide from his hands, rattling down over his legs to the floor. He stared at his uneaten toast smeared with jam. His fingers gripped the edge of the kitchen table like claws.

His son. His precious son. He would not let anything jeopardize that boy. He had been careless with his wife. He had lost his wife. He would not lose his son.

## 2
## Lucky

She remembered opening her eyes to find Mrs Hayashi crouching beside her in the dark. She remembered being strapped to a stretcher making its bumpy way up a footpath out of the ravine, the same way her grandmother's body had been carted out six weeks before. She remembered hearing a police officer talking to the ambulance driver. "She was lucky," he said. "The branch got the worst of it."

The word that stayed with her was "lucky."

*

"It's true," said Joe. He was sitting beside her, still wearing his jacket, staying only a few minutes. "You *are* lucky." She was not in her bedroom, not in her bed. Had someone said it was Swedish Hospital? She tried to remember, while he told her how he had gone down where it happened, seen the shattered branch which the bat had struck instead of her head. Joe's cheeks were unshaved, his brown eyes sad with concern. His fingers knotted helplessly in front of him.

"You gotta wonder about guys like that," said Joe. "I mean, we're talking first-class psychopath. Why would you want to break open someone's head? Wonder why he stopped after just one whack."

"Sure glad he did," mumbled Pepper with effort.

*

"What did you say, sweetheart?" said Mom, bending over her. "I didn't hear you, Pep. You're glad what?" She adjusted her daughter's blankets around her shoulders, brushed back a lock of wayward hair.

Pepper opened her eyes at the sound of Mom's voice. Joe had vanished. She wasn't in the hospital anymore. She was home again. Only her mother was there, and the first sight of her mother's face shocked her. Her cheeks had sagged with wrinkles, her eyes had sunken deeper into her skull. She looked worse than she had when Grandma died. "You were saying something, honey. You were talking in your sleep."

Pepper blinked. "Where's Joe?"

"Joe? He visited you yesterday in the hospital. You're confused. You've been sleeping." Her mother adjusted the ice pack. The bedroom windows behind Rose were dark with afternoon rain. "It's the pain pills. They make you groggy. Lie back and rest."

"Have I been taking pain pills?" said Pepper. "No more pain pills, Mom. I've got studying to do."

"Nonsense!" scolded Rose. "You're in no condition—"

"I've got a nasty headache, that's all," said Pepper. "Aspirin will be fine. Headaches go away."

"I'm worried about more than headaches. God gave you back to me, but you've still got to go slow and easy—"

"Wrong, Mom. I'm going to class on Monday."

She acted brave, like nothing had happened, but headaches were the least of the after-effects. Her faith in other people had been destroyed. She would never trust people quite the same way again. What one person could do to her, others could do. She had experienced human nature at its worst. She knew now that evil was real. She had proof.

By Monday morning she was bravely, stubbornly striding across the courtyard of the Center for Urban Horticulture on her way to Isaacson Hall. Her hair covered the cut and the swelling on the side of her head. Nothing hinted that Pepper had been the victim of an attack other than a sad darkness in her eyes.

Not many noticed her eyes. She kept them turned away. The hardest thing was looking at people. To think that her attacker was walking around in the same world with her terrified Pepper. She had never seen his face. She wouldn't know if she were standing in the same room with him.

She tried to walk into the graduate student room quickly and casually, the same as she always did.

"Pepper, we heard. How awful!" cried Madeline Wong, rising from behind her computer screen and hurrying toward her. Maddy was a fellow graduate student who studied at the desk beside Pepper's. "I can't believe you came back so soon. If someone attacked me and dragged me into the ravine, I'd be out for the quarter."

"I was lucky," mumbled Pepper.

"The newspaper didn't actually mention—" Maddy stepped closer to her, spoke under her breath, voice faltering with genuine concern. "Did he try to—?"

Pepper shook her head. "I was lucky."

# 3
## Memorabilia

On her way home that afternoon, Pepper noticed two policemen on horseback emerging from the mouth of the ravine at the end of the soccer field. Before she got to the corner, she spotted a policeman on a bicycle zipping down from the field house. A blue-and-white squad car came slowly rumbling past the children's slide and swings.

Pepper shuddered. The perpetrator was still out there somewhere. She was constantly on guard. Would she know him if she saw him? Would some instinct warn her? She wasn't sure.

She scooped the mail out of the Merlino mailbox on the post where the street dead-ended, then trotted up the stairs to the front door and let herself in. The house was silent.

"Mom?"

No answer.

She was thirsty, and headed straight down the hall to the kitchen. She noticed one of the letters was addressed to her. She looked to see who it was from and stopped dead in her tracks, halfway across the linoleum floor. With trembling fingers she ripped open the envelope and stood reading the letter, in shock.

She had been accepted into the doctoral program of the College of Forestry at Oregon State University in Corvallis. The acceptance letter was late arriving due to a cancellation. It offered a partial scholarship for tuition and a position as a teaching assistant, with a far lower stipend than she'd expected, but it was a real offer. It was a new life waiting to be snatched up and accepted. She had been slapped in the face with an actual decision — the choice of really leaving Seattle.

She went up to her room, unloaded her textbook-jammed backpack, changed into more comfortable clothes. She hardly knew what to do with herself. She couldn't think straight. Leave Seattle? Move to Corvallis? To distract herself, she decided to channel some of her nervous energy into cleaning up Grandma's clutter of letters, souvenirs, and memorabilia. She'd surprise her mother. The last thing Mom expected would be to find Pepper helping her take care of a thankless task.

She stepped out of her bedroom and heard a floorboard creak down the hall.

"Mom?"

No answer.

Pepper stepped into the hallway, flicked on the lights, and headed straight for her mother's room. "Hey, Mom, I thought I'd start cleaning out Grandma's—"

Her mother wasn't there. She looked in her grandmother's old room, her footsteps echoing hollowly across the wooden floor. Not there, either.

Grandma's bedroom was a guest room now. All her things had been crammed into the large closet. Time to dive in and get started! Lugging cardboard boxes out into the middle of the room, she sat down on the floor, her back to the neatly-made, lifeless bed, and set to work sorting through yellowing Christmas cards, bundles of letters, and other long-saved treasures.

She was glancing through a rubber-banded collection of old photographs when one caught her eye, making her set aside the rest.

It was a photo dated 1958 of her grandmother as an attractive woman in her thirties, standing in front of a bloom-covered rhododendron in the back yard. Beside pretty Carmen Merlino, his arm tight around Grandma's waist, drawing her toward him, grinning mischievously, was a handsome young man. Carmen's smile was forced. She looked uncomfortable. Clinging to the other side of the young man was a little girl whom Pepper immediately recognized as her mother, smiling radiantly, the happiest little girl in the world, looking up at the young man with worshipful eyes.

"Uncle Gabriel—" she whispered.

"The devil himself!" said her mother behind her.

Pepper leaped to her feet, heart pounding. "Mother, you scared me half to death."

"Sorry," said Rose, standing in the bedroom doorway. "I thought you heard me." Her poor mother was a wreck. Wrinkles of fear had been carved into her face. She had a blank, preoccupied stare.

"Where were you, Mom?" said Pepper, giving her a peck on the cheek. "You didn't answer."

"I was down in the basement. I didn't hear you."

She snatched the picture out of Pepper's hand and ripped it in half, tearing Uncle Gabriel down the middle.

"The devil himself, eh?" echoed Pepper. "What a great-looker. Bet he drove the girls crazy."

Rose did not look amused. "The most charming man I've ever known." Her voice was reduced to a weak whisper. "Oh, how he could cast a spell!" She tore the photo into shreds and sprinkled the glossy confetti onto the hardwood floor at her feet.

"Mom, what's wrong?"

She was staring down at the ripped shreds of glossy photo. "Selfish as a cat! So pleased with himself you could practically hear him purring. He used to babysit me while Mama was at work. He used to get me laughing." She started to smile, remembering. "I think when I was little I was in love with him." The smile died halfway across her face. "I thought I'd gotten rid of all those old pictures."

Pepper knew her mother well enough to see that she was just barely keeping her emotions under control. Something about Uncle Gabriel was making her come unglued. Pepper decided to risk her anger. "Why does he upset you so much. Mom?"

Rose looked up sharply, eyes bright with emotion. "Upset me? I used to adore him. Then he brought evil into my life."

Pepper touched her gently. "What do you mean?"

"Not what you think," said Rose. "Worse. He taught a ten-year-old girl how cruel and unfair the world could be."

"Mom, what did he do to you?"

"He took away my happiness. He changed me into what I am."

"What do you mean?"

"Your Uncle Gabriel destroyed everyone he touched. He destroyed Mama. And he destroyed me." She took a deep breath. "You should rest. You've had a terrible shock, and you're still recovering."

Rose turned and walked away down the hall, leaving Pepper with shredded bits of photo scattered at her feet.

# 4
# Eyes Open

Billy stood looking down over the railing of the old wooden pedestrian bridge. That was as close to the ravine as he was permitted to go.

School was over for the day and ordinarily he'd be down in the trees somewhere drawing, but suddenly everything was complicated and scary. No one was safe, not with that menacing man out there somewhere.

The boy's shoulders were hunched against the wind, hands stuffed deep in his parka pockets. The maple leaves around him were a riot of soggy color. He was no longer allowed to swing on the rope dangling underneath the bridge.

Arms folded on the green railing to make a prop for his chin, Billy stared down gloomily into the bamboo thicket, trying to understand how such awful things could happen. Billy's father didn't believe in God, but sometimes Billy wanted to try, especially times like now. How could God allow it? From beneath the bridge, a smashed and splattered pumpkin face grinned back up at him toothily, the victim of holiday frenzy. That broken pumpkin face seemed to know the answer to his question. Violence was the ugly secret of life. It was everywhere. There was no escape.

He didn't notice the footsteps crossing the trestles. He didn't look up as Pepper approached him from behind.

"You shouldn't be out here alone."

He spun around. "Oh, it's you," he faltered. "Hi."

Pepper stopped beside him, admiring the view, her backpack strapped to her shoulders. "Dangerous place to be daydreaming."

"I wasn't daydreaming," he said defensively. "I was thinking. I'm okay. I'm safe. I keep my eyes open."

"Could have fooled me," said Pepper. She smiled at him. "Sometimes having your eyes open isn't enough. You didn't hear me coming, did you?"

He hadn't.

"As your concerned neighbor," she continued, "I advise you to be a little more careful. Especially after what happened to me down there. This isn't the safest place to be."

"I'll be careful," said Billy. He had an overwhelming need to make his fear specific. "Tell me — did you — did you see who did it?"

"It was too dark, too sudden," said Pepper. "Believe me, there's nothing I'd like to know more."

"Are you all right?" He couldn't hide a tremble in his voice. He was afraid to hear the answer.

"All right?" said Pepper. "Well, I'm not sure that's the word. It doesn't exactly describe having someone take a swing at you with a baseball bat. But it could have been worse. Which is why I want you to keep your eyes open. I don't want anything to happen to you."

# 5
# Questions

Pepper had just sunk down into an armchair and allowed her eyes to close — exhausted after a long day on campus, first in the laboratory and then in the greenhouse — when an unexpected rapping startled her to her feet.

She opened the door to find Wanda Skinner glowering in righteous indignation. "What an outrage against civil liberties!" she announced as she strode inside. "Makes me angry every time I think about it. What a contemptible act of sexual hate against women."

"Hi, Mrs Skinner," said Pepper.

"Wanda," she corrected. "I had to see how you were."

"Thanks," said Pepper. Her eyes closed, as though the mere sight of her neighbor exhausted her. "I'm fine."

"I won't tire you," said Wanda. "I just want you to know that not all of us are silly enough to believe what we read in the newspaper. What happened to you has nothing to do with any homeless man in the park. I happen to know that for a fact."

Pepper stared. "You do?"

"I was out on my deck the night it happened. Watching."

"Watching?" Pepper whispered with difficulty.

"I'm always watching," said Wanda. "I've lived in Ravenna Springs most of my life. I like to know what's going on in my neighborhood. In my desk by the window I keep a pair of binoculars. Some people call it spying. I call it watching. I've got a perfect view of your house."

Pepper's eyes widened. "You spy on us?"

"I watch. Just being a good neighbor, keeping an eye on things. I saw the lights in your house go off that night. But then I saw something funny. After all the lights were out, I saw a man come out of your house."

"A man — out of *our* house?"

"Yes, a man. Whoever it was didn't want to be seen. Whoever it was, I saw him rustling down there in the bamboo." Wanda put her hands on her hips, as though assuming a fighting position. "That was no home-less man who attacked you. That was no trick-or-treater. He came out of your own home."

"That's impossible! Are you saying a man was in our house that my mother and I didn't know about—?"

"A man *you* didn't know about," corrected Wanda.

Pepper blinked, digesting that. "Are you suggesting my mother knows who attacked me?"

"I'll tell you what I'm suggesting, dear." Wanda leaned closer to her. "Somebody's up to something. And someone knows about it." She clutched Pepper's hand. "I don't know who yet. Or what. But I'll tell you what I do know. As a concerned Seattle citizen, as a Ravenna Springs neighbor, I intend to find out."

# 6
## Seven Notebooks

"Sometimes I think the reason I came to Seattle," said Joe, "was to paint Ravenna Park." He had a sketchbook under his arm, a handful of charcoal pencils in his vest pocket, a camera slung around his neck.

He and Pepper were walking through the ravine, bumping shoulders, shuffling slowly along the main trail through the dark columns of trees. The bright, shallow waters of the creek rippled beside them. Jackets zipped to the collar, they were heading straight into a chilling, wet gale of wind that was tearing off the last of the maple leaves, flinging them crackling and tumbling at their feet.

"I saw the ravine the first time I came to Seattle," said Joe. "Made a huge impression. A slice of wilderness right in the middle of the city."

After almost thirty hours in bed over the weekend, Joe had shaken the worst of his flu. Other than a persistent cough and an occasional throat-clearing, he was back on his feet. "Years later in Chicago I couldn't get it out of my mind. I swore that I'd paint it before I died. And when I took the plunge and moved to Seattle, the first house-for-rent I looked at — well, I'm still living in it now, right on the edge of the ravine."

"Clearly where you belong," said Pepper.

"I've got seven notebooks filled with pencil sketches — enough for an entire series of oil paintings."

"I'd love to see them," said Pepper. "I bet I know every one of the places you sketched. Oil paintings, too?"

She could see at once that she had touched a wound. Joe was suddenly paying too much attention to the creek beside the trail. "Not yet," he admitted. "But I've got enough studies to create an entire show. I just haven't started painting yet. I can't decide on exactly the right style."

"The right style?" said Pepper. "That's holding you back? You know what my Grandma would say to that? You need a kick in the pants."

Joe burst out laughing. "Oh, is that Grandma's secret?" He was amused. "You think that would solve the problem?"

"I'll tell you how to solve the problem of style. Try one style, and if that doesn't work, try another style. The real problem is doing it. That's why I've come into your life, Joe. To kick you in the pants. It's a law of the universe — paintings do not exist until the artist paints them. So, show me the places. I want to see which ones you chose."

He led her from one site to another, from the high, graceful spans of the 20th Avenue bridge to the squat, massive arches of the 15th Avenue bridge. The grassy playground in front of the fieldhouse, with its tall Lombardi poplars. The red-barked cedars against the golden-leaved maples. The giant tangled root-wad of a tree tipped over in the creekbed.

"Paintings waiting to happen," he said.

"Don't wait. If you've got a gift, then give it. You never know how long you've got."

"Scary to think you could have been killed," said Joe. "I can't get that out of my mind. It shakes me up."

"You think it shakes *you* up," she said.

They laughed together nervously.

"Coming close to death changes you. Once I found out I was HIV-positive, I started giving up on long-term projects. Why bother to start what I couldn't finish? I thought a lot about suicide. Why not just end my career right now? One way or the other, it doesn't matter. You end it yourself or a virus does the work for you."

"Doesn't matter?" said Pepper. "Of course, it matters. How can you talk like that? Life matters more than anything."

"You think what we do in life is important?" said Joe skeptically. "I hope you're right." He hesitated on the trail. "Let's stop here."

A weathered log had been sawed down the middle and anchored flat-side-up as a bench. Wire fencing separated the bench from the nearby creek. The wires had been snarled and bent, stretched and ripped by irritated animal claws. The creek-bed was clogged with rippling green beds of watercress, edged by mossy boulders. The bench was overlooked by three tall, bony cedars. He saw the exact view he wanted. He photographed it from several angles. Then he sat down on the bench with Pepper beside him, and started sketching in the first bold lines.

He scowled at the shallow creek. "An artist could spend his whole lifetime trying to do water right."

"You're a perfectionist," said Pepper. "I'm an optimist. I've been one ever since I was a kid. I never recovered from Catholic School."

"Does anyone?" They chuckled together. He sketched in the large rocks obstructing the current in quick, jagged strokes. "You mean, you still have moral values? Beliefs?"

"Corny as it sounds," said Pepper. "I believe in the whole Good versus Evil thing. Not as an epic war. Not in the black-and-white way the nuns teach you. I mean real Goodness — as in compassion for other living beings."

"Goodness as in helping." Dark, emphatic lines suggested the towering cedars.

"That's it!" said Pepper. "My Grandma had that kind of goodness. Active goodness. You have choices to make, and you make the right one.

You have a chance to put your power somewhere, you have one life to do it in. You choose. You can maybe make things better. Or not. I want to be like my Grandma. I want to put my energy on the good side. To do the right thing, no matter what anyone says, like Grandma did."

He had to laugh. "For you it's so real. For me, Good and Evil are sort of a fairy tale. One I wish I believed in. You stop believing in goodness after watching a good man die a slow, horrible death."

"Death comes to us all. You need to remember how to live, Joe. You've got to figure out why people go on living."

"Art is the only reason I've got," said Joe.

"One reason's better than none," said Pepper. "I hope to show you a few more reasons."

He looked at her. "If anyone can do it, you can. A friend can be a good reason."

"Glad to hear you think so." Pepper laughed. "The feeling's mutual."

She could hardly believe the emotions going through her. She enjoyed his company so much! He had somehow slipped past all her defenses. She found herself thinking about him throughout the day. You'd think she was falling in love! She began wondering how she was ever going to tell him that she was considering leaving for Oregon State.

Instead she rose to her feet, dusted herself off, changed the subject. "I should be getting back. I've got a few phone calls to make. I've finally found someone who knows about that ravine that got buried in Cowen Park. Someone who has a private collection of photographs."

# 7
# Ferry

The ferry dock slid away behind her. Seagulls circled overhead, screaming. The skyscrapers of downtown Seattle began shrinking, becoming smaller and smaller against the gray November sky.

Pepper clutched the icy railing. She could feel the chill through her gloves. The stinging, salty cold of Puget Sound reddened her cheeks as the little pedestrian-only ferry churned its way across the black water toward Vashon Island. Pepper couldn't make herself stay inside where it was warm, in the coffee shop with its chattering regulars. The water drew her, that salty smell of life and death. She needed to stare down into the icy depths, into that heaving, shifting darkness.

Somehow, she felt sure, this entire tragedy had begun in the conversation she'd had with her grandmother right before she died. Somehow Pepper had unwittingly triggered it, her questions had awakened some terrible memory of the year 1960 and the filling of Cowen Ravine. But what had she said? What was the secret memory she had disturbed?

What Pepper needed were more facts about that other, filled-in ravine.

She'd consulted a forty-year-old handwritten history of Cowen Park provided by a brisk, efficient librarian in the Special Collections room of Allen Library. The director of the City Archives had shown her old maps of both ravines. She had spoken on the telephone with a woman at the Seattle Parks Department who had given her the telephone number of a descendant of the original Reverend William Beck who first purchased what became Ravenna Park in 1898.

As a result of her phone call, the Vashon dock seemed to glide toward her to meet the ferry.

*

"I'm always surprised anyone remembers Cowen Ravine at all," said Franklin Denny Beck, a nicely-kept man in his seventies, the great-great-grand-nephew of Reverend Beck. "Hasn't even been forty years yet, and already it's just a memory."

He wore a straw-colored sportcoat without a tie, his shirt collar unbuttoned. His cheeks were childishly rosy, as though they had forgotten to age along with the rest of him. His pale, thinning hair was neatly combed, like a well-tended garden.

"I'd never heard of it until recently," confessed Pepper.

He'd picked her up at the ferry dock and driven her through the wind-swept trees of the island, then up a maple-crowded winding dirt driveway toward a single-story house on a rise over the water.

"Well, I'm ready to answer any questions you have about the City of Ravenna. That was the original name, you know, for the whole three hundred acres. It was going to be a little independent city. With one special part set aside to be wild."

He escorted her into a spare, ultra-modern living room of polished natural wood. Pepper found herself facing a wall-size window overlooking the waters of Puget Sound. The other walls were crowded with framed black-and-white photographs.

Facing his guest, he backed toward the mounted photos without looking at them. "Here's the Reverend Beck himself, the one who started it all. This one is my father, with his brothers and cousins." He pointed, scarcely glancing in their direction.

"There's a little boy in our neighborhood named Billy Beck," said Pepper hopefully. "He lives near the ravine."

He smiled vaguely, shook his head. "Too many Becks for me to keep track of." He continued up the wall. "Here are some of the famous big trees." He singled out one with his finger. "This Douglas fir was two-thirds the height of the Space Needle." He pointed at another. "Look how small that woman is standing beside it. These trees were so big they had names, you know." He pointed. "President Roosevelt." Another photo. "Robert E. Lee." Another. "Adam and Eve. They all disappeared mysteriously. Happened during World War Two. Somebody just went in and logged them."

Photo after photo. The park she loved, but wilder. Ravenna Creek in 1900, looking more like a river, so deep it was up to the knees of six little girls in bathing suits.

"The pictures you're interested in would be these." A sequence of framed photographs were hung above the television. "It was a beauty, Cowen Ravine." He tapped one photo on the wall, then another. "This is a covered observation deck back in 1909 — see how it looks out over the trees. And this one from 1913 — here's the 15th Avenue bridge when it was just a wooden footbridge. Here's Cowen Ravine itself. Look at that! Soon no one will remember it at all — but here it is, in all its glory. Small but quite lovely, as you can see."

The photos depicted a miniature, fern-framed Northwest version of Eden.

"All gone now," he sighed. "My great-great-grand-uncle had an incredible dream. Maybe it was too good for this world. His little City of Ravenna got swallowed up by a bigger city. His lovely slice of wilderness — well, it's been dug up, chopped down, re-planted. A sewer line's been run through the middle. It's been so altered and rearranged it hardly looks like the same place. The real ravine no longer exists. Today's ravine is a re-creation, entirely artificial."

"Artificial?" She felt like she'd been slapped in the face.

"The ravine was butchered back in the thirties. The Volunteers of America chopped their way through the original trees. It made jobs for the unemployed, you see. What's left today is a planted reconstruction. It's a park pretending to be wild."

"That's a completely negative way of looking at it," said Pepper. "It may not be as it was before, but that doesn't mean it's artificial. It's healing. It's in recovery."

"Ah, is that what it is?" said Beck, with a sad smile. He stepped across the room to the other side, and gestured toward photos farther down the wall. "Here are some pictures of the actual fill-in." Tractors tipping over trees, pulling down trees with chains. Cement slabs of torn-up highway. Truckloads of dirt being dumped. Grinning workers posed before fallen maples.

One young man in particular.

Pepper almost walked past it, then took a step backward and looked again. Then she froze. Her heart began hammering. She looked closer, scrutinizing it. She checked the names listed in the caption. When she came to his name, she gasped.

"Is something wrong?" asked Beck in concern.

"Yes," said Pepper. "Something is very wrong."

He looked where her finger was pointing. His features lost their open cheer. "Ah, yes. I should have noticed. A relative?"

"My great-uncle," she said. The same cocky, grinning young man she'd seen in the photo in Grandma's room. "When was this taken?"

He squinted up close at the documentation under the glossy photo. "In 1960." He spoke with uncomfortable reserve. "I was there at the fill-in. He wasn't someone you could forget."

"You actually remember him?"

He looked uneasy. "If I may speak honestly—?"

"Please do."

"Every crew has someone like your great-uncle," said Frank Beck, scowling at the picture. "No offense, but he was a real pain. We knew him as Gabe. Always clowning around, never where he was supposed to be. Endangering others with his carelessness. Always acting like he was on something. If I remember correctly, he just took off one night. Never picked up his last pay check. No one ever knew why he got out of town so fast. Let's just say nobody was surprised. He was always up to no good."

Pepper couldn't turn away from the photo. Uncle Gabriel seemed to be looking straight into her eyes. Sneering over his own personal secrets, posed in front of a tractor, with his hand up against a fallen tree as though he had just pushed it over, brazen and confident, wearing a shiny black leather jacket.

# 8
## Lemon Squares

"It's a mistake," said Rose. "It can't be him."

"I saw it myself. How can you be so sure, Mom?"

"Because he couldn't have been in Seattle, that's why." She stripped the sheets off the bed mercilessly, with a ferocious yank, as though they'd been caught performing indecent acts, hurling them balled-up into the corner to be washed. "How could he have worked in Cowen Ravine and not known that he had inherited the house? It doesn't make sense. Uncle Gabriel wasn't like that."

"I've seen the photo myself. It's him."

"Show me."

*

138

It took Pepper three days to complete the transaction, from arranging for the photocopying to actually picking up the enlarged prints when they came over on the ferry. She caught a bus back to the U. District. She didn't feel the cold, didn't notice her red overcoat blowing unbuttoned as she walked home from the bus stop. Pepper was so excited about getting a chance to show the pictures to her mother that Wednesday afternoon that she didn't see Wanda Skinner until the interception was complete.

"There you are!"

Pepper stopped in her tracks, caught.

"Perfect timing," said Wanda. "For a walk together."

"Actually," said Pepper, "I'm anxious to get home—"

"And what have we here?" said Wanda, sliding the slim package out from under Pepper's arm. "Enlargements! Must be something worth seeing. May I take a peek?"

"Well, actually I—" Pepper hesitated. Knowing how much her neighbor would be delighted to see the fill-in photos made the opportunity to show them irresistible. "They're pictures of Cowen Ravine, before it was filled in."

"Goody!" exclaimed Wanda. "I didn't feel like walking, anyway. I just baked lemon squares." She grabbed Pepper's arm, steering her toward the bridge. "We can taste them over coffee and take a good look."

Which is what they did, in Wanda's living room, with the enlargements spread across the coffee table. Reproductions of authentic photos of the I-5 construction crews dumping soil and debris into Cowen Ravine.

"Wait a minute," said Wanda, popping a sugar-dusted yellow chunk into her mouth. She drew one picture closer. "Look at this photo caption. It says one of these men's name is Merlino."

"That's my great-uncle," said Pepper coolly. Wanda Skinner didn't miss much.

"Is it?" said Wanda, screwing up her lips in thought. "Now doesn't that make him your grandmother's brother?"

"He was."

"Really? Well, that's odd. Maybe I've got the story wrong, but I thought your grandmother's brother just sort of wandered off and died."

"So did we all," said Pepper, somewhat surprised at the depth of her neighbor's knowledge. "You knew Uncle Gabriel?"

"Of him," qualified Wanda. "Everyone in the neighborhood knew Gabe." She studied the photo more intently, her finger moving down the glossy surface until it was pointing toward one of the workers. "That's him, all right." The dirt-smeared young man grinned back at her confidently. "I'll tell you what I think. I think your uncle is back in town."

"That's impossible," objected Pepper. "He's dead."

"I don't think Gabe died. He came back in 1960. There he is!" Wanda rubbed her hands together, delighted with her sleuthing skills. "He's come back. That's who tried to hurt you Halloween night."

"Uncle Gabriel? But why would he want to?"

"For the same reason your grandmother got so upset — whatever that reason may be."

"But by now he'd be in his seventies!"

"So?" said Wanda. "I know some strong seventy-year-olds. And we're not the only ones who think it's Gabe."

"Who else does?" asked Pepper guardedly.

"Your mother."

"How do you know what my mother thinks?"

"Don't believe me? Let's ask her."

"Don't you dare!" said Pepper. "Wanda Skinner, I should never have showed these to you. You leave Mom out of this—"

"Don't worry. I'd never dream of bothering your mother." Wanda bit into another lemon square. "Although I do intend to find out what happened. I refuse to live in fear. This is my neighborhood, and I have a right to know. I would think you'd want to know, too."

"I do, but—"

"As far as I'm concerned, your Uncle Gabriel is a dangerous man and your mother is hiding something. But that's for you to find out. It's none of my business."

"Don't you upset her, Wanda," said Pepper. "She's upset enough. She's not going to our cousins' for Thanksgiving. She wants nothing to do with anyone. She's retreating into her own little world. I can hardly talk to her. I finally agreed to go to my cousins' without her."

"The poor woman's alone for Thanksgiving?"

"It's her choice to be alone," said Pepper. "You leave her that way."

"Oh, absolutely," said Wanda.

Pepper rose, gathered up her photos, slipped into her overcoat. "I'd better get home. I'm driving to Eastern Washington tonight with my cousins."

"Have a wonderful time," said Wanda, dusting the powdered sugar off her hands. "Eat yourself silly. You're so skinny you can get away with it."

# 9
# Dead Branch

"Mom?"

She found her in the living room, staring down through the picture window at the trees in the darkening ravine.

"Mom, you didn't answer."

Rose turned around. "Oh, there you are."

"You all right?" The heat was going full blast. Pepper shrugged out of her overcoat, dropped it across the sofa and approached her. Rose had her arms folded across her chest, like someone who was too cold.

"I've decided to have that branch removed," said Rose, pointing at the large, bent tree limb that seemed to be pointing back at her through the glass. "It's just an ugly reminder. I don't want to see it anymore."

"It reminds you of Uncle Gabriel?"

"I can still hear that laugh of his when he'd hang there and scare Mama so bad. I'm getting rid of his stuff in the basement, too. I should have thrown it out years ago." She stared at the window. She seemed to forget that Pepper was standing beside her.

"I've got the photos I was telling you about, Mom. I want you to look at them. They prove Uncle Gabriel wasn't dead in 1960."

141

Rose smiled sadly. "They couldn't prove any such thing," she said. "But I'll look at them."

Together they pulled out kitchen chairs and sat down on either side of the fruitbowl. Pepper emptied out the manila folder onto the kitchen table. Glossy prints slid across the placemats. Rose reached out and glanced at one. Pepper could see the change come over her mother's face.

"It is Uncle Gabriel, isn't it?" said Pepper.

"That doesn't mean anything," said Rose, putting the picture back down, looking at another, then another. "So what? So he drove a tractor or a dump truck. Do you know how many jobs he had? He never lasted longer than a week."

"These pictures prove he was here," said Pepper, "here in Seattle, when everyone thought he was dead and missing. It shows that he could have inherited."

"It shows nothing," said Rose. "Who knows when it was taken? It's just a picture of a selfish, charming man. He had no interest in anything but himself. So what if he was in Seattle? He wanted nothing to do with us. He never helped Mama. To all intents and purposes, he was dead. Pictures don't prove anything. Pictures don't tell you the truth."

Pepper reached out for her mother's hand, so that Rose turned for a moment to regard her. "What is the truth, Mom?"

"The truth," said Rose, releasing her hand from her daughter's hold, "is buried. Leave it that way."

"Sooner or later, people find out."

"Not always. Enough of this nonsense. Get your things together, before your cousins get here."

As though on cue, a car honked a cheerful series of toots outside the house.

"Here they are." Rose scrambled rapidly out of her chair. "Go answer the door. I'm going up to my room. Tell them I'm sick. I don't want to see them. I don't want to see anyone. What I really need to do is get down on my knees and pray."

# 10
## Thanksgiving Offerings

Wanda Skinner walked carefully to keep it all balanced. She carried an open-topped cardboard box containing a steaming casserole dish of whipped garlic potatoes (topped with melted white cheddar), an aluminum-wrapped plate of turkey selections, a small covered pot of gravy, a small bowl of cranberry sauce, and a plastic-snap container of her famous walnut-apple stuffing. Balancing the box on an upraised knee, she knocked loudly and firmly on the front door of the Merlino house before taking hold of the box again with both hands.

She'd heard the car honk several hours ago, and watched Pepper run out and get inside. The Merlino house had been quiet ever since. She was feeling quite justified in breaking her promise to Pepper. After all, no one should be left alone at Thanksgiving. Wanda had two dinner invitations for tomorrow, both of which she intended to keep. Everybody should have at least one. In her assault on the Merlino house, she came armed with an arsenal of mouthwatering offerings for the holiday tomorrow. How could anyone not give her a warm welcome?

She balanced the box on her knee, and knocked again. She wouldn't stay long. She'd be quick and to the point.

No one answered. She listened. No television inside. No music. No voices. Rose Merlino was being awfully quiet in there. Wanda tried the doorknob. The door wasn't locked. A slight pressure, and it swung open.

"Hello?" she called into the silent house.

No response.

"Happy Thanksgiving, neighbor—"

Wanda cautiously took a step inside, closing the door behind her. "Anyone home?"

The house was hushed, motionless.

"Rose Merlino?" she called into the emptiness. "Listen, I'm putting some food in the kitchen. You have a wonderful Thanksgiving."

She hurried down the dim hallway, finding her way. Snapping on the overhead kitchen light, she arranged her casserole dishes on the drainboard. Her sharp eyes took in as much as they could on the quick trip through — the gleaming copper bottoms of the pots, the handsome knife collection above the sparkling drainboard, the perfectly-arranged fruitbowl. Then she quickly headed back toward the front door.

"Just warm it up in your microwave, and you've got a Thanksgiving dinner," said Wanda into the emptiness.

She hesitated at the foot of the staircase. Where could Rose Merlino have gone? Perhaps she'd come at an inconvenient time. Perhaps she should leave. Wanda turned to go out the front door.

Rose Merlino stood in front of it.

"Looking for me?"

Startled, Wanda rapidly regained the scraps of her composure. "Well, yes, I was. I'm Wanda Skinner. I met you before. I live just on the—"

"I know who you are," said Rose. "I know where you live."

"Yes, well, good to see you again." Wanda reached out her hand in preparation for a handshake. Rose's hand never came forward to meet it. Hand outstretched and dangling, Wanda became irritated. "I brought you some Thanksgiving dishes. Left them in the kitchen. I'm not in any rush for the containers, but I do want them back."

Rose took a step closer, peering at her in confusion. "What made you think I didn't know how to cook?"

Wanda was horrified. "I thought you'd appreciate a neighborly gesture. Clearly I was mistaken!" The woman's thanklessness provoked Wanda into speaking her mind. "That night, the night your daughter was attacked under the bridge — I saw a man go down there."

Rose eyed her. "Did you really?"

"Yes. And I know where he came from. He came from your house."

"My house?" said Rose.

"Yes," said Wanda with conviction. "After all the lights were off. A man came out of your house and went down into the ravine."

Rose regarded her. "How interesting! Whoever it was must have been *beside* the house. No one was in it but me. I appreciate your concern. It's good to have such an observant neighbor. We all need to look out for each other. What else did you see?"

Wanda had intended to go on, to ask for the truth about Uncle Gabriel who should have inherited the house, who didn't seem to be very dead. She didn't. A cold warning glinted in Rose's eyes. Wanda for the first time became nervous. An awkward silence thickened between them.

"That was all I saw," muttered Wanda. "Maybe he wasn't inside your house, after all. Maybe he was *beside* the house, like you say. It was dark. I could be wrong. You could be right."

In an awkward panic, Wanda backed out the front door, muttering apologies. "I assume you like garlic, being Italian. I always put a lot of garlic in my mashed potatoes."

Rose closed the door in her face.


# 11
## Prowler

That night Wanda Skinner felt uneasy. She left the television on, newscaster addressing the empty living room, volume turned up to fill the apartment with voices and noise while she did the dishes. Then she nodded off for a short nap in front of the television, awakened sometime after eleven, and revived herself with a hot cup of lemon tea.

She was writing a letter to her sister when she thought she heard a door close somewhere inside the house. She walked down the hallway, glancing in the rooms. Nothing. She checked the front door. Locked.

The telephone rang. She snatched up the receiver.

"Hello?"

Click. Bzzzz.

She replaced the receiver and crossed back through the house, scolding herself for nervousness. Wrong number. Nothing to fret about. This was the nineties — rude people didn't apologize. They just hung up.

She crossed over to her desk by the window. There it was, across the ravine — the Merlino house. A light flickered in one of the upper windows. Wanda reached into her desk drawer and took out her binoculars. She focused them on the window. A shadow crossed the lighted square. Wanda turned the focus knob. She could hardly believe her eyes.

The shadow of a man. What man would be inside the Merlino house, prowling around in the dark?

She could get a better view from outside the house. She unlocked the back door, binocular cord around her throat, and strode halfway across the porch. Though it was chilly outside, she could certainly see better. But she'd be able to see better yet from the deck.

The boards of the deck creaked beneath her feet. She focused the binoculars across the ravine. He was gone. The window remained brightly lit, with no human figure in the small square of light. Pepper wasn't home. No one ever visited Rose. Someone was in the house.

But who? And where was he now?

She was so busy focusing on the window across the ravine that she didn't hear anyone on the deck behind her until she heard a board creak. Wanda spun around with a gasp.

A man stood in the shadows watching her.

"You there, what do you think you're doing?" she demanded angrily. "Get off this property right now."

No response. No movement.

"Who is that?" she demanded, heart hammering, trying to sound fiercer than she felt. "I'm calling the police."

No answer.

"Gabe Merlino, is that you?" she hissed bravely. "Have you come back to cause more trouble?"

The shadow took a step toward her.

Not until that terrible moment did Wanda realize, in the midst of her indignation, how completely vulnerable she was, standing with her back to the ravine, with a stranger between her and the house.

The shadow hurtled toward her.

It happened so fast she scarcely had time to scream. Wanda bolted backward, hit the edge of the deck railing, lashed into the air with her outstretched arms, and went over. Suddenly there was only crackling leaves, snapping twigs, tumbling stones, and a sparkling gleam from the wet rocks below.

CHAPTER SEVEN

# December Terror

## 1
### *Obake*

A week after Mrs Skinner's accident, on a chilly December afternoon after school, Billy happened to glance up at the house he was passing on his way to the ravine. There, in an upper window, was old Mrs Hayashi, signalling to him, motioning him to come inside.

Billy hesitated, then turned off the sidewalk, up the tree-darkened walkway, and politely knocked at the door. She opened it before his knuckles could strike the wood a second time.

"Mrs Hayashi?" said Billy. "Are you all right?"

She nodded and gestured up the stairs, gliding ahead of him into the shadows. Billy had never been inside before. He passed a small shrine with a brass gong. The thickly-carpeted stairs muffled his footsteps. At the top was a shallow bronze dish containing three bare twigs. She stepped into a room bright with the winter afternoon. He hesitated outside the door, awkwardly shuffling in the hall, nervously rattling the zipper up and down the front of his parka.

"Come in, Billy."

He hesitated, then stepped into a room of needlework hangings and lacquered bowls. She was seated by the window, her delicate, bony hands resting on crocheted doilies. She looked fragile, weaker, but her smile was as warm as ever.

She gestured toward the window. "Look."

Billy looked. The ravine dropped away below. There was the log where his foot got stuck.

"The best watercress used to grow down there. In the old days, if you want watercress, you go down to the creek, you have a knife, you cut watercress."

"I've heard the watercress in the ravine isn't good to eat," said Billy. "And you're breaking the law cutting through those fences. You should stop."

"Better in the old days," said Mrs Hayashi. "But the old days are gone. I went down there to get watercress—" She pointed down through the glass. "That's how I met the old one. The one who trusts no one."

"The one who died?"

"That one, she's always watching. Eyes of a hawk." She tapped the side of her head. "Funny up there. The Merlinos always keep to themselves. The young one, she's your friend?"

"Pepper? Yes, she's my friend. It was terrible what happened to her. I suppose you've heard," he said hesitantly. He didn't know how to phrase it. "About Mrs Skinner."

Mrs Hayashi nodded sadly.

Billy swallowed. "I think — it was probably the same guy who hurt Pepper. I think there's someone scary hanging around the park."

Mrs Hayashi nodded again. She rose and crossed the room until she stood framed in the doorway, silhouetted by the hall light, like a carved ancient goddess.

"I saw him do it," she said quietly. "From my window. I saw him hit her. A baseball bat." Billy could feel her eyes boring into him, looking right through him. "I was watching from this window the night it happened. I saw who did it." Mrs Hayashi leaned toward him and said softly but clearly, "Oh-bah-keh."

Billy blinked at her. "What?"

"I said *obake*. The Japanese word for 'ghost.'"

He shook his head. "You're wrong. He isn't a ghost. He's real, Mrs Hayashi. It's a man."

"A man before," she said solemnly, "now *obake*. No feet."

"Of course he had feet!" said Billy uncertainly.

Ada Hayashi smiled. "Japanese believe the way you know a ghost for sure — it floats. No feet. It just fades away down there."

"Some of those weeds in the ravine are up to your knees," said Billy. "Anybody could look like he didn't have feet."

"He comes back," said the old woman knowingly. "Many, many years ago he comes back. Now he comes back again. I see him from the window. I see him hurt the young Merlino." She looked directly at Billy. "He looks the same. Thirty, forty years, he doesn't change. The old woman's brother, he comes back just like before. Something very wrong. He's *obake* now. Even his jacket still the same. Still the shiny black jacket."

The blood drained out of Billy's face. "A black leather jacket?"

# 2
# No More Questions

Pepper could see the cold, crisp silhouette of Mount Rainier up ahead, a darker gray of volcanic rock against the gray of early morning, brooding over the black waters of Lake Washington.

She admired the view as she ran along the Burke-Gilman Trail. What had once been the old Northern Pacific Railroad line had been converted into a city-spanning running and biking trail that passed close to her home and then cut across campus.

It was too dark now to run in the ravine before her morning class. Besides, with the terrrible things that had been happening there, she was content to run her alternate route for the dark months.

She missed the ravine. She missed feeling safe there.

Anonymous phantoms jogged past her in both directions, faceless, unidentifiable. Bicycle lights bobbed and weaved toward her like tiny, bright UFO's, accompanied by the whirr of wheels.

Her thoughts were in turmoil, moving as fast as her feet but in all different directions. Another person attacked! Who would be next? How could she leave for Corvallis? Would Mom be safe alone? How could she tell her? How could she tell Joe? Which was another problem. Whoever dreamed friendship could mean so much?

He was a man she admired, a good and attractive man whose laughter and conversation she enjoyed. Period. Who cared what his sexual preferences were? For that matter, she'd have a hard time explaining her own, the number of suitable men she'd rejected, the number of budding relationships she'd left behind her. She was a solo act, too brainy and independent for her own good. She and Joe were both unicorns, neither quite fitting into the world. They perfectly suited each other.

She turned around at the overpass to Husky Stadium, and started looping back toward home.

With every footfall hitting the asphalt, she tried to sort out her feelings about Joe. Since it clearly wasn't a romance, what was it? Maybe it was something without a name. Did all significant relationships have to fit into pre-ordained slots?

At the intersection she left the Burke Gilman Trail and jogged the last few blocks up 25th Avenue before swerving over toward home. The streets were gray with morning, slowly brightening. A neighbor was up walking her dog, another was starting his car. There, in the midst of all that ordinariness, Mrs Skinner's house looked just as ordinary.

It was directly across the ravine from Mom's house. To think that the woman had been attacked on her deck, in full view of Pepper's bedroom window, gave her the chills. If she hadn't been at her cousins, if she had been home, she might have glanced out her window and seen—

Wanda Skinner's house was up ahead. Someone was on the bridge, looking at the house. Pepper slowed to a walk, still hot and wet from running. At the end of the bridge, she recognized the boy. She crossed halfway out to where Billy stood looking at the Skinner house.

"And what are you doing up so early?"

"Couldn't sleep," said Billy.

Underneath his baseball cap, what she could see of his face seemed much older, the skin chalky, with cavernous shadows around the red-rimmed eyes.

"You look upset," said Pepper. She stood beside him on the bridge, resting her arms on the railing. "Is she a friend of yours?"

"No way," said Billy. "She always yells at us every time we ride our bicycles too fast. She called the police on us once. I don't like her. But I didn't want anything bad to happen."

"None of us did, Billy." She squeezed his shoulder affectionately. "Has she come home from the hospital yet?"

He nodded. "She's home. I saw the car drive up. I think it's her sister. The license plates are from Ariz—"

The front door of the Skinner house unexpectedly opened. They both turned to look.

Mrs Skinner sat stiffly in a gleaming wheelchair, being manipulated through the doorway with some difficulty by a heavier, wilder-haired sister who was also trying to steer two suitcases with bumping and nudging and clever footwork. Billy and Pepper hurried up the porch stairs to help her.

"Thank you, dears," said Wanda's sister. She patted Billy's head. "If you could put them in the trunk of the car."

"I hope you're feeling better," said Pepper to Wanda, taking the bottom of the wheelchair and easing it down the front stairs. "We heard—"

Wanda Skinner regarded her solemnly. A bruise darkened the left side of her forehead. Her right leg was in a cast. She looked harrowed, her graying blond hair disheveled as though it would never be tamed by a comb again. She tried to scowl, but it only made her look afraid.

"Don't believe everything you hear," she rasped. "And don't ask questions."

"Wanda, I've got to ask you," said Pepper. "Did you break your promise to me? Did you pay a visit to my mother?"

Mrs Skinner suddenly released her bony grip on the wheelchair's arm and seized Pepper's hand.

"Don't ask questions," she repeated in an urgent whisper. "No more questions. You know enough, believe me. Sometimes it's better not to know. Now I know he's out there. Now I'll never stop worrying. He knows where to find me." She gripped the metal arms of her wheelchair as though they were brakes and she couldn't stop. "That's why I'm leaving. This is Brenda, my sister." Brenda made reassuring sounds. "I'm going to live with her for a month or two. Brenda says it doesn't rain in Arizona."

151

\*

Billy and Pepper watched the car drive away.

"Boy, did she look scared," said Billy. He knew the feeling from experience. "You could see it in her eyes."

"Oh, now — she didn't look that scared!" said Pepper, playing it down, noticing the tension in his voice. "She's a tough old crab. She'll be noisy and feisty and back on her feet in no time. I only wish I had tried a little harder to stop her from doing something foolish."

"Stop her?" echoed Billy. "How could you stop her from falling off her own deck? It wasn't your fault some man broke into her house."

For a moment Pepper almost didn't answer his question. "I think Wanda saw something that night," she said vaguely. Billy stared at her, waiting. She reluctantly continued. "She knew I'd be gone. She went over and talked to my mother. She got my mother all scared. And then — well, no one knows exactly what she did after that. Somewhere between leaving our house and getting to her house, she met someone else."

"What do you mean?" said Billy.

"I'm saying that Wanda Skinner may have stuck her nose into something that didn't concern her. She was never one to back away. She might have gotten herself in trouble—"

Billy's face seemed to become gray in the morning light. "Trouble like what happened to you?"

Pepper had tried to avoid it. "Possibly. My poor mother is so upset she hardly makes sense. It's like she can't think straight. She's always looking over her shoulder. She keeps forgetting what she's doing. She left the oven on last night. She keeps making mistakes at QFC, then worrying about them at home. All she can talk about is Grandma falling, and what happened to me, and now what's happened to Wanda. I've never seen her in this condition. Poor Mom. She's a real tough-guy type. It's hard for her to let down her guard and admit she's scared."

Billy nodded solemnly. "I'm scared, too."

Pepper took his hand. "It's hard not to be. There are so many good reasons to be afraid."

# 3
# Treasure Box

Rose got off work at QFC at three, and by four she was at home alone, pacing. As the afternoon grew later, she found herself waiting for Pepper to get home, trying not to listen to the sounds of the empty house. She sponged the drainboard clean, wiped out the inside of the microwave, polished the stove top and the refrigerator door. She tightened the faucet so it wouldn't drip. She moved her damp clothes from the washer to the dryer. She kept busy, trying not to stare out the window at the bleak, gray winter sky, at the skeletal branches stripped of their leaves. At Uncle Gabriel's branch.

Those pictures! Those terrible photos Pepper had found — as if the one up in Mama's old boxes of junk hadn't been bad enough! Now these others of the Cowen fill-in. Just seeing that face again, that arrogant smile, that cocky, knowing look in the eye. She had to get that face out of her mind. She glanced at the kitchen clock. Her daughter would soon be home.

Pepper was still on campus. The quarter was coming to an end. She was caught up in all kinds of December deadlines, finishing up classwork, writing up fieldwork notes, meeting her thesis deadlines. She would be home before dinner, but when exactly not even Pepper knew from night to night. Rose snatched up the morning newspaper, glanced at the headlines, saw nothing she hadn't already read several times, and flung the pages crackling back into the armchair.

She abruptly stopped and listened.

Nothing.

Rose reached in the towel drawer, pulled out her secret flask, and took a long swallow. She was always nervous now when she was alone in the house. She could sense a change in the atmosphere inside those walls, an ominous threatening. The house was no longer securely under her control.

She knew she had left the kitchen perfectly clean when she discovered the smudge mark on the refrigerator door. She stopped abruptly in her tracks, staring. Dirt and grime were smeared around the polished handle on the cold, clean whiteness. As though someone with filthy hands had not washed them before opening the refrigerator.

Had Pepper been taking care of the trees again in the park? Was her daughter already inside the house, leaving a messy trail behind her?

"Pepper, are you home?"

No answer.

The frequent words of her mother came back to her, the exasperated tone. "Gabriel Merlino, don't you dare get my kitchen dirty." That was the way Carmen had started talking to him after their mother died, as though she were no longer his sister but really a little mother scolding him into shape. "You get over to the sink, Gabriel Merlino, and wash your hands before you touch one more thing. I mean it, don't you dare—"

Rose could remember Mama's fiery eyes as she scolded the charming brother who never paid her any attention, the handsome uncle who teased his pretty little ten-year-old niece, the selfish monster who had disappeared and would never come back. No matter how hard she tried, Mama hadn't quite been able to control her brother. Gabriel had been untameable, a slippery charmer with a heart of ice, so delighted with himself that everyone else was, too.

Rose shook her head at the memories. She could vividly recall playing with Uncle Gabriel in the days before he ran away. Wrestling with him on the sofa when he changed the television channel. Watching him sneak booze when no one was looking. Watching him shave in the bathroom. He had even kissed her a few times, once when he hadn't shaved and his cheeks were rough. As a little girl, Rose had fervently believed that he was the handsomest man alive.

The thought of him now made her clench her teeth, force him out of her mind. She hated him! What he did to Mama. What he did to her.

She grabbed a sponge and quickly began rubbing at the dirty smear. The refrigerator door was sparkling again and she was rinsing the sponge out in the sink when she heard something downstairs. She turned off the tap water and listened again. She reached toward the faucet to turn it back on when she heard muffled laughter.

Someone was in the house with her.

Reaching for the cutlery rack, Rose slid out the biggest knife, gripped it firmly, and walked straight to the stairs. Snapping on the overhead light, she went halfway down before she said, as boldly as she could, "Who's down here?"

No answer.

She didn't really have to ask the question. She had recognized that sniggering, mocking laugh. Only her Uncle Gabriel had ever laughed like that. Why couldn't she get him out of her mind these days? He was driving her crazy.

At the bottom of the basement stairs, she stopped. In her earliest memories, the basement had always been Gabriel's domain. He had lived his last years in the house downstairs, demanding privacy, keeping all hours, doing secret, forbidden things, door locked, sometimes alone, sometimes with others that Rose never saw, only heard whispering, laughing.

She snapped on another light. That was when she noticed the closet door was slightly open. Had Pepper opened it? Neither of them had any reason to go down there. She opened the closet door the rest of the way, knife clutched and ready. She pulled the overhead drawstring.

One box had been tugged partway free of its usual location on a lower shelf. She tried to push it back, but something was blocking it. She set down the knife and shifted the box to get a better angle. In moving it, she pinched her finger against the wall. She gave a little yelp, and yanked her hand away.

The box fell lose, splattering its contents across the floor.

Magazines. Dozens and dozens of magazines. Slithering and sliding over each other as they tumbled out at her feet. Magazines with shocking, provocative covers, lurid stares, far too much glossy skin. She groaned and snatched up her knife, backing away from the closet, kicking at the magazines. She slammed the closet door on them. She was trembling, her breath coming in quick, shallow gulps.

Magazines that belonged to Uncle Gabriel. Magazines of naked people doing shameless, sinful things that good people like Rose would never think of doing.

There it was, again! She froze. Somewhere down in the basement with her, that same arrogant chuckle. She whimpered and backed toward the stairs.

"Who's down here?" she said, voice cracking.

No answer.

With a nervous glance up the staircase, she spun around, hurried up the stairs and slammed the door at the top, refusing to let herself break down in tears.

She would wait in the kitchen for Pepper to come home. In the kitchen, with all the lights blazing.

# 4
## Night Line

At first Pepper thought the ringing came from her alarm clock. She was groping for it blindly when a figure stepped silently through the doorway and approached the bed. The figure bent over her slowly, without making a sound. Something was being lifted over her throat. Pepper was about to scream when she realized she was being handed the telephone.

"For you," said her mother, unhappily awakened, her voice gravelly with sleep. "He said it was urgent."

Pepper fumbled with the receiver, waited for her mother to go back to bed. "Who is this, please?"

"It's me," said Billy. "I looked up your phone number."

Pepper blinked in surprise, recognizing his voice, then glanced at her watch, illuminating the dial. "Do you realize what time it is?"

"I'm sorry," said the small voice at the other end, "but I had to talk to you. I'm afraid."

"Afraid?" She was at once supportive. "What is it, Billy? What's scaring you?"

"I've been having these nightmares."

She sighed with relief. That was all it was. "After what you saw," said Pepper, "nightmares are only natural. Have you been dreaming about my grandmother falling?"

"No. Sometimes I dream about the ravine. But mostly it's a guy I'm scared of." He took a deep breath. "He lurks around outside, always watching me. He wears a black leather jacket."

Pepper gasped. "He wears what?"

"A black leather jacket, with the collar up."

"That's what the guy was wearing who hurt me in the ravine," said Pepper. "A black jacket. Mrs Hayashi saw it, too." She was thinking about another leather jacket — the one worn by Uncle Gabriel in the photo from 1960.

"It's him. I know it's him," said Billy. "The one who hurt you. The one who scared Mrs Skinner. That's the reason I'm calling. I just had a nightmare. A bad one. He was at your house. Outside on the deck, waiting — waiting to hurt someone."

His words chilled her. The very thought that her attacker might still be stalking her— "Billy, it was just a dream." She clutched the phone tightly. His voice seemed feeble and far away.

"It's more than a dream. It's like a warning." He tried to find the right words. "He's going to hurt someone in your house. No one believes me. Dr Griffin doesn't. My Dad doesn't."

"I believe you, Billy." The words were easy to say because she said them with complete conviction.

"My Dad wants to understand, but he can't. He won't listen to me anymore. Please, if you could just talk to him."

Suddenly muffled scratching sounds, as though the phone were being dragged under a blanket. A man's voice in the background.

The dull buzz of a broken connection.

# 5
# Dr Griffin's Reality

"You're afraid these dreams are premonitions of something terrible that's going to happen?"

Billy wasn't exactly sure what she meant. "They could be."

"Is everyone else in your neighborhood afraid now, too?"

Billy nodded.

An unspoken, unacknowledged tension had quietly settled over Ravenna Springs. No one knew what to expect next, or who would be hurt next, or who they could trust. Neighbors stopped being quite so friendly to neighbors. Someone who lived among them had turned treacherous. Someone was deceiving them.

Billy was almost beside himself. He looked down at his feet all the time now, avoiding people's eyes. He had developed a new habit of chewing on his fingernail.

"Billy, you're making your finger bleed," said Dr Griffin.

The boy snatched his finger out of his mouth and pushed his hand under his leg, as though sitting on it might keep it out of reach.

"You think it's him, don't you?"

Billy nodded.

"Do you think your neighbors are having bad dreams about him, too?"

The boy shook his head. "No."

"Why do you think you're dreaming about him?"'

"I don't know why," he said, adding impulsively, "but I don't think they're dreams anymore. Dreams are different. These are too real."

"They only seem real," Dr Griffin corrected.

"Dreams can't swing a baseball bat," said Billy. "Dreams can't push you off the edge of your deck."

Dr Griffin could feel his panic, barely restrained. "Dreams are only dangerous if you believe in them, Billy. But they can have a real message. Sometimes they try to tell us something. Something that frightens us. Something we're trying to forget."

"These aren't dreams," said Billy. "These are real."

"That's just what they're not, Billy," said Dr Griffin, looking him straight in the eye. "I can tell you that for sure. Not real at all."

Billy stared at the floor, polite, unbelieving.

An edge of urgency crept into Dr Griffin's voice. "Billy, the mind can do amazing things. But it's up to you to control your mind. Because it can work against you. It can interpret things incorrectly. Your Nightmare Man is a trick that your mind is playing on you. It's up to you to take control of your mind, Billy."

*

He took the elevator down to where his father was waiting in the car on the corner. He slid into the passenger seat and fastened his seatbelt as Paul Beck pulled out into the sluggish river of idling cars. Downtown traffic, usually congested at that time of the afternoon, had been worsened by Christmas shopping. It was a slow-motion, inch-by-inch automotive parade from stoplight to stoplight.

"Well, how did it go?" he asked his son, keeping his eyes focused on the cars around them.

"Okay."

"Feel like you might be making some progress?"

"I don't know."

He wanted to ask more. He glanced at Billy, and hesitated. "Is she giving you any help with being afraid?"

When he didn't hear an answer, he took another quick look away from traffic in his son's direction. The boy was looking frail lately. These nightmares were taking their toll on his health.

"I'm still afraid," he admitted honestly, adding bravely, "But not as much."

"You've got bags under your eyes, pal." He reached out across the car seat, covering Billy's hand with his own.

# 6
# Psychic

The steady drone of rain that evening had unexpectedly lulled the boy to sleep. Paul Beck watched in silence from the kitchen doorway. The sight broke his heart.

Billy had fallen asleep at the kitchen table. He had been slow finishing his dinner, and in the process had simply slumped forward. One arm extended messily across the table. His head had fortunately missed his plate. Breathing soundly and deeply, slumped over, propped between table and chair, his unrested body was hungrily soaking up minutes of desperately-needed recuperation.

The boy never woke up to see his father watching him, never noticed when his father left. Paul got as far as the living room before the ache inside doubled him over. He didn't make any sounds. He didn't want the boy to know how worried he was. He refused to let himself cry. If he ever let himself break down and acknowledge the pain, he wasn't sure he could put himself back together again. He had to be strong enough to save the mind of his son.

He was halfway through his second beer. The day had darkened. A familiar, well-groomed news commentator filled his fifty-inch television screen with her personable, trustworthy smile, interspersed with clippings from the day's tragedies. The rain pounded outside.

The doorbell jolted him back to the present moment.

Paul lurched to his feet and headed for the door in his stockings, drawstring dangling out of his sweatpants, shirt unbuttoned, shirttails untucked, bristly jaw tense with anxiety, unruly hair tormented by the raking of worried fingers. He opened the front door to find himself facing an attractive young woman he'd never met before, standing on his porch under a dripping umbrella.

"Good evening, Mr Beck," she said. She looked up at him, cheeks damp and flushed, bangs of black hair wet against her forehead. "I hope I haven't disturbed you." Raindrops glistened on the olive skin of her cheeks. "My name is Pepper Merlino. I'm a neighbor of yours. My grandmother — she was the one who fell from the bridge."

"Right, of course," said Paul. "Please come in." She lowered her folding umbrella and shook it, then wrapped it up and left it on the porch. He stepped aside, ushering her past him. "I hope Billy hasn't been over there bothering you."

"I like Billy," said Pepper. "He's no bother. That's why I'm here." She took several steps down the hall. From there she could see Billy sleeping at the kitchen table. She stopped at once and backed away.

"Let him sleep," she whispered.

"He's exhausted, poor guy," said Paul. "He's afraid to go to bed at night."

"He's afraid with good reason," said Pepper. "That's why I'm here. I think your kid is dealing the best he can with some pretty intense and frightening stuff. He calls them dreams, they seem like dreams, but I think they might be more than that. I think he's aware of things that you and I miss."

Paul didn't like the sound of it. "Things we miss? Oh, no. You mean like ESP?"

She nodded. "That's exactly what I mean. I think your son is psychic, Mr Beck." She spoke clearly and simply, sensing he did not want to hear what she had to say. "He called to tell me a dream about the man who attacked me."

"He phoned you? I'm so sorry. Please, believe me, what happened to you has absolutely nothing—"

"Billy is not mentally troubled," said Pepper with confidence. "That boy is saner than either of us. You weren't there when it happened. I was. He's a very sensitive kid, and he's been hooked into some kind of psychic link with something very frightening that he doesn't understand."

"I disagree one hundred percent," said Paul. "My son is not having paranormal experiences." His eyes were closed, voice steady. "This is why I don't want him around you. I don't want his head filled with — with this kind of nonsense. My son is in psychological denial after witnessing your grandmother fall to her death. He's in a traumatic fugue state. It's happened before to other people. It's a well-documented psychological condition."

"Whatever you say," she said, retreating down the hallway. "If that satisfies you. Your attitude is not very helpful to Billy." She opened the door. "Well, I had to try. I didn't expect you to believe me." The sound of drumming rain rumbled in the entryway.

"I appreciate your concern," he said. "I really do." He blurted the words out suddenly, before he could bite them back. "Thank you for caring about my boy."

"I know you don't believe me," she said without bitterness, stepping outside onto the porch as she opened her umbrella. "All I can say, Mr Beck, is you should believe your son before you believe a psychiatrist."

"Call me Paul," he interrupted.

"It wasn't easy to come here — Paul. I would much rather have stayed home tonight. I came here because I think my message is important. Urgent! Your son is telling you the truth."

He stepped outside onto the porch beside her. He quickly became dotted with raindrops. He didn't seem to notice. "Miss Merlino, I love my son—"

"Call me Pepper," she interrupted.

"I love my son, Pepper, more than anything else in the world. I screwed up my marriage. I'm not going to screw up my kid. I want what's best for Billy. And sometimes I think I know what that is."

She reached her umbrella up over him, sheltering his head from the rain. "Sometimes," she said, "sometimes even the very best parent, even the most loving parent, can be wrong."

# 7
# Downpour

"He seemed like a nice man, but a very worried man."

"I think he'd like to string me up by the thumbs and hang me from the bridge."

With Bobo running on ahead of them, Joe and Pepper walked shoulder to shoulder, lost in conversation. She had been unable to leave campus that afternoon until almost four. Crossing through the park on her way home, she'd heard Bobo's unmistakable bark ringing through the trees. Her path and Joe's had converged. They had continued on together past both their houses to the ravine's other end.

"An attractive man," added Pepper, glancing at Joe.

"A hunk," agreed Joe. "But a grumpy one."

They entered Cowen Park and the trees at the far end of the grassy baseball field.

"This is where it was, Cowen Ravine," said Pepper. "We're standing on top of it."

Ignored for a moment, Bobo took off across the ballfield. "Come on, Bobo," called Joe, "get over here!" The big Airedale bounded toward them across the grass.

They started back, heading down under the 15th Avenue bridge on the main trail through the ravine. Bobo zigzagged ahead of them, exploring banks of ferns on one side, splashing through the creek on the other. They noticed it was getting darker. Neither of them mentioned it for fear of shortening their time together.

"Sorry I'm such dull company," said Joe. They had been walking in silence past the frog ponds toward the deepest part of the ravine. "I think I need a nap. Didn't get much sleep last night."

"Up late painting?"

"Up late screaming." He smiled lamely at his own humor. The smile died quickly. "Afraid I'm going off the deep end. I can't seem to stop having these awful dreams. Crazy, but true. Worse than any nightmares I've ever had in my life."

"Nightmares?" Pepper looked at him assessingly. "How odd. So is Billy."

"Really?" Joe paused. "He mentioned that something was scaring him. Hope his dreams aren't as bad as mine." The subject made him nervous. He was about to change it when a thought occurred to him. "I don't suppose he dreams about some guy in a black leather jacket?"

Pepper stopped in her tracks and stared at him. Then she laughed. "So he told you, right? This is a joke?"

Joe shook his head. "Billy dreams about him, too?" He shuddered. "I keep having these horrible dreams about some guy in a black leather jacket. I get so scared I wake up in a sweat."

Pepper laughed nervously, in spite of herself. "I've never heard of people dreaming the same dreams. It sounds too weird. How could it possibly happen?"

"It couldn't, if they were just dreams. They're more than dreams."

"That's exactly what Billy said!"

163

"Something is in my mind, Pepper. Something I can't get out, that won't leave me alone, something I don't understand. I feel threatened by something that scares me—"

The first hard-hitting raindrops caught them by surprise.

"Oh, no! Where did all this come from?"

"Yike! We're going to get drenched."

"Head for my place," said Joe. "Come on!"

They ran for it. In moments they were encompassed by sheets of rain. They squealed, shouted, half-laughing, half-wailing. Bobo lunged about them on either side. They tried to escape down the main ravine trail, but were soaked by the time they got to the footpath leading up to the bridges.

Halfway across the rain-drenched bridge, Pepper stopped in her tracks in shock, staring at the back of Joe's house. She was too wet to worry about getting any wetter. The familiar house was transformed. It gleamed at them through the rain, a fantasia of winking, blinking Christmas lights.

"You decorated!"

Joe grinned. "You noticed."

She walked the rest of the way across the bridge and around the house in a daze of admiration. Lights were blinking everywhere — along the eaves, down the gutter-pipes, around the windows, over the doors. Lights outlined each bush and shrub along the front walkway, like luminous, overlapping connect-the-dots. While she praised his elaborate handiwork, Joe slid the barrier aside in front of the garage and secured Bobo in the studio. Then he led Pepper up the glittering walkway and opened the front door, stepping aside for her to go first.

She gasped in delight.

Evergreen branches were festooned over the mantelpiece, doorway and windowframe, interwoven with knots of holly and ivy and loops of wide satin ribbon striped red, gold and green. Clinging to the ribbon were little wooden rocking-horses and teddy bears, silver bells, candy canes, painted nutcrackers and frosted glass reindeer and snowmen, all of them highlighted by delicate strings of tiny lights. Presiding over the mantelpiece, between two mighty Christmas candles, one red and one green, perched a fat bronze baby angel with a ribbon bow on his head.

"Do you do anything halfway?" Pepper was turning around in circles, open-mouthed at the delirious detail.

"I treat every Christmas like it's my last," he said, then suddenly added, "I'm sorry. You're soaked. Anyone with manners would have taken your wet coat and turned on the heat and brought you a towel before you catch cold."

Standing there dripping while the first rumble of thunder rattled the windowpanes, she watched Joe slap his hand at the thermostat as he hurried into the hallway. In that brief moment of waiting, Pepper happened to notice a book on the endtable by the armchair, the glossy cover gleaming fitfully in the sparkle of the lights. Now green, now red. She reached out one wet finger to tilt the cover around to face her, so she could read the title.

*After Death Experiences.*

# 8
# Sleepwalk

Billy went to bed soon after dinner.

Rain beat at his bedroom window. He watched the drops ripple down the glass, like invisible fingers trying to write him urgent messages. He dreaded having another nightmare, but he was too tired to stay awake.

The boy sank into a deep sleep almost at once. For the first part of the night he didn't dream at all. He dropped into pure unconsciousness. After days of insomnia, nights of terror, his catatonic slumber was a welcome relief to his exhausted body. But in the depths of his dreamlessness, he heard something.

Billy sat up in bed.

The house was still. The television wasn't on. His father was softly snoring down the hall.

He folded back the covers. In his pajama bottoms and a white undershirt he shuffled into his slippers and left the bedroom. He made his way down the hall, lingered momentarily outside his Dad's room, and then forced himself to walk on.

Soundlessly he padded down the stairs and into the kitchen. He slowly crossed the linoleum tiles until he was facing the back door window. He drew aside the curtain. The back porch was empty. Beyond the porch he noticed a shadow in the back yard detach itself from one place and glide to another.

Billy could make out the shape of a man. The figure seemed to glance over his shoulder in the boy's direction. Billy never got a chance to see whether the man had feet. He felt sick with fear. He recognized the turned-up collar of the leather jacket. The man was heading for Pepper's house.

Billy wanted to run back to his room and dive under the covers. He couldn't. Someone had to stop that man. He had dared to hurt Pepper once. No matter how scared he was, Billy was determined to stop him before he could hurt her again.

Without going to the closet for a jacket, he opened the back door and stepped outside. He didn't feel the rain that quickly soaked him, the icy wind slicing through his T-shirt. He set off slowly and methodically down the back stairs. Stiffly, unsurely, he walked past the bright, blinking lights of Joe's house, becoming more drenched every minute, and descended the cement stairs to the high wooden bridge. His T-shirt clung to him wetly. His pajama bottoms sloshed and flopped.

Blindly his hand reached out for the wet, green railing.

Sound asleep, heading toward the Merlino house, Billy started out across the trestles.

# 9
# Unpredictable

Later, huddling in Joe's spare bathrobe in front of the fire by the Christmas tree, waiting for her clothes to finish tumbling in the dryer, she asked Joe about the book. A glass cup of hot egg nog warmed her hands. All around her, laceries of tiny lights twinkled cheerily.

"That?" Joe sat beside her, also in a bathrobe. He picked it up. "One of Todd's old books. Pretty interesting stuff." He handed her the dog-eared paperback.

Pepper glanced at the blurbs on the back cover, riffled through the pages. "Believable?"

"Now, I didn't say that," Joe qualified. "Believing is something else." He took a sip from his steaming cup. "I have a hard time believing anything. So maybe not always believable. But thought-provoking."

"Like, for instance?"

"Like, it's about — how to describe it? — all the different types of experiences that people rule out and call impossible. The things they say don't happen. Don't exist. Can't be proved."

"You mean like psychic stuff?"

"Like psychic stuff." He opened the book at his marker. "People have very definite ideas about how far reality can go. It's all cultural. We see what we believe we can see."

"What we're taught we can see."

"Right," said Joe. "Some things are accepted by one culture as natural. Another culture says they don't exist. Take the topic I'm reading about now. What's it called?" He looked in the book. "It's called psychometry. Ever heard of it?"

"No. What is it?"

"I'd never heard the word before, either. But I'd heard of the phenomenon. It means sort of like 'psychic detection.' It's the way someone can touch clothing or personal belongings and get in psychic contact with a missing person. The police use it, sometimes. You know, hire a medium to touch a shoe or a shirt from a missing kid, for instance, to establish a psychic link. Some people would find that hard to swallow."

"People find the idea of psychic powers disturbing," said Pepper. "Psychic powers are just one step away from ghosts."

An awkward silence.

"I don't believe in ghosts," said Joe. "But there's something wrong with those dreams of mine, Pepper. Sometimes they really are more like hauntings. Like I'm reliving something. But I don't know the reason why. And I don't know the cure."

Pepper looked on helplessly. Joe got up from the sofa and fed the fire while she sipped her hot drink. He waited till the flames roared up, then sat back again beside her. "It's the unpredictable that people fear. It's the experiences that take them outside of what they know."

The crackling bright warmth of the flames toasted their legs, flushed their cheeks.

"That's the scariest thing about loving," said Pepper. "People are so unpredictable. You think you know someone. Then they turn out to be someone else. That's why I like you, Joe. The more you open up to me, the more I enjoy your company. I love talking with you like this. It makes me feel almost drunk to be so relaxed with you."

"Maybe you *are* drunk," suggested Joe. "Maybe the hot egg nog has something to do with it."

"It has nothing to do with egg nog," said Pepper. "I just didn't realize how much I wanted a real friend."

That got through his defenses. His arm gave an answering squeeze around her shoulders.

They snuggled closer together before the fire. They talked softly. Sheets of rain pounded in a dull roar at the windows. The flames crackled. They ran out of words.

Between the hot egg nog, the warm fire, and the growing trust between them, Joe and Pepper ended up falling asleep on the sofa together in each other's arms.

*

She woke up to Joe's mumbled cries. He was moaning in his sleep, his forehead wet with sweat. His hand was clutching at her. Pepper drew her bathrobe together and gently shook him awake.

"Joe, you're dreaming."

He woke with a jolt, his eyes snapped open. Then he sank back into the pillows with a groan of relief.

He fell immediately back to sleep. Troubled, she eased gently off the sofa without waking him and quietly moved into the night-darkened kitchen for a drink of water, disturbed by the sight of Joe's suffering, wracking her brain for an answer to this mysterious epidemic of bad dreams.

Rain streamed down the windowpanes. Draining her glass, she glanced out the window over the kitchen sink.

In the light from the streetlamp, in the midst of the downpour, she saw a small figure set out across the ravine on the narrow wooden bridge. What appeared to be a shadowy dwarf was moving very slowly, guiding himself with one hand trailing lightly along the railing. Why was a dwarf crossing the bridge at one o'clock in the morning in a rainstorm? When the dwarf paused briefly, she recognized him as Billy.

He was wearing only a T-shirt and pajama bottoms. He was thoroughly drenched. He was moving at the wrong speed, as though he were drunk.

She ran back into the living room and jostled Joe. "Wake up!"

"Wha—?"

"Come in here, quick. Look!"

He stumbled to his feet, adjusting his bathrobe, aware of her urgency, following her. Together they watched from the kitchen window as the boy slowly, blindly groped his way through the downpour toward the middle of the bridge.

"It's Billy," said Joe, his eyes snapping wide open. "Something's wrong. That kid's not awake."

"Oh, my God, that's it!" whispered Pepper. "Joe, look — he's going straight toward the place where Grandma fell."

All they had time to do was tighten their bathrobes around them, cinch the cords snugly around their waists. Pepper bolted out of the house with Joe right behind her. They hurried down the wet, slippery cement stairs around the side of the house, and out onto the narrow wooden bridge. Their bathrobes were sopping before they got there.

"Don't scare him."

Together they approached him cautiously. The boy seemed to sense their presence. He slowed down to a shuffling pause, his fingers tapping on the wet railing in confusion.

"Billy, it's just us," said Joe. "No need to be afraid. Just Joe and Pepper come to give you a helping hand. What do you say we go inside, where it's a little dryer?"

Together Joe and Pepper took hold of him, each of them gently gripping one of his arms. Together they guided him back off the bridge toward Joe's house.

# 10
# Psychometry

Pepper turned over the boy's hand on the kitchen table, palm up. "Looks like you got a splinter from the bridge railing."

Billy drew his hand back. "I had that before."

Joe remembered. "You mean when you cut your hand?" Billy nodded. "That still hasn't healed?"

"It's as bad as your eye," said Pepper.

The thought made Joe uneasy. He changed the subject. "We should call his father," said Joe.

Toast crumbs and smears of raspberry jam decorated the table surface between them. At two in the morning, with rain still rattling and droning at the windows, Joe had fried up something halfway between an omelette and a fritatta, with some frozen pasta sauce thawed and tossed in for flavor. Whatever it's technical name, it had lasted only a few minutes after he put it on the serving platter.

Billy's wet pajama-bottoms and T-shirt were tumbling in the dryer downstairs, along with the two drenched bathrobes. He wore one of Joe's sweaters that came down to his knees. Pepper was now wearing her freshly-dried shirt and blue jeans again, and Joe was wearing another T-shirt and sweatpants. They looked like a scruffy, sleepy, all-American television-sitcom family eating breakfast together on Saturday morning. They did not look like three frightened neighbors from different homes brought unexpectedly together in the middle of the night.

"Please don't call my father," said Billy.

"But he *should* be called," said Joe. "He has every right to know where you are."

"But calling him would just upset him," said Billy. "He's already worried enough about me."

"Then we should take you home," said Pepper.

"I don't want to go home," said Billy. "I don't want to go to sleep. I'll just have more nightmares."

"I know how you feel," said Joe.

"Both of you having bad dreams!" Pepper's eyebrows lowered into a thoughtful scowl. "Let me ask you boys something. Would this describe the man you're dreaming about? Approaching thirty, good-looking, cocky, black hair, black eyes, black leather jacket."

"That's him!" they both echoed.

"For some reason that I can't understand," said Pepper, "you're both dreaming about my Uncle Gabriel."

"But why should Billy and I have bad dreams about your uncle?" said Joe. "That doesn't make sense. What do Billy and I have in common?"

"We're both artists," said Billy, venturing a guess. "We both live near here."

Suddenly the chapter Joe had been reading in his *After Death Experiences* came back to him. The chapter on psychic detection. On psychometry.

"We have one other thing in common," said Joe slowly. "One very odd, particular thing." He reached out and took hold of Billy's hand, turning it over to the small tear in the pad of his right palm. "You and I both got injured at that old log. Look, you can still see the cut in the corner of my eye. And my eye hasn't healed yet, either."

Billy looked.

"Maybe that's the answer," said Joe. "If there's anything to this psychometry stuff, then maybe the nightmares we're having are caused by some kind of psychic vibes that we got from splinters of the tree trunk. Maybe something terrible happened there. And now somehow Billy and I are contaminated. That's why we're being haunted."

Billy listened, wide-eyed with dread.

"It makes a weird kind of sense," said Pepper. "If anything so out-to-lunch can be called sense."

"Maybe Billy and I are replaying in our dreams something that really happened. Some event that left a psychic scar behind. That could be why I dream about someone knocking on the door at night."

"You hear it, too?" said Pepper. "So does my mother!"

"So do I!" said Billy.

"The watching man in the shadows."

"Yes!"

"Falling off the bridge."

"Yes!"

"Being buried in the ravine."

"Yes!"

"Now, wait a minute," said Pepper. "Psychometry explains the dreams, but it doesn't explain the rest. The man who attacked me was no dream. The man who scared Mrs Skinner off the edge of her deck was no dream. There's more than psychometry going on here. Something much more dangerous."

"And it's somehow connected with your Uncle Gabriel," said Joe. "What if your uncle was buried in the ravine? Buried under that old, vine-covered log, where both Billy and I got hurt."

"A fascinating theory, but one we could never prove," said Pepper. "The land on this side of the bridge isn't really part of Ravenna Park."

"Not part of the park? Then what is it?"

"This whole finger of land that breaks off from the main ravine — this is private property. Unusable land. The neighboring houses are all built around it, and no one tends it, so it goes wild and blends into the park."

"So that log down there is on private property?"

"The corners and ends of a number of private properties," said Pepper. "You'd have to get a surveyor down there to know exactly who owned what."

He sighed. "Well, there isn't time for a surveyor. This problem isn't going away. It's just getting worse. I don't think there's any choice about what we have to do next."

Rain pattered against the glass, drummed on the window-ledge, rattled in the gutterpipes. Both Billy and Pepper stared at him, waiting for him to continue.

"There's only one way to solve the mystery. Sooner or later," said Joe quietly, logically, "we're going to have to find out the secret of that log."

172

"Believe me, it's not a good idea to go down there digging," said Pepper. "You saw what happened to me when I tried it. Besides, it has to be against the law."

"I'm willing to take the chance," said Joe. "Every clue in this mystery is pointing in the same direction. It's time we took a look at that log. As far as I'm concerned, tonight's the night."

"Tonight?" said Pepper. "Couldn't we wait for a little more light and a little less weather?"

"That's what makes it ideal," said Joe. "With all the police surveillance, not getting caught will be a trick. No one in their right mind will be expected down there tonight, sloshing through the mud in this rain."

"You have a point," said Pepper. "Besides, at any other time my mother would see us before we got halfway there. It has to be late at night. But it's asking for trouble." She hesitated. "I'm going with you."

"Not after what happened to you."

"No one's scaring me away from this ravine."

"Count me in, too," said Billy, in a faltering voice.

"Out of the question," said Joe. "You've already had one nasty experience down there." He got up from his chair. "Your clothes should be dry by now. I'll get them." He headed downstairs into the studio.

"I'm not afraid," lied Billy.

"I can tell you're not," said Pepper. "You've got a lot of guts. But you can't go with us. What Joe and I are going to do is too risky. We'll walk you home first."

"But it's only right that I go." Billy tried to look brave and confident. He didn't allow himself to think about what happened last time. "I'm the one who started all this."

"Well, you've done your part," said Joe, coming up from the studio, handing him his dry T-shirt and pajama bottoms. "We'll take it from here. Put your clothes back on. And you'd better borrow the sweater — and these socks, too." He turned to Pepper. "For you, I've got a jacket and boots."

Soon she was pulling on Joe's extra boots and gloves, both much too large, bundling up in Joe's other parka. Each of them got a shovel out of the garage downstairs.

"Better take this, too," said Joe, handing her a flashlight. "One ought to be enough. We don't want to attract attention. Let's stick together, now. First we stop off at Billy's. Then we find out what's under that log."

The three of them took one last look at each other, smiling nervously. Then Joe locked the door behind them and they set out into the wet night.


# 11
# Into the Wild

The rain was a steady pattering all around them.

The street was deserted, everyone inside and asleep. They stopped on the sidewalk in front of Billy's house. All the lights were out. They followed Billy around back.

"Let me give you my phone number," said Joe. "In case your father asks about where you've been. Or whose clothes you've got. He can call me if he wants to." He jotted it on the back of a cash machine receipt, and handed it to the boy. Billy crumpled his fist around it to keep it dry.

He didn't say anything, no thanks, not even goodbye. He simply bounded away from them suddenly, across the grass of the back yard. Together they watched him use a maple tree beside the house, then the garage roof to get quickly and silently back into his bedroom.

"Well, that's taken care of," said Joe. "Now the hard part."

Keeping the flashlight pointing down at the wet sidewalk, he and Pepper headed back to the ravine. They crossed the narrow wooden bridge single-file, looking like two Joes, both wearing his jackets and boots. From the other side, they quietly descended the main footpath down between the roots and rocks into the wild end of the ravine.

One by one, their feet sank up to the ankles in the sludge. Splashing their way up the shallow, rocky creek, they reached the vine-covered log. The moment they stopped moving, the ravine became ominously quiet.

In the stillness, they could hear someone sloshing toward them. Pepper tried to conceal her panic. Joe snapped off the flashlight. The splashing footsteps got closer. Joe signalled her with a finger before his lips.

They could see the tall bamboo reeds rustling. The stalks parted. A figure stepped forward, nylon parka gleaming in the rain. Joe aimed the flashlight.

"Billy, is that you?"

"I had to come."

"You scared us half to death," said Pepper.

"Sorry."

"So you're the stubborn type?" said Joe, lowering the flashlight, turning it off. "Can't take no for an answer, eh? Welcome to the club. As long as you're here, you might as well stay with us." Picking up a branch off the ground, Joe poked under the thick netting of intertangled vines draped over the log. "Whatever we're looking for, my guess is — it's under there."

Pepper had herself tightly under control. She refused to let herself give way to fear. "So, where do we start digging first?"

"That's where my foot got caught," said Billy, pointing. "There's another branch underneath. My heel got wedged between the branches."

Joe reached under the net of vines, and took hold of the hidden, lower branch. The moment he touched the log, he felt an icy jolt which he tried to ignore. "Let's see if we can move it." Pepper joined him. Tugging together, they tried to pull the log to one side. "Won't budge. Those vines are holding it right where they want it."

"If anything was ever buried underneath it," said Pepper, "it must have come in from the side."

"Only one way under there," said Joe grimly. "Guess it's time to put these shovels to work." He stepped up to the log first, and jabbed his shovel into the mud.

"Get away from there!"

The beam of a powerful flashlight accompanied the cry, slashing down through the darkness.

Rose Merlino stood on the wooden deck behind her house. Her blue raincoat flapped open. A clear plastic scarf tried to contain her turbulent black hair. She aimed the flashlight beam like a flamethrower.

"You heard me." She called down angrily, stopping them in their tracks. "Get off my property right now, all of you."

"Mother, it's me," said Pepper.

"You and the others, too," said Rose. "You have no right to be digging down there."

"Mrs Merlino," said Joe, stepping forward to face her, "we don't mean to cause you any worry—"

"I don't care what you mean to do," said Rose. "Now you listen to me. Leave or I'll call the police."

"Mother, calm down," said Pepper. "There's no need—"

"Get off my property this minute!" barked Rose. She was beside herself with emotion, spearing them with the beam of her flashlight, going from face to face. She held the light on Billy, her eyes widening as though seeing him for the first time. "You! The horrid boy who caused my mother to fall. Go away — now — this minute!" She shifted the beam into the face of her daughter, making her squint in the brightness. "As for you, Pepper Merlino, I'll speak to you inside."

## 12
## Daughter Defiant

The back door swung open and Pepper stepped into the kitchen, still wearing Joe's old black parka and muddy boots. Rose turned to face her, blue raincoat hanging open, cheeks flushed with barely-suppressed rage. "You're filthy! Look, you're tracking mud all over the floor. Take off those horrible boots before you take one more step."

Pepper sat on the edge of a kitchen chair, tugged off one big boot after the other, shrugged off the sopping jacket, peeled off waterlogged socks, rolled up wet cuffs. Then she spoke.

"You should be ashamed, the way you talked to that poor boy!"

"So you side with the neighbors now?" Rose cried. She didn't notice that her own wet raincoat was leaving a trail across the glossy floor. "What do you think you're doing down there? Since when did my own daughter turn against me?"

"Our neighbors aren't against us," said Pepper patiently. "Our neighbors just have a healthy fear of the mysterious psycho who's terrorizing

176

Ravenna Park. They think you know who the prowler is. I hope they're wrong. I pray to God my dear mother knows nothing about it."

"Of course, I don't," said Rose, turning away from her. "And those people have no business snooping and prying. Let me tell you, there's a price for digging up old secrets. You can't just trample through private property and get away with it. You can't just—"

"Enough!" Pepper lost her temper. "I'm tired of you telling me what I can and can't do. You won't have to put up with me much longer." That was the moment she decided. "I've been accepted into a doctoral program at Oregon State. I'm through with Seattle. I'm moving to Corvallis."

"You're what?" Rose was stunned.

"You heard me. I've been offered a position as a teaching assistant. I'm moving out. I'm finishing this quarter and leaving."

"Leaving? And then?"

"I've got enough to survive on until I start teaching. Then I'll have three or four years to get my degree."

"I'm going to lose you?" Rose stared at her daughter. All the fire had gone out of her. "I don't understand what's happening. You can't just pick up and go."

"Yes, I can," said Pepper. "That's exactly what I'm doing. Mom, you knew I was applying to doctoral programs."

"But that was before. After Grandma died, I assumed you wouldn't leave me all alone, that we'd spend time together."

"Well, you assumed wrong," said Pepper. "I helped you with Grandma. She's gone. It's time to get on with my life."

"You're really moving away, just like that?"

"It's possible to survive outside Seattle."

"But I can't survive without you," said Rose, sinking into a kitchen chair. "Am I supposed to not notice you're gone?"

Pepper was embarrassed. "Mom, don't be so dramatic. It'll be a relief. You won't be fighting with me all the time."

"Is that what you think of me, really?" said Rose. "Just fighting with you?"

She loved her mother enough that she didn't like hearing the pain in her voice. "Now, I didn't mean it that way."

Her mother's eyes darkened with injury, walling her out. "Do you think I fight with you because I hate you?"

"Oh, Mom, please don't—"

Rose had been hurt. She wouldn't back down. "I fight with you because I love you."

Pepper knew her mother's techniques. She had to take a stand, or her mother would swallow her alive. "Sometimes you love me too much!"

Rose flinched, then simply stared. She could endure criticism, loneliness, rejection, but she couldn't endure having her love flung back in her face. She glared at her daughter. "The sooner you move out, the better."

The words were so cruel! They hurt Pepper just enough to make her blurt out, "Fine. I'll move out as soon as I can. But before I do, since you love me so much, tell me the truth for once. Do you love me enough for that? To tell me what really happened? What's the big secret? What are you hiding?"

"The truth?" Rose made a derisive little snort that sounded like laughter. "There's no truth to tell. There are no secrets."

"No secrets, huh?" said Pepper. "Glad to hear it. So tell me, did Uncle Gabriel come back?"

A horrible silence

"Uncle Gabriel?" said Rose, obviously flustered. "Forget Uncle Gabriel. What does he have to do with anything?"

"That's exactly what I want to know, Mom. Are you ever going to tell me the truth? What is it I don't know?"

Rose avoided her direct gaze. "Uncle Gabriel is dead and gone. Better to forget all the horrible little details of the past."

"It's my past, and I want to know the details," said Pepper. "You say you love me, but you're always keeping secrets from me. What is it you won't tell me? I'm your own daughter, and you act like I'm some kind of spy in my own family. Why don't you trust me?."

Rose Merlino broke down. Her sobs were silent heavings of the shoulders. "I do trust you. I just don't want to make you unhappy."

"Mom, tell me what really happened," said Pepper, softening. "The truth won't make me unhappy."

"Yes, it will, believe me. You think the truth won't change you? The truth — it changes everything."

She started to sob again. Pepper put her arm around her mother, walked with her into the dark living room, over to the sofa, where she turned on a lamp and helped her mother sit down. She tried to comfort her. There was no comfort for Rose.

"You're right, of course," said Rose through her tears. "As usual, you're right." She patted her daughter's hand. "You deserve to know the truth before it's too late, before there's no one to tell you. I've been lying for so long."

"Mom, when someone loves you, you don't have to lie."

"Oh yes, you do," said Rose. "Love means lying all the time! If someone loves you, you have to lie to protect their feelings."

"Mom, that's not true." Pepper took her by the shoulders. "When you love someone is when you *don't* have to lie."

"If only that were so!" said Rose, with a bitter imitation of a laugh. "You can't love anyone without lying."

"Love me without lying," said Pepper.

"I can't."

"You can. Nothing you say can make me love you less."

Rose's cheeks were lined with tears of defeat. "You have to promise me something first. You have to swear — this is between you and me alone. It's no one else's business. I mean it, Pepper! Do you promise to tell no one what I tell you?"

"Mom, be reasonable."

"Someone else is at risk here. The reputation of someone I love very much. Promise me never to repeat any of it. Promise!"

"I promise, Mom."

"Good. You deserve to know the truth. You need to know. About the night Uncle Gabriel died—"

# 13
## Inheritance

Carmen Merlino didn't have enough money the Christmas of 1960 to really decorate the house. She had done her best for the sake of her ten-year-old daughter, Rose. She had cut some holly and evergreen boughs from the edge of the ravine, pinned them along the mantelpiece, put a candlestick at either end, and strung popcorn and cranberries into cheerful holiday loops which she and Rose had draped through the fir needles and leaves, from candlestick to candlestick.

The kitchen was hot with baking, windows fogged with steam. Rose was making a careful selection of cookies for the central platter, arranging the biscotti and pizzele. Carmen was washing her hands in the kitchen sink. Because the water was running, she didn't hear the rat-a-tat.

"Someone knocked at the door," said Rose.

"What, honey?" Carmen turned off the water.

"Somebody's out there."

"I don't think so," said Carmen. "It's just the wind. It's so windy out there." Her mother's face clouded with worry as she dried her hands on the dishcloth. She walked across the kitchen and swung open the back door. Rose remembered how confident her mother had been that no one was there. Rose saw her expression change.

"Gabby!" she cried.

He was lounging against the doorframe casually. He smirked at her. "Guess who's home for Christmas."

Brother and sister embraced silently, briefly, and drew apart. He started through the back door into the kitchen, glanced away from his sister, and saw her. He halted, grinned, and opened his arms. "How's my pretty little Rosie?" She flung herself into his embrace. She adored her Uncle Gabriel.

Carrying her in his arms, he stepped into the kitchen — a mysterious, shabby young man in a shiny leather jacket, his boyish features weathered by life, dried out and soured, though leaving him still attractive in a lanky, cocky way.

"Everyone thought you were dead."

"The walking dead, that's me." His eyes had a hard glint that she was too young to understand.

"Where in the world have you been?"

He pointed out into the damp darkness. "I'm your new neighbor. I'm driving a tractor at the other end of that ravine." He snickered, and kissed Carmen on the cheek. "Good old sis. Happy to see me? Mmm, what smells so good in here?"

"You're just in time for Christmas Eve dinner."

"I must be psychic," said Uncle Gabriel.

"Please, stay!" urged Rose, using the words as an excuse for clinging to him.

"If you really want me to stay," said Uncle Gabriel, "you have to give me a kiss."

Rose quickly did so, before her mother could object.

"Rose, please, go upstairs," said Carmen. "Give Uncle Gabriel a little breathing room. I'll call you for dinner."

Rose obeyed her mother grudgingly, but behind her bedroom door she listened intently, peeking through the keyhole. Her mother had followed him up to the bathroom.

"You can use this towel, and this one."

"Give me a kiss, Carmen. Show me that you're happy to see me."

Carmen pulled away from him. "Stop teasing, Gabriel. And leave Rose alone. Stop charming her, I mean it."

"Just natural charm," said Uncle Gabriel. "Can't turn it off." He pulled off his shirt over his head. "Guess I'll clean up."

Her mother pulled shut the bathroom door, cutting off the sight of him. She turned away from the bathroom, biting her lip. A few minutes later, Uncle Gabriel and her mother went downstairs, and talked in soft voices. Then he went down into the basement, to his boxed-up belongings where he found old clothes left behind the year before. Her mother put the clothes he'd been wearing in the washing machine. Rose opened her bedroom door a crack. She could hear her mother in the kitchen. Rose went downstairs.

"He's come back," her mother whispered sadly. "Not quite a year. He's back too soon, honey. This ruins everything for us. Oh, it's not fair! We're going to lose the house."

Uncle Gabriel came upstairs from the basement, his black hair still wet. He sat down at the table with them. Carmen said grace. He ate like a starved animal. Bit by bit, he told his story.

He'd only been back in Seattle for a couple of days. He'd landed a temporary job as a driver for the I-5 freeway construction, unloading cement debris and surplus dirt into what had once been Cowen Ravine.

"So I didn't find out until yesterday that Dad was dead."

"Last year," she said. "Not long after your big showdown."

Rose giggled.

"You two stop kicking each other under the table," scolded Carmen. "Afterward you can help open Christmas presents."

Not until after he had finished another serving of meatballs and sausages did he tell her why he'd come. "I wouldn't have bothered you, except — well, I picked up some old mail yesterday and found out about the house. I mean, that it's mine."

"Yes," said Carmen. "Papa wanted you to have it."

"Well, that's why I'm here." He bit into a slab of garlic bread. "I do want it. And looks like the legal side is all worked out. So, I guess I'm going to move in. I just wanted you to know that. I mean, it does belong to me, the house. So I'm taking it."

At first she couldn't speak.

"Well, that'll be wonderful," she forced herself to say in a quavering voice. "We can be a family again. Rosie will love having her uncle here."

"I don't think so," said Gabriel, finishing off his wine. "Tell you the truth — no offense, Rosie — I don't need children complicating my life. I've had enough of family, thank you. And I don't need my older sis bossing me around, either. So, don't even think about it."

"But what about us?"

"What about you?" He used the half-eaten end of garlic bread to mop his plate of pasta sauce. "I suppose you'll have to move. That's none of my business."

"Move? Where?"

"That's your problem, sis, not mine. I take care of my problems. You take care of yours."

"Rose and I can stay here. We can clean for you, cook—"

"Out of the question."

"But Gabriel, I'm your sister. Surely you're not going to just throw us out."

"I'm not throwing you anywhere. You just don't live here anymore."

Her desperate glance darted in the direction of her daughter. "And what about your dear little niece? You're taking away a ten-year-old's home."

"I'm not taking anything. Listen, maybe when I get things squared away, you can both move in. But not now. I need to be alone. I need elbow room. I don't need family baggage. Sorry."

"Sorry? You're sorry?"

"Actually, I'm leaving. I'm busy tonight. But I'll be back."

"No, Gabby, wait—"

Rose was terrified. Right before her eyes at the dinner table, her little world had come apart. She had watched and listened as her wonderful, handsome uncle snatched her home away. He grabbed his leather jacket and disappeared out the back door. "Merry Christmas, Rosie!" he called over his shoulder. She watched her mother run after him down the dead-end street.

"Mama!" she had screamed, forgotten, left behind.

"Rose, go up to your room this minute!" called Carmen, before turning to run after her brother. Rose watched her from the doorway, whimpering with frustration. Then she disobeyed her mother. She dashed out the back door after them

Her mother had caught up with Uncle Gabriel halfway across the old wooden bridge. She grabbed him by the collar of his leather jacket and spun him around.

"Look me in the face. I helped raise you like a mother. I worked long hours to keep food on the table. And you're throwing me out in the street."

"I'm not throwing you anywhere."

"How can you be so cold-blooded?"

"I'm not doing anything wrong to you. I told you, I'll help you when I can. It's just that—"

"I'm your sister!"

"That's not my problem."

She struck him. The blow was harder than she thought.

"Hey, cut that out!"

"You deserve worse!"

Rose watched them from the stairs leading down to the pedestrian walkway, staring in fear. They were reckless and furious with each other, as only brother and sister could be.

"I deserve some respect."

"You deserve—" She'd run out of words. She shoved him in the chest, this time much harder. It caught him off-balance. The blow knocked him backward.

Rose had run down the stairs to the end of the bridge. Staring helplessly, she gave a shriek. She never believed that her mother meant to do it. Her mother was a good woman. Her mother was a saint, the best mother in the world.

Her uncle screamed as he toppled off the bridge. It was an awful sound, filled with pure hatred. He was so mad, so furious to fall, so enraged to be defeated in such a simple, stupid way. Rose would never forget the fury of that cry, or the terrible sound when her uncle's body hit the ground.

# 14
## The Wonderful Truth

Pepper sat sunken into the cushions of the armchair, listening as her mother's story came to its terrible end.

Winter silence gripped the neighborhood. It was almost three in the morning. No cars were passing on 25th Avenue. No dogs were barking. The rain had eased to a steady, whispering drizzle, accompanied by the pattering of drops on millions of twigs and branches and needles, dripping, dripping. Only one light was on — in the living room of the Merlino house.

Pepper stared out the picture window over the ravine. The glass was black with night, reflecting her own face back at her.

"Grandma?" said Pepper. "My good, wonderful Grandma — killed her brother? Killed him in a fight over this house—"

"You are never, ever to speak a word of this," said Rose. "You promised."

"I'll keep my promise," said Pepper.

"Now you see why I didn't want you to know," said her mother. "Why should you have to carry something so ugly inside? I lied to you, God forgive me, but I did it for Mama's sake. I wanted you to love Mama, not to be afraid of her." She was exhausted. She had lived through it all over again. "I didn't want you to think of your Grandma as a murderer."

"But she wasn't a murderer," said Pepper. "It was an accident, wasn't it? Wasn't it?"

"God knows, not me," said her mother. "I'm sorry you made me tell you. You won't be happier knowing. Now you'll spend the rest of your life lying. Lying to everyone you love. You'll lie to protect her, just like I did. But you can't lie to God. The wonderful truth — it's better buried and forgotten! You see why I tried to hide it from you?"

Pepper nodded. Too late she understood. She rose abruptly, shook herself, brushed herself off. "So, what happened then? The two of you didn't bury him down there, did you?"

"You don't need to know."

"Yes, I do, Mom."

"I've told you enough. More than enough."

But Pepper wanted the rest of the story. She wanted answers. "Go ahead, I can take it. What are you afraid to tell me? Is he buried under that log?"

"I've said all I'm going to say. Don't make yourself more miserable than you already are."

"This is what you were always talking about together, you and Grandma, isn't it? Your little whispers and secrets. And you're still protecting her."

"She did it for me." Rose was staring back into the past. "No mother could have done more."

185

"Done more?" Pepper didn't see it that way. "Done what? Excuse me, Mom, but an accident is one thing, if that's what we're talking about. Or are we talking about murder? A mother's love is all very nice, and accidents can happen. Or are you telling me that Grandma killed her brother to get this house?" Her mother didn't answer. Pepper wished she'd never asked. "How can you go on living here?"

"How could I live anywhere else?" Rose shook her head, with a bitter smile. "The young always think they can judge."

"Thank God I'm leaving," whispered Pepper. "Thank God I'm escaping."

# 15
# Afraid to Sleep

He stood on the sidewalk across the street, ignoring the rain, watching Billy grab hold of a low maple branch, swing his way up onto the garage, and vanish behind the house. Rain dribbled down through the bare twigs, gargled down the gutterpipes, pecked at Joe's cheeks. A light snapped on upstairs. Billy waved from his window over the front porch. Joe turned around for home.

He was so preoccupied he scarcely noticed his own Christmas lights, blinking at him faintly through his mental fog. He entered through the basement studio door, patted Bobo on the head, left his muddy clothes on the doormat, and walked straight into a hot shower. He couldn't get Pepper's mother out of his mind. He stretched out on his bed, arms folded behind his head, staring at the ceiling, trying to understand. What could have possessed Rose Merlino to yell at them like that? The same way her mother had yelled at Billy. Were both women mentally ill? Or did they have reasons for keeping people away?

He almost sank into a doze, then jolted awake. He sat on the edge of the bed, covering his face with his hands. He was afraid to fall asleep. He got up off the bed and paced the hallway, tense, exhausted, then drifted toward the kitchen.

He slumped over at the kitchen table in his underwear, trying to read the newspaper without causing it to rattle from the trembling of his hands. An hour later he was still there, staring at a half-empty carton of milk and crumbs in an empty cookie package.

Red-eyed, sleepless, he scratched at his bristly jaw.

Would he ever get used to the nightmares? He propped his elbows on the kitchen table, covered his face with his hands. He couldn't pay next month's rent. He'd have to place more ads, take the first caller. Dreading the very sight of his bed, trying to put off sleep as long as he could, Joe went downstairs to his studio.

Bobo looked up from his rug in confusion. Joe scratched behind the dog's ear. With a couple of half-awake tail wags, Bobo sank back into peaceful dog-dreams, so different from the dreams of his master.

Joe turned on the electric heater, propped a blank canvas on his easel. He took a step back from the canvas, and stared at it.

"Seven notebooks full of sketches — but no paintings. What am I waiting for? Why do I bother calling myself a painter? What makes me think I have anything to contribute? Why do I bother staying alive? If I had time for only one last painting, if I knew I were going to die at dawn, what would I paint?"

# 16
## Goodbye

She hadn't seen Joe for two weeks.

Their friendship was ruined. How could she be honest? She had made a promise to her mother. She could never reveal what she'd learned that night, never tell Joe and Billy the true cause of their nightmares without betraying her grandmother.

Joe had phoned twice. She hadn't returned his calls. One look at Pepper, and he'd realize something had happened. One word, and he'd know she was lying.

She had packed, made arrangements with graduate housing at Oregon State, bought her plane ticket. She'd finished her lab assignments, prepared for a written exam, earned the second-highest grade in the class. Her faculty advisor had okayed the revised third chapter of her thesis. She'd completed the appropriate paperwork for withdrawing from the university. All personal belongings had been removed from her desk in Isaacson Hall.

Pepper counted the days. She was eager to leave it all behind. Her new knowledge of the family had contaminated and ruined all her fondest memories, transforming the past, fouling every impression she had of Grandma. Could that loveable old woman have actually killed her own brother so she could steal his house?

She put off telling Joe until the last possible moment. She had planned to do it by telephone, so that he couldn't see her face. In the end, the need to return his borrowed parka and boots caused her to phone and leave a message that she'd be stopping by. He didn't return her call. Two hours later, she bundled up in her overcoat and scarf, gathered up the parka and boots, and walked across the bridge.

His outdoor Christmas lights were blazing. The front drapes were drawn. She knocked, peered in the window. No signs of life in the living room. She sighed and circled around the side of the house to the kitchen door. In passing the garage workshop in the basement she noticed a bright light downstairs.

He must be in his studio on the other side of the garage, wearing his headphones, working on some project. She approached the garage, slid the blockade aside far enough to edge through, and found herself abruptly staring into a big, brown, hairy face. Her ears rang with a bark as loud as a revolver shot. The paws hit her in the chest. Suddenly she had her arms full of dog. She wrestled him down, patted him on his big head, and stepped around him into the studio.

"Joe?"

No sign of him. The rest of the studio was dark. Two bookshelves crammed full of art books towered over a wash basin, a work bench, and shelves of color-coded paint-jars. One high-intensity overhead lamp was focused on the only lit object in the basement, his easel — an oil painting of the Ravenna Park fieldhouse against a stately row of poplars. She stared at the painting. It was breathtaking. It captured a certain feeling about the park that she knew perfectly. Not until her second look did she notice, in the background, a brown Airedale romping over the grass. She smiled.

"Where is he, Bobo? Where'd that guy go?"

She walked several steps past Bobo.

"Joe?"

A flash of light. She gasped, took a step backward. Another overhead lamp had snapped on. It spotlighted another painting on an easel further into the studio. The waters of Ravenna Creek, three shallow waterways rushing together just before the tumbling white froth of the little falls. In the background, the old wooden pedestrian bridge. Beneath it, half-hidden behind one of the trees, a small boy was intently drawing.

"Gorgeous!" she cried. "Hey, what's going on here? Hello—"

Another lamp snapped on. A third painting. The main ravine trail, coming down from Cowen Park. The magnificent spans of the 15th Avenue bridge overhead, like the massive entrance gate of a lost kingdom. Beams of morning light shafting through the spans. In the distance, on the trail, a small detail — a woman jogging.

A shadow rose up out of the armchair. He was unshaved, red-eyed, in T-shirt and sweats. "Hi, stranger."

"It's been a while."

"You could say that," said Joe. "Ever since our little digging party in the ravine."

She avoided his eyes, ignored the comment. "Which reminds me." She handed him the parka and boots. He set them aside, hardly glancing at them. She kept her eyes focused on the easels. "These paintings, they're incredible." She took another look at him. "Are you okay?"

Joe took a step closer, into the light. His eyes were overflowing with tears, but he was smiling. "I can't pay my electric bill, and they're threatening to turn off my water," he said. "I haven't got a housemate to help pay the rent. I have nightmares and visions that are driving me crazy. I should be feeling sorry for myself, and I'm not. I'm so happy I'm crying. Thanks to you." He gestured toward the paintings. "I've got a wonderful new friend who gave me a kick in the pants when I needed one. I've been painting for two weeks. I can't stop!"

He went from painting to painting. "See this? And this? My own version of Impressionism, Northwest-style. What Seattle has given me. What I found here that brought me back to life. I can paint this. I can pay back the happiness. Look at this — bet you know right where it is."

"No wonder I haven't heard from you," she said, smiling.

His smile faltered. "But you have. Twice. You didn't call back."

She turned away her eyes. She didn't let him see her face.

"Pepper, why did your mother threaten to call the police on us?"

"My mother is a touchy subject." Pepper turned away from him, her features hardening into an unreadable mask. "Don't start on her. She's already driving me crazy. I can only take so much."

Joe threw caution to the wind. "If she knows something about this prowler, she should say so. I know the old 'blood is thicker than water' thing. I'm Italian, too. But this isn't just pranks by neighborhood kids. If Uncle Gabriel is back in town and angry, the neighbors deserve to know. He's going to kill someone next. She needs to report him—"

"My mother has nothing to do with this," snapped Pepper. She closed her eyes quickly, to keep the tears from showing. "I didn't come here to talk about my mother. I came to talk about me. And you. Somebody needs to say something. This whole thing between us is about as crazy as it can get. So it's just as well we nip it off now."

He was shocked, suddenly scared. She could see it in his eyes, the vulnerability, the panic. "Nip it off? I don't understand."

It couldn't be posponed any longer. "Joe, I've been accepted into a doctoral program at Oregon State. I'm leaving Seattle."

He stared at her. "Is this some kind of joke?"

"I know, hard to believe." She smiled half-heartedly. "Strange but true. I'll be living in Corvallis. It's not that far."

"Is this the plan for next year?"

"No, actually — I've got my ticket. I fly out Sunday morning."

"This coming Sunday?" Joe's features went slack. "Before Christmas? You can't be serious."

"I've completed this quarter at the U, and now the rest of the year I'll finish off there, and start my fieldwork in the fall."

*Three Paintings*

"Sounds like you've got it all figured out."

"So that's why I'm here. I wanted to say goodbye."

Joe's mental wheels were spinning. "This is all going too fast for me. I think I must be missing something."

She gave his hand a squeeze and turned away. "I wish you success."

"Pepper, wait, this isn't possible. You're my best friend. How can you just casually announce you're walking out of my life? We've got something unique. We understand each other. We trust each other. I thought we both needed each other!"

She never knew at what point she finally broke down crying. Her cheeks turned red, streaked with silent tears. "I'm sorry, Joe. My days in Seattle are over. I don't mean to hurt you. I've learned a lot from you. You're an incredible man. I've enjoyed knowing you so much!"

"Don't leave," he said quietly.

"Don't hate me," she said. "I've got to leave. Or that house will eat me alive, the same way it swallowed up my grandmother and mother. That house — I can't live there anymore."

"Why not?"

"This is my chance to escape, Joe, and I've got to take it."

"What happened?"

"I've got to leave Seattle behind."

"You're not telling me something."

"I'm telling you goodbye."

Fighting against the tears filling her eyes, Pepper impulsively hugged him, kissed him on the cheek. She clung so tightly that at first it seemed she wouldn't let go. Then she pulled decisively away, turned her back on him, and walked out of his life.

He stood in the doorway long after the door had closed, stopped in his tracks, like an electrical toy that had come unplugged. The first sob came choking out of him as he swung out his hand and angrily slapped the switch, snapping off the three spotlights he'd rigged a few hours before as a surprise for his wonderful friend.

CHAPTER EIGHT

# Christmas Eve

## 1
## Missing

On that terrible Christmas Eve, Paul Beck noticed his son's increasing isolation, his lack of eye contact, his silence, his withdrawal. He detected the danger signals the moment Billy came downstairs as only a father could, but since Billy had not been himself for months, Paul chose to ignore them. Instead he smiled, and acted like it was going to be a perfect Christmas.

Billy seemed troubled over something, deep in thought. Paul found him in front of the picture window in the living room, none of the lamps turned on, half in shadow, staring out through the glass at the wind-lashed, rattled branches.

"What are you doing in here all by yourself?"

"Oh, hi Dad. Thinking."

"Thinking, huh? Come in the kitchen with me. You can think while you're keeping me company."

Billy obediently slumped into one of the kitchen chairs. He stared at the tabletop as though it were a glowing television screen.

"Are you all right, pardner?"

He looked up. "I'm fine."

"Good." He filled himself with Christmas cheer. "That fire looks like it could use a log or two."

Billy left the room and built up the fire in the fireplace.

"Good job. While you're at it, those presents under the tree look pretty messy. Why don't you straighten them out? You can see if there are any for you."

He arranged the presents under the tree. Paul noticed his lack of response to the ones marked with his name, as though the name belonged to someone else.

"You can light the candles on the mantelpiece, if you want." He suddenly looked around him, turned in a circle, slapped at his pockets in frustration. "If you can find the matches."

Billy found the matches. He lit the candles on the mantelpiece.

Paul made the mistake of asking him if he'd like to listen to a CD of Christmas music.

"No, thanks."

"Well, you might as well set the table then. Dinner is almost ready."

He set the table.

Then, in that one brief moment before Paul could think of another task for him, Billy drifted upstairs.

Paul thought nothing more about it. He had enough on his mind orchestrating a traditional holiday dinner, even if it was only for two. He was soon completely caught up in the minute-to-minute schedule of oven doors and serving bowls, stirring pots, listening for the ding of the microwave. He hadn't taken the time to reach out to Billy. Well, kids had moods. He would talk to him at dinner. There was plenty of time.

The wind that night was icy and stinging, rattling holiday decorations, tugging at wires of Christmas lights, driving the brief flurries of rain almost horizontal, forcing everyone inside to be merry.

Though Paul was bravely attempting cheerfulness, trying not to worry about his son, it was a low-key Christmas Eve at best. His sister had moved to Boston. His brother had been relocated to Georgia. Somehow the Becks had fallen through the cracks among the other relatives. They had Christmas Day plans tomorrow with two uncles, a big holiday dinner in Tacoma. But they were alone that Christmas Eve.

At least the cooking ordeal was almost over. Paul was ready to sit down to dinner and enjoy the rest of the evening. He looked forward to

Billy opening his presents. They would laugh together. Laughter was what the kid needed. Laughter was better than any psychiatrist's couch.

"Billy, it's dinner-time," he called up the stairs toward his room. "Better wash your hands and get ready, pal."

No response.

Paul was hungry. "Some pretty great smells down here." An awkward silence. He smiled. The poor guy was so tired lately, he'd probably dozed off.

He bounded up the stairs toward the boy's bedroom.

Billy might be sound asleep. Or wearing his headphones. "Come on, pal, time to chow down," said Paul, and opened his son's door.

The bedroom was empty.

An icy breeze sliced into the room from the crack of the window not quite closed. The inside windowsill was splashed with raindrops.

"Billy?"

No one was there.

He stood there staring into his son's room, confounded, unable to venture a guess. How could his son mysteriously disappear on Christmas Eve?

"Billy!" cried Paul, as though maybe he hadn't called him loudly enough. He flung open the closet door. He dropped to one knee and looked under the bed. He had to be there. He'd never come back downstairs. Paul began dashing from room to room, flinging open closets, shouting, calling, pleading. He ended up back in Billy's room, staring at the raindrops on the inner windowsill.

"Why would he run away?" thought Paul. "I mean, where would he go?" He began pacing back and forth, occasionally pounding his fist into his palm. "It's that guy in the park. He's been hanging around Billy. Tell me one good reason for a forty-year-old man to be hanging around an eleven-year-old boy. Give me one good reason!"

Then it dawned on him. Hadn't he just seen a phone number somewhere?

He strode over to his son's desk and snatched up the number scrawled on the back of a cash machine receipt. Striding back down the hall to

195

the telephone, he stabbed in the numbers, his finger viciously jabbing the buttons, one by one, as though accusing each button of unspeakable crimes.

# 2
# Alone

No lighted windows brightened the Merlino house. It brooded in the dark at the far end of the ravine, only one edge of it lit by the neighborhood streetlamp. Nothing moved inside. From the house next door came the weak blink of red and green lights against the drawn curtains. Voices spoke in the stillness. The concerned, loving voices of relatives speaking into an empty electronic silence.

"Merry Christmas, Rose. It's your cousin, Linda." That familiar hearty cackle. "I should scold you. You haven't returned one of our calls. Are you coming? Can we expect you? I hope so."

"Hi, dear. It's Aunt Lorraine. You did get our invitation? I'm sure you got many. We haven't heard from you. We'd like to."

"Are you there, Rosie? Merry Christmas from Uncle Carl and Aunt Lena. Just wishing you the best, hon. But I would like to add a thought. We were taught to return calls when I was a girl. You should try it. We miss you."

The silence was interrupted by a soft human sound from the direction of the armchair. In spite of its desolate appearance, the room had one resident. Rose sat alone in the darkness, her face wet with the tears she would never let anyone see. Her vodka was beside her. There was no mother or daughter to hide her flask from anymore. The message tape on her answering machine had come to an end. She pressed *Rewind* and listened to the messages again.

Those familiar voices! They were proof. Proof she wasn't alone, she wasn't forgotten. People remembered her. There was still a Rose Merlino living in Seattle, daughter of Carmen, mother of Pepper, even though Carmen and Pepper were gone and weren't coming back. All those people leaving messages couldn't be wrong. Those people were family. They loved her and wanted her to join them at Christmas. They didn't want her to be left alone in that terrible house.

She had no choice. Rose couldn't leave. The house had claimed her. Besides, she wasn't alone. She would never be alone, not there. And she would never leave it. She had no intention of moving to some sensible, cramped condominium to grow old. She would not be growing old.

Something had disturbed the secret. Something had irritated the ancient wound that had never healed. She found herself thinking about him lately. It was that boy's fault, that cursed boy who had stuck his foot where it didn't belong!

Too late to accept invitations. Too late to reach out to relatives. She had chosen to stand by her mother, to match her mother's love.

Footsteps outside.

She rose silently from the armchair, listening. Then she quietly crossed the carpet and started toward the kitchen.

So softly she almost didn't hear it came a faint rapping at the back door. She froze, listening, waiting for the sound to repeat itself.

Footsteps crossed the deck outside.

She bounded upstairs and rushed down the short hall to the drapes overlooking the back deck. She thrust the curtains apart. No one. She stared down at the deserted, winter-stripped deck, at the dark, leafy crack in the earth she knew was the ravine. Not a breath of movement.

She heard footsteps circling around to the other side of the house. Someone was out there.

The telephone was downstairs. Her mother had insisted on having only one. Rose had always meant to buy more phones. She hurried quickly and quietly back down the stairs. She would dial 9-1-1 immediately. She could see the telephone attached to the wall by the coat-rack. In just a moment she was going to feel very silly. She reached the bottom stair. Now just straight across the hallway carpet to—

Halfway there she glanced through the dark kitchen at the brightly-lit back door.

His face was looking in the window.

# 3
## In Danger

Billy should have been washing his hands for dinner. He had no reason for wandering upstairs, no reason for going into his bedroom, no reason for looking out the window to see the man in the back yard looking up at him.

He quickly backed away from the glass. It was scarcely dark, and he was already waiting. No use trying to hide. He had come for Billy, and would not leave until he got what he came for.

Not unless Billy changed the rules. Not unless he stopped running away. Not unless the boy faced his fear. The battered remains of his eleven-year-old pride had taken all the abuse he could endure. "Every night I wake up scared. I don't want to be scared any more."

He opened the closet door and pulled out his blue turtleneck sweater. He tugged it down over his head until his arms thrust out the sleeves.

He returned to the window. The man was no longer standing below. The boy looped a leather cord around his neck. At the end dangled a small plastic whistle that could be heard blocks away. He slid his grandfather's old jackknife into his pocket. Then he eased open his bedroom window and clambered out, one leg after the other.

He half-slid, half-scrambled onto the garage roof. From there he could grab the lowest maple branch. He swung down onto the grass, landed with a thud, caught his breath, peered in all directions. No one in sight. He cautiously approached the side of the house.

No one there, either.

Billy walked to the dead end of the street. As he did, the palm of his right hand began throbbing. The pad beneath his index finger began to feel swollen and hot.

The wind was rising. Windowpanes rattled in their frames. Screen doors clattered and jiggled. Fir needles shivered frantically.

No sign of the man.

Billy darted down a sheer, twisting footpath that descended through twigs and exposed roots to the ravine bottom. He crossed under the bridge without looking up. He trudged along beside the creek bed without noticing that he was sloshing through puddles and leaf-clogged muck. His right hand throbbed. His eyes were on the fallen maple trunk ahead.

He stopped in front of it. He reached out the hand with the tiny, unhealed wound and touched the crumbling bark. That's all it took, and he knew. Somehow that tree trunk was at the center of it all. The night wind hissed through the bare branches around him like a high-pitched singing. The answer was here, if he only knew the question.

Suddenly Billy looked up, out of the depths of the ravine, at the Merlino house.

Something moved outside the house, something glided away from the wall — a human figure — a man who stopped and stood there on the deck, as though he were looking straight at Billy.

Once again Billy refused to give in to fear. He made his way slowly up the side of the bank, toward the figure waiting above.

By the time he scrambled and clawed his way up behind the house, the man was gone. A light suddenly brightened an upper window. No other sign of life disturbed the hush. No music. No voices. No Christmas cheer. He climbed the short walkway and quietly circled around to the front of the house, then back around the other side. No one. He stepped out onto the deck. Each step he took across the slats of the flooring made a hollow footfall.

Billy looked up at the second floor of the house. He thought he saw someone move in the lighted window. A shadow cut briefly across the light. A curtain rustled back into place.

The man was inside.

Billy left the deck behind, and climbed up the stairs curving around the side of the house. Ahead was the back door. He was trying to figure out how to get inside when he noticed that the door was open a crack. He reached out and gently touched it. The door swung wider, revealing a dark kitchen opening into a shadowy hallway. He was halfway down the hall when he heard the back door click shut behind him.

Billy spun around.

Nightmare Man was standing in the doorway.

For one hideous moment, the boy tried to make his legs work backward, tried desperately to put as much distance as possible between himself and the man blocking the door.

The man lunged at him. Billy wailed and tried to leap aside, but not fast enough. The man's hand gripped hold of him by the collar.

Billy seized his whistle to blow on it. He felt the cord with the whistle ripped away from his neck. He tried to reach into his pocket for the jackknife, but he was jerked roughly off his feet. The man's elbow clamped around Billy's neck, cutting off his air, hauling him down the echoing hallway, limbs flailing more and more weakly.

# 4
## "Where Is My Son?"

Joe had just taken the pasta off the stove and was draining the boiling water into the sink in an explosion of steam when the phone rang. He didn't hear it. He wasn't really paying attention to his cooking, which was unlike him. He couldn't think straight. All he could think about was Pepper's abrupt, inexplicable departure out of his life.

He had put together something that resembled a sauce, the best he could do in his condition. Gently bubbling on the range, it should have been full of delicious surprises, broccoli, olives, mushrooms, celery, sausage. Tonight, on Christmas Eve, it contained nothing but tomato sauce.

He was so busy pouring it over the hot rigatoni, so preoccupied mourning his loss, that he almost didn't hear the telephone ringing the second time, either. He picked up the receiver and tucked it between neck and shoulder.

"Merry Christmas."

"Let me speak to my son this minute."

"Who is this?"

"This is Paul Beck. Put Billy on the line."

He was so confident that Billy was there! Had the boy told his father he'd be at Joe's house? The kid didn't strike him as the lying kind. "Billy isn't here. Did he say he would be?"

"He didn't have to say anything. Are you going to let me talk to my son, or do I call the police?"

"Police?" echoed Joe in disbelief. The man was as desperate as he sounded. "What happened? Please tell me. Is he all right?"

The concern in Joe's voice rattled Paul's confidence that he was on the right track. "How should I know?" His voice cracked. "That's why I'm worried."

"But where is he?"

"That's why I'm calling you."

"But he isn't here."

"Well, he isn't here, either," said Paul Beck with a forced levelness of voice, "but he's going to be soon. I intend to get him back fast, no matter what I have to do."

Joe knew immediately where the boy had to be — either he'd gone back to the log, or gone to spy on the Merlino house. That blasted kid!

"I'm asking you, do you know where Billy is?" said the boy's anxious father. When Joe didn't answer, he lost his temper. "Listen, I've had enough of this. I'm not eleven. You can't fool me. It's time someone told you to play with boys your own age."

Joe hung up.

He was trembling. His eyes were stinging with rage. How dare that man insult him! But something else was even more upsetting than the blow to his pride. The boy was in danger.

# 5
# Convergence

Paul Beck was pacing with nervous frustration. The house wasn't big enough for the strides he needed to take, the energy he needed to expel. He ran his hand back through his hair. His forehead was damp. He loosened his collar. He cracked his knuckles. He pounded his fist helplessly into his palm.

He had to get out of the house. It was the one place Paul was sure the boy wasn't.

He turned off the oven, the stove, took the green beans out of the microwave, stirred and covered everything and left it all right where it was. So much for Christmas dinner! He grabbed his red goosedown parka out of the front closet before bolting outside. Fighting his arms into the sleeves, he locked the front door behind him. Then he began loping down the street into the icy wind, his footfalls ringing hollowly on the pavement, past the neighborhood basketball hoop, craning his neck to look in every direction. The Hayashi house wasn't particularly noticeable, mostly hidden behind two big maples that crowded and darkened the house till it was scarcely visible. The old woman seemed to materialize on the lawn, stepping out of the shadow of the trees.

"Excuse me, I'm looking for my son, Billy," he began awkwardly. "He's disappeared. Less than an hour ago. I — I don't know where he can be." The words tumbled out. His voice shook. He folded his arms tightly across his chest. "I can't lose my son. I can't let anything happen to him. I can't."

She cut him off by gesturing across the ravine, as though she knew what he wanted. He looked where she was pointing.

"Yes, of course!" said Paul. "The Merlino house. That's where he's gone. That has to be it."

He was unsure whether he ever thanked her or said goodbye. He only knew he was running as fast as he could to the end of the street, where the thickets of undergrowth began, where a dozen steep, cement stairs led down through the trees to the pedestrian trestle bridge suspended over the ravine. He lunged down the stairs at a reckless pace and was about to bolt out across the narrow bridge when he saw that he wasn't the first to arrive.

Halfway across was the man who kept hanging around his son.

*

Joe stopped at the sound of approaching footsteps, turned and stared. Billy's father kept coming. Joe waited for him, his teal-green parka flapping open, one black glove gripping the railing, red scarf blowing loose at the neck.

"So, where is he?"

Joe could feel the man's words like an aggressive shove. "I told you I don't know."

The man's eyes were like razors, slashing, slicing, looking for weaknesses, cracks, clues. "Heading somewhere in a hurry?"

Joe eyed him, irritated, bristling. "I've got an idea where he might be." He could distinguish the log in the darkness below. The boy wasn't there. That left only one other place.

The boy's father scowled. "So now you suddenly remember where my son might be? How is it you know so much about my son?"

Joe could feel his cheeks turning red. For a moment the two men were almost touching.

Joe regarded him nose to nose. "Why do you want to make me fight you?"

The wind sliced through their coats, mercilessly cold. It stung their cheeks. It tugged at the flaps of their jackets, tore at their collars. They both regarded each other through eyes narrowed to cautious slits against the blast.

"Nobody is going to hurt my boy," said Paul.

"I'm trying to help you find him," said Joe. "I think I know where Billy might have gone."

"So do I," said Paul.

Neither of them spoke. They both simply turned to look in the same direction, at the Merlino house.

# 6
# Crucifix

With his red parka flapping open against the winter night, trying to trust the man he most suspected, Paul Beck ran the rest of the way across the bridge with Joe Strozza bounding up the concrete stairs behind him. They turned up the short walkway through winter-stunned crysanthemums, shrivelled and wilted, to the three stairs leading up to the front door of the Merlino house.

"This is where I think we'll find him," said Joe.

Paul knocked on the front door. No answer.

"Maybe I'm wrong," said Joe. "But I was sure he'd come here."

Paul knocked again, louder this time. He turned the doorknob. To his surprise, the door swung open. He and Joe glanced at each other.

"Do we go in?" said Paul.

"We don't have any choice."

They quietly stepped inside.

"Merry Christmas?" called Joe into the emptiness. "Hello?"

Not a sound. No signs of life except for the half-hearted twinkle of red and green lights reflecting through the windows from the house next door. They walked guardedly down the gray entrance hall. Other than a puddle of light around the lamp in the far corner, the shadowy living room hardly seemed lived in. Every piece of furniture was relentlessly clean and tidy and squarely in its place.

"Mrs Merlino?" called Paul, more boldly.

No answer.

"Do you think she's here?" said Joe, in a voice bordering on a whisper.

Paul was scowling. He looked around at the austere neatness, at the severe, dustless interior. "She's not the one I'm worried about."

Not until then did Joe notice that someone had made quite a mess. The fireplace was jammed with a mound of papers and boxes spilling over onto the hearthstone. Piles of magazines, old underwear, notebooks, photos, T-shirts, letters, the detritus of a lifetime.

"Somebody's cleaning out old memories," said Joe.

Paul wasn't interested. "Billy!" he called into the house's echoing hollowness. "Billy, are you in here?" No response. He turned indecisively to Joe. "I hope he isn't doing something stupid. Why did we think he would be here? Where could that crazy kid be?"

As though in answer, a floorboard creaked in one of the rooms above them.

"Sounds like someone's home," whispered Joe.

Paul nodded. With a meaningful glance at each other, they approached the staircase leading to the upper floor. Neither of them ventured a guess as to who that stealthy someone might be. Why would

Rose Merlino not answer their call? Was Billy hiding in fear? Or was it someone else? Someone they were not expecting.

Together they began quietly ascending the stairs. They paused midway in the darkness. Another floorboard above them groaned. He and Joe both looked up toward the landing.

"Watch my back," said Joe, continuing up the stairs. "I don't want any surprises from behind."

"I'm coming with you," said Paul. "He's my son." He glanced down the upstairs hall. He turned just in time to see a door close at the hall's end, cutting off the gray spill of moonlight.

He touched Joe's arm as they reached the top of the stairs.

"I've got a funny feeling about those rooms down at the end," Paul whispered. "I'll catch up with you."

Joe gave a nod, and continued cautiously straight ahead toward the creaking floorboards. Paul turned down the hall in the other direction. He approached the room where he had glimpsed movement. He reached out and touched the door.

It swung open into Rose Merlino's immaculate bedroom.

Christmas lights from the neighbors' house shimmered through the window glass, blinking on the bedroom walls. Paul snapped on the light switch. The first thing he saw was an enormous crucifix hanging over the bed's old-fashioned ornately-carved mahogany headboard. On one side of the bedstead hung a picture of Jesus, on the other one of Mary, each delicately pulling open the bared skin of their chests to show inside a bright red suffering heart.

A rumpled blue dress had been flung across the white bedspread. A pair of shoes lay tumbled on the throw-rug. At the foot of the bed was a padded kneeler, facing the crucifix.

The empty bedroom opened into a small bathroom, its door partly open. Paul cautiously approached the light switch. The blaze temporarily blinded him. White tiles and little soaps and an oval mirror. No one lurking behind the shower curtain.

Paul heard a step behind him. He quickly poked his head back out into the bedroom.

"Billy?"

No one. He was developing a case of the jitters. He felt like a snoopy intruder. Besides which, he was wasting his time. Billy wasn't here. He was quickly walking out of Rose's bedroom, crossing by the foot of the bed, when he noticed a slight change in his peripheral vision which brought him to an abrupt halt.

The ungainly crucifix was no longer over the headboard.

He turned around in circles of astonishment, facing the hall door, the bathroom door, the closet door. No one was there. He turned to face the window. The bedroom light snapped off.

He spun around.

The intruder stood silhouetted in the lighted doorway.

"Hey," said Paul, "turn the lights back on."

At first he thought it was Joe. But it wasn't. Paul took a step toward him, heart thudding wildly.

"Who are you?" Paul tried to shout. His voice came out trembling.

The man didn't answer. One arm shifted slightly. Paul glimpsed what looked like a large carpenter's tool with sharp right angles. As the man sprang toward him, Paul realized that the weapon raised overhead, coming down in an angry arc, was a crucifix.

It hit him in the head. Paul dropped to his knees.

The last thing he saw as he crumpled forward was the man's black leather jacket. It was him. The man Billy had tried to tell him was real.


# 7
# Leather Jacket

The headache tightening across Joe's temples became localized in a tiny, throbbing pain in the corner of his left eye. He fought down the panic inside.

"Billy?"

He listened to Paul's footsteps moving away down the hall. He was getting the strong feeling that no one else was there. The upper floor of the house felt as empty as the lower. Every footstep, every rustle of his parka, seemed to disturb the peace. His hunch about Billy's whereabouts had proved entirely wrong. If they were smart, they'd vacate the premises immediately before they had a lawsuit on their hands. Before his eye began hurting any worse.

He could hear Billy's father poking around down at the end of the hall. He would be stomping up to Joe soon, demanding an explanation. Joe wished he had an explanation to give him. What could have possessed Billy to take off on Christmas Eve, of all nights?

He glanced around the guest room at the top of the stairs, peeked out the window, snooped in the closet. No trace of Billy.

Paul shouted something from down the hall.

Time to round up his anxious neighbor and get out of there. Being in someone else's house, especially uninvited, made Joe increasingly uncomfortable.

A grunt was followed by a heavy thud at the end of the upstairs hallway. Had his volatile neighbor broken something?

"Paul?" he said.

When no one answered, he stepped out of the guest room. No one in sight. He listened. A strained silence throughout the house. Then he heard a footstep that seemed to come from the next room. He sighed with relief. There he was!

"Paul, I think we should go now. There's no one here."

No response. Joe took three strides down the hall and stepped through an open door into a small storage room.

"What did you find that's so interesting?"

No answer. His hand slapped at the wall until it located the light switch. It clicked back and forth, without effect. He could see Paul at the other end of the room, standing in the shadows beyond the crowded boxes and jammed old furniture. His back was toward Joe. He seemed to be staring down into the ravine through the window.

"Come on, let's go," said Joe. "Before somebody sees us."

He took another step into the darkness of the storage room, and then stopped in his tracks. There was just enough light to see that something was wrong with Billy's father. He had changed. He wasn't wearing the same jacket he'd worn before. Too late Joe realized it wasn't Billy's father at all. He found himself facing a man in a black leather jacket.

Joe gave a sharp, brief cry. The man of his nightmares! "You, there! Who are you? What are you doing here?" he stammered.

The man turned slightly. Feeble light from the hallway gleamed on his upraised jacket collar. One sleeve of his jacket swung out of the shadows. In his hand was a large crucifix, gripped like a weapon.

He came at him suddenly.

Joe stumbled backward, groping desperately for squeezing room between the wedged-in armchairs and the sideways vanity, tripping over an old coffee table. He fell, hit the floor behind him, kicked and scrambled his way into the hallway but couldn't quite manage to get up on his feet. The man from his nightmares just kept coming. Out of the room, into the hall, straight at him. He was unstoppable. The crucifix swung up into the air, up over Joe's head and down—

An arm coiled around the man's neck from behind. Another arm grabbed the crucifix, twisting it with a wrenching turn. It slipped free, clattering down the stairs. Suddenly there were two nightmare figures locked in combat, stumbling backward toward the staircase. Scrambling to his feet, Joe watched in horrified disbelief. Tangled together in a furious knot of swinging limbs, they lurched off the edge of the staircase, missing the top stair, falling, bumping and careening, one over the other, tumbling headlong. Joe ran down the stairs after them, staring in shock as both figures came to a stunned stop on the hallway carpet below.

A bar of moonlight slashed through the hallway from the kitchen. Joe's rescuer was flung to the floor there, illuminated in the faint blue light.

"Pepper!" Joe couldn't believe his eyes.

The man in the leather jacket had fallen nearby. He tried to scramble free. Pepper lunged on him, regaining her hold. An angry, desperate thrashing about on the hardwood floor, jabbing elbows, clawing fingers. Joe circled, trying to reach in and grab the man from behind. Something was wrong with his face. Wrong with his body.

Joe reached out blindly behind him and flipped the light switch at the foot of the stairs.

Pepper gave a jolt, as though she'd been stabbed in the stomach. She pulled away with a sob and began to cry.

Her mother lay sprawled on the floor, the glossy black jacket flopped open at her sides. She regarded Pepper and Joe wordlessly, gasping for breath, dazed, like a drugged animal that could at any moment become vicious. Her face was flushed and swollen as though she'd been crying.

Pepper towered above her, red overcoat torn open and missing several buttons, red beret clamped down askew on her head, plaid red-and-green scarf hanging in disarranged loops around her throat. She wrapped her arms around her mother, propping her up. "Mom."

"What happened?" mumbled Rose. "What am I doing down on the floor?" She took a wild-eyed look at the leather jacket she was wearing. "Oh, my God! Why am I wearing this?"

"Mom, did I hurt you? I'm so sorry—"

"Why did you knock me down?" she demanded. "Why do I have this jacket on?"

"Mom, you were trying to hit Joe," said Pepper. "Don't you remember? You were going to bash him over the head."

"Bash him?" Rose laughed nervously. "Why would I want to bash anyone? You're not making sense. Why am I wearing Uncle Gabriel's jacket?"

"You were wearing it when I came in. Mom, you must have put it on yourself."

"That's impossible," said Rose. "I was praying when you came in. I was deep in prayer, and then I heard a noise."

Pepper was crying and shaking her head in disbelief.

"Don't look at me like that," said Rose. "You don't understand. You think you do, but you don't."

"I understand what I saw," said Pepper in a whisper.

"You don't understand anything," said Rose.

Gently, patiently, Pepper steered her mother away from the staircase into the living room, with Joe on the other side of her for support. Joe remembered Billy's father and glanced back up the stairs.

"Paul!" he called.

No answer.

Had he found his son and taken him home? "Billy's Dad must have left," he explained to Pepper. She wasn't really listening.

They guided Rose toward the picture window over the ravine. The sofa was large enough for all three to be seated.

"Mom, why were you attacking Joe?"

"He has no business being in this house!" snapped her mother. "And you!" she said to Pepper. "You break my heart. You leave me thinking I'll never see my daughter again."

"Why would you never see me?"

"You got what you needed out of me. You were throwing your old mother away."

"How could you even think such a thing? Mom, why do you always believe the worst?"

"Because the worst is what happens." Rose was half-hidden in the shadows. "Because this world, that's what it's made of — all the bad things people didn't believe could happen." When Pepper reached toward the lamp, she brushed away her daughter's hand. "Well, what are you doing here? Where have you been?"

Pepper shrugged uncomfortably. "In a motel out at Sea-Tac Airport. I needed time to think."

"Time to think?" Rose smiled in quiet contempt. "You can't think in your own house? Seems a little late for thinking, when you've got your plane ticket. Well, think again. I suggest you head straight back to the airport. Get out of here quick, before something bad happens. You don't live here any more. This is my house!"

Pepper stared at her incredulously. "Mom, what's come over you?" She studied her face, trying to read answers there. "I came back because I was worried about you. I kept feeling you were in danger."

"You don't know how dangerous he is," said Rose. "Can't you feel him? Uncle Gabriel is getting stronger all the time."

"Well, he'll have to deal with me now. I'm staying in Seattle. I've got work to do in the ravine. This is my home, here with you."

"You're not safe here. We've stirred him up, disturbed his resting place. That's why he killed Mama. That's why he wants to kill me."

The ravine had become an indiscriminate blackness on the other side of the living room window. Pepper knelt before her mother, holding one of Rose's hands in both of her own.

"Why would Uncle Gabriel want to hurt you, Mom?"

"Because he hates me so much!"

"Hates you? But why? Because your mother killed him?"

"Mama didn't kill him."

"But you said Grandma killed her brother."

"That's not what I said."

"But you said—"

"I said she knocked him off the bridge. I didn't say she killed him."

# 8
# Good Girl

Ten-year-old Rose stood helplessly staring at her mother. Carmen had collapsed to her knees, slumped against the bridge's wooden wall, afraid to look over the side. She hugged herself, doubled over, sobbing.

"Don't cry, Mama," said Rose, watching Carmen's ordeal wide-eyed. She was so scared she could hardly force the words out of her mouth. "Please don't be sad. I love you, Mama."

She pulled free of her mother's grasp and broke into a run toward the other end of the bridge, toward the footpath leading down into the ravine. When her mother realized what Rose was doing, she called out, "Honey, come back here. Don't you dare go down there!"

"Don't worry, Mama," cried the girl over her shoulder. "I'll find him." That was what a good girl would do. He might need help right away. She might need to call an ambulance.

Forcing herself not to be afraid, Rose began making her way down through the dark trees. She placed each foot carefully, working her way down the bank, stepping onto an exposed root here, a protruding rock there, then past the scaffolding of bridge supports, through the blackberry thickets and bamboo. She groped her way, with occasional splashes into shallow, icy water, toward where her uncle had fallen.

He wasn't there.

She looked quickly first in the obvious places. Then she looked again slower, more carefully. She searched on both sides of the bridge. No trace of him anywhere. Standing there stymied, uncertain which way to go next, she was about to retrace her steps when she heard crackling in the leaves and a dragging sound. She froze, and listened. The approach of snapping and breaking twigs. She looked in terror around her. It sounded like maybe he was crawling, but she couldn't tell from which direction. Her injured, angry uncle was dragging his broken body toward her through the underbrush.

Now silence. She stepped cautiously backward.

A hand closed around her ankle. She nearly screamed, before she managed to kick away the limp, half-curled fingers. The motionless body of her uncle lay stretched beside the hand.

Rose stepped away from her uncle's body, staring at it with an involuntary shudder. When she looked up, her mother was standing across from her under the bridge.

"Uncle Gabriel is dead," said Rose miserably.

Her mother knelt down beside the body and stared at him. "Your uncle was an evil man," said Mama. "He was going to take away our house from us. He's better off dead. Now you and I still have a home. We've been saved."

Rose didn't hear what her mother said. Carmen shook her. "Stop crying, Rosie. He was going to hurt you."

"Yes, but—!" protested Rose.

"Hush!" said her mother. "If anyone finds us down here with him, they'll take me away. They'll put me in jail for the rest of my life. You'll never see me again."

Rose stared at her mother in horror.

"Help me," said Carmen. "We've got to get him away from here. We've got to find a way—"

Looking around the ravine, her mother noticed a fallen tree trunk just a short distance upstream. "That log," she said to her daughter. "Come on, help me drag him over there."

Mother and daughter hauled his body over the rocks by the arms and legs, over to the tree trunk, where they slumped him over the log. "We'll bury him under here," said Carmen. She tried to rip away some of the vines interlaced around the log. She couldn't. She swore, and for just a moment broke down in tears. She recovered herself, clenched her teeth, determined. "I'm just going back up to the house to get a shovel out of the garage," said her mother. "And a flashlight."

"I'm coming, too."

"You stay here."

"Mama, don't leave me."

"You've got to keep an eye out. Make sure no one comes snooping. I'll be right back." With that, her mother was only a shadow scrambling up through the other shadows.

Rose found herself alone in the darkness, standing beneath the trees with the body of her uncle. She tried not to look at the log where he was stretched out. He looked like he was sleeping or passed out drunk. His head had rolled so that his eyes were looking at her.

Her mother was taking a long time. Rose hugged herself, stamping up and down with the cold. She accidentally bumped against the log. The body was jostled. The hand slid over and touched her.

Uncle Gabriel's eyes struggled open. They were wild with fear and pain and confusion. His hand closed around her wrist. He pulled her down close to him.

"Rosie, it's me," he said with gasping effort. He reached out suddenly and grabbed her other arm. His fingers dug into her, gripped too tightly. "Be a good girl, sweetheart. Nothing to be afraid of." He flinched, shuddered on the log, gritting his teeth. He was slowly dragging himself up closer to her, closer. "Your uncle needs a doctor, Rosie." She kicked at his legs, to no effect.

"Get away from me."

"You've got to help me, Rosie," he said. "Don't be afraid of me."

She pulled an arm free, grabbed at a branch to pull herself away from him. He dragged her back. "Gotta get out of here."

"Let go of me!"

213

"Your Mama wants to kill me," he said, breathing hotly in her face. "But not you, Rosie. Not you—"

She jerked away from him, staring at him wide-eyed. She reached down and pried up a rock.

He saw her grip it. "Put that down!" He saw her raise it. "Rosie, don't!" She came a step closer. He grabbed her wrist.

"Drop that rock, or I'll—"

She struck him on the side of the head. His grip on her wrist tightened. He tugged himself partway up. His other hand closed around her neck. His fingers tightened into the flesh of her throat. She struck him again, harder.

"No — no!"

And again.

He collapsed back onto the tree trunk. He shuddered and lay still. A line of blood came out of the corner of his mouth. Blood darkened the log behind his head.


# 9
# Haunted

The hissing, icy wind battered at the picture window, trying to join the three miserable people huddled inside. Rose still sat on the sofa but she was alone there now, back stiff, staring straight ahead, scowling across the coffee table at the black picture window as though viewing her past there. Pepper knelt on a small throw-rug at her mother's feet. Joe was awkwardly standing, backed against an armchair somewhat apart from them, staring in shock.

"I never told Mama," said Rose. "She came back with the shovel, and gave me the flashlight. She told me not to watch her digging. When the digging stopped, I turned to look. At first I thought Mama was hugging him, but she wasn't. She was hauling his body up off the log. She let it fall over into the hole, and then started shoveling dirt in. I tried not to look. Once I saw his hand sticking out of the dirt. The only thing Mama didn't bury was his wallet. And his jacket."

"The next morning, we acted like nothing had happened. Nobody ever suspected. I used to wake up crying. Mama would come into my room and say, 'You didn't do anything. Don't you worry, my little Rose, you didn't do anything.' But I knew what I had done. I did it for her, but I did it.

"I remember a school official came to the house once to ask Mama if anything had happened to me. I had stopped talking to all my friends. Mama told him I was fine.

"No one ever found Uncle Gabriel's body. No one noticed he'd disappeared. He was just another guy with a bad attitude who drifted into town and drifted out again. The house became Mama's legal property. Our secret tied us together for life. That secret always separated us from you."

"Oh, Mom, if you'd only told me!"

"I wanted you to escape the Merlino curse," said Rose. "I wanted you to be happy. And you could have been — until that boy ruined everything. He disturbed Uncle Gabriel. He brought him back. That's why Mama fell. Her brother pushed her. That's why she yelled his name."

"But she didn't," said Joe. "The word she shouted was more like 'happy' or 'help me.'"

Rose shook her head. "She only called him Gabriel when she was mad. Most of the time she called him Gabby." She smiled sadly. "As for the rest, the very idea that I would attack Joe, that I would try to hurt anyone — it's ridiculous. Now, if you'll excuse me, I'm going upstairs to pray. I need some time alone with God. Sometimes prayer is the only thing that can bring me peace."

She walked away from them. At the foot of the stairs, face-down on the carpet, lay the crucifix from her bedroom wall. Snatching it up off the floor, she clutched it to her chest as she hurried up the staircase.

Her footsteps quickly crossed the length of the ceiling. Her bedroom door slammed shut behind her.

Then came the scream.

Pepper and Joe bolted up the staircase, flung open the door of Rose's bedroom. They stared down at the body stretched on the floor at the foot of the bed.

"This man!" cried Rose. "Here, in my room—"

"It's Billy's father!" cried Pepper.

Paul was groggy, confused, struggling to get up. "Can you give me a hand?" He reached up to Joe, who hauled him onto his feet. "I'm a little wobbly." He sat down abruptly on the bedside, one red hand holding his head.

"Paul, you're bleeding. Wait a minute, stay still — let me look at it." Joe examined the matted hair on the side of his neighbor's head. "Lucky for you, it doesn't look deep."

"It hurts like hell," said Paul. But the sharpness of his reply was belied by an odd expression on his face.

"You're smiling?" said Pepper in bewilderment. "You just got your head broken open, and you're smiling. What don't I understand?"

Paul's smile, pained and wincing, grew larger. "My kid was right," he said. "And so were you." He gripped Pepper's hand. "Billy doesn't need a shrink. I just saw the man he's afraid of. He was no dream. He clobbered me. He knocked some sense into me—" He faltered as he took another look at Rose. "That jacket — that's who attacked me."

"Don't be absurd," said Rose. Her lips twisted in contempt. "That's ridiculous. I just got here."

"I have a feeling," said Joe, "you're not the only one she's attacked."

"That's a complete lie!" objected Rose.

"Is it?" Joe continued. "I think you sincerely don't know who attacked your daughter. But that doesn't change what happened. The man who did it — is you."

"You're out of your mind!"

"Halloween night," said Joe, "although you may not remember it, you put on that jacket and went for a walk in the ravine."

"No!" cried Rose. "Are you accusing me of hurting my own daughter? What kind of mother do you think I am?"

"Mom—" Pepper was quietly crying. "When Mrs Skinner came over that night, did you put on the jacket?"

"You, too?" cried Rose, glaring at her daughter. "Why are you telling these lies about me?"

"I think, Mrs Merlino," said Joe, "something is happening that you don't understand. Something out of your control. Something is loose in this ravine. It's infected me. It's infected Billy. But it's worse with you. You just don't realize it."

"You're talking nonsense."

"You're being haunted."

"Haunted?" Rose snorted. "What's that supposed to mean?"

"I think the spirit of Uncle Gabriel is so strong now," said Joe, "he's learned how to take over completely. He's using you. That's why you don't remember putting on his jacket. That's why you don't remember what you did to Paul — or what you tried to do to me."

The very thought hit Rose with a physical jolt. "That is not true," she said. "You think I'm possessed? Absolutely not. God protects good people. He would never—"

"Mom," whispered Pepper. "I think I know how it might happen. Maybe it's when you pray."

"When I pray? You think God would allow such—?"

"Maybe, when you pray, you go into a trance. Maybe that's when Uncle Gabriel takes over."

Her mother stared at her, speechless. Then she strode angrily out of the room and down the stairs.

"Mom!" Pepper hurried after her.

Paul surged up onto unsteady feet. "I just want to find my boy and get out of here."

"I don't think you're going anywhere," said Joe. "I think I should call an ambulance.

"I'm fine," said Paul. He took two steps, and his knees buckled out from under him. Joe managed to catch him, easing him back against the dresser for support.

"Lean on me," said Joe. "We're heading downstairs."

"No," Paul protested weakly. "I've got to find my son."

# 10
## Burning Memories

Pepper could hear the wind intensify, whistling in an angry hiss against the front windowpane, rattling the glass behind her mother. Hobbling together, Joe and Paul reached the bottom of the stairs, and slowly approached.

"It's so cold tonight," said Rose, staring out the night-blackened glass overlooking the ravine. She hugged herself. "Such a cold Christmas. Cold as the Christmas when it happened." She shivered and turned to the fireplace, with its overflowing contents. "That's what I need to warm me up. A fire always lifts your spirits."

"Mom, that doesn't look like such a good idea—"

Snatching up a can of lighter fluid from the far side of the woodpile, her mother gave several long, streaming squirts, drenching torn-down posters and bundles of receipts and mounds of letters and schoolbooks, shirts and socks, model airplanes, athletic trophies. Then she reached confidently into the leather jacket's front pocket and pulled out a gleaming metal lighter.

Rose clicked it into flame, bent over and touched it to an exposed paper. The flame caught. "Yes, see — a nice fire." With a whoosh, the mound of belongings in the fireplace leaped into flames which began to crackle and dart, shiver and burn.

"That's a pretty big fire," said Joe disapprovingly.

"Mom, that's totally unsafe," said Pepper. "Okay, that's enough, you've made your point. Give me that."

Before Pepper could take the lighter fluid away from her, Rose squeezed the dispenser again, squirting it across the mound of belongings in the clogged fireplace, dousing papers and notebooks and underwear. The flames shot up in crackling tongues over the mantelpiece.

"Mother, please!" sobbed Pepper, jerking the lighter fluid out of her mother's grip. "You're scaring me. That's enough."

She wasn't the only one scared. "Where is my son, Mrs Merlino?" demanded Paul. "I'm through waiting. Where can I find him?"

The silence was interrupted by a muffled thudding from somewhere else in the house.

"Oh, my God!" whispered Paul. "Listen."

"I hear it, too," said Joe.

Rose watched them both quietly, without saying a word.

"It's him, isn't it?" said Paul. "That's my son you've got locked up somewhere in this house!" Paul's cheeks flushed with rage. "How could you do that? He's just a kid!"

"Not just any kid," said Rose. "The kid who started it all."

"Are you going to tell me where he is," said Paul, glancing nervously toward the roaring fireplace, "or do I have to find him myself?" He stepped impulsively forward, staggered, nearly fell.

Joe caught him. "You're in no condition to go anywhere."

Rose gasped softly, cocked her head slightly to one side, peered out the black window. "Listen — can you hear it? That creaking sound. It's that branch up there." She pointed through the picture window at Uncle Gabriel's branch.

The room seemed to grow darker. A blast of icy wind rattled the window glass.

"Listen to it now. Look how far that branch is bending! The wind must be incredibly strong—"

The crack was loud as a gunshot. The branch outside the window snapped at its base and swung down in a broken arc. The free end speared the windowpane.

A spider web of shattering. A showering explosion of glass fragments. An unexpected blast of wind roared into the living room. Flames leaped from the overcrowded bulge of the fireplace, eating hungrily up the side of the flapping curtains.

"Mom!" screamed Pepper. "Watch out."

Flames, agitated by the wind, lashed out across the hearthstone, climbed up over the side of the armchair.

"Oh, my God — get back!"

The wind licked the fire across the sofa's back, snatched up burning papers from the fireplace and scattered them, whipping them up into the air, blasting them down the hall. Burning debris swept up the staircase. Crackling ashes dipped down the basement stairwell.

"It's him." Rose looked around her at the spreading fire. "Tonight's the night it happened. Christmas Eve."

Pepper tried to pull her mother away. "Come on, Mom, please, we need to get out side. We need to call the Fire Department."

Rose pried loose her daughter's hand. "You should never have come back."

A sob shook Pepper's body. She looked at her mother as though a ravine were cracking open between them. "Mom, I love you so much—"

Rose smiled weakly. She pushed the girl's hand away. "And I love you, Perpetua. My love for you has kept me alive. Unfortunately, my love for my mother came first, and it ruined everything. Sometimes in life there aren't enough choices, and none of them are good ones."

The flames roared hungrily. One end of the living room was shivering with fire. Smoke made it hard to see.

"There's no reason to go on," said Rose. "No one will ever be happy now. God forgive anyone who thinks they can take just one small step into the darkness. Get out of here fast, before it's too late. I have a matter to settle."

"Please, Mom—"

"Uncle Gabriel!" shouted Rose toward the jagged gap in the window. "I know it's you." In answer, a soul-chilling blast swept through the room, lashed the burning curtains, fanned the flames from pillow to pillow, across the carpet.

"Come on, Mom, we've got to get out of here."

"I'm not leaving. This is where I belong."

Pepper tried to grab her, but Rose eluded her and started with a determined stride up the staircase. Pepper lunged after her.

"Pepper, come back!" cried Joe.

She turned to him midway up the staircase. "Find Billy," she called. "I'm going to get Mom."

# 11
## How He Died

Joe quickly hooked Paul Beck's left arm over his shoulders, and heaved him up onto his feet. "Come on, let's get you outside."

"No!" Paul protested. "I can't leave my son. I've got to—"

Moving backward, Joe bumped open the front door with his shoulder and hauled Paul out into the windy night.

"Will somebody call 9-1-1?" shouted Joe toward the neighbors' front window. A shadow ran for the phone. He turned to Paul. "You stay here. I'll find Billy. I promise."

Easing Paul back onto the fender of a parked car, propping him up securely, Joe bounded back across the front lawn toward the house, swung open the door. The living room was ablaze. No sign of Pepper or her mother. And then he heard it. The feeble, persistent, desperate pounding that came from somewhere else in the house.

It came from the basement.

He made for the kitchen. The air was so thick with smoke Joe could hardly see where he was going. A draft of wind was being sucked downstairs, along with tumbling sparks. He plunged down the smoky stairwell, descended the stairs as fast as he could make his feet move.

At the bottom he froze, listening. "Billy—!"

An old sofa lined one wall, taking up much of the floorspace. Several tall file cabinets cut off the view on one side. Two gleaming white cubes down the other side were the washer and dryer. The water heater rumbled. On the far side of a pile of storage boxes was a closet door. Feeble thuds came from inside.

The closet seemed so far away. But he would get there. Even if he had to crawl.

He didn't remember dropping to his knees.

He found himself crawling on the floor, light-headed, coughing, groping his way through the blinding smoke with a thudding in his ears. It sounded like someone slamming an enormous hammer against the walls, again and again. He realized the sound was his heart-beat.

So, this was how he died.

He had come to Seattle to die, but he'd expected to wither away in a hospital bed, to gradually lose the desire to eat, the desire to move, the desire to live. Not to be burned alive. Joe hadn't cared about living when he came to Seattle. Now he cared. Once he'd been prepared, but not anymore. He let out a cry of protest. He wasn't ready to die!

Joe scrambled weakly, dizzily, back up onto his feet.

His hands reached out in front of him. He couldn't see. He tripped over the end of the sofa. He rapped his knuckles on the hard edge of the washing machine.

Eye pain. The closer he got to the thudding noise, the more his eye throbbed.

Fire roared all around him. He was gagging on the smoke. He tugged open the far closet. Inside, crumpled into a sweaty lump on the floor, was Billy, cheeks wet with tears, hands tied behind him, a rag stuffed into his mouth. The boy turned toward him wide, glassy eyes. Joe yanked out the rag, flinging it aside.

"You okay?"

"I want my Dad," he whimpered. He was trembling. Joe couldn't untie the knots.

"I'll get you out of here," he said, scooping the boy into his arms. "Don't worry, I've got you now."

The old sofa burst into flames.

Clutching the boy to his chest, Joe staggered back toward the basement stairs.

The boxes and storage containers leaped into a crackling blaze.

Turning Billy's face away from the heat, he strode through the smoke to the foot of the staircase. It took every bit of determination he had. Flames roared hotter, closer, licking at Billy, scorching the hair on Joe's arms. He took one step after the next. He had come so far, risked so much. He refused to be defeated.

The stairs burst into flames behind him. There would be no going back.

The heat around the staircase was searing. Step by step, he managed to get the boy to the top. But to open the door! That was another matter. He tried to shuffle the boy into one arm, reaching for the doorknob, trying to turn it. The boy began slipping. Joe was losing his grip.

The bottom of the staircase was now solid flames.

He coughed, gasping for breath.

Smoke — so much smoke! And a door at the top of the stairs that wouldn't open.


# 12
# Uncle Gabriel

"Mom, we have to get out of here."

Her mother stood at the foot of the bed, staring at the bare place on the wall where the crucifix had once hung. Pepper came up behind her, embraced her. She could feel her whole body tremble.

"Mom, please come with me."

"I can't." She shrugged free of Pepper's hold. "I belong here. Can't you feel him? You think he's dead, but he's not."

"He'll have to deal with me first," said Pepper, "because I'm not leaving you behind."

"Go. This is between Uncle Gabriel and me."

"No one's harming you while I'm here," said Pepper, "living or dead."

The bare wall where the crucifix had once hung burst into flames. The portraits of Jesus and Mary with their exposed hearts shriveled into flaking, crumbling strips of black ash. The bed went next, as though a bedspread of fire had been thrown over it.

And then — there he was, standing in the flames.

The man who had stalked Joe and Billy in their nightmares. The face Pepper had seen in the photos. It was her mother's shameless, dangerous uncle, Gabriel Merlino, unshaved, shifty-eyed, belligerant, who had been knocked off the bridge by his sister, struck dead with a rock by his niece. Flames licked all around him. He didn't seem to feel a thing. He looked at Rose and smiled knowingly.

Then he turned toward Pepper, charming, seductive. "Be a good girl." The words echoed in Pepper's head, resonated, took over her complete attention. They were all she could hear. Her defiance, her resistence, drained out of her. "Don't be afraid of me." She forgot all about the fire. She couldn't look away from those eyes, couldn't resist the undertow of that voice. "Your Mama wants to kill me. But not you — not you — not you!"

Pepper couldn't turn away from him.

Rose slapped her. Pepper staggered, shocked awake. "I love you, honey!" Rose cried, her words filled with sorrow and maternal love. Then she gave Pepper a sudden, rude shove backward and slammed the bedroom door in her face.

Pepper screamed and battered at the door with her fists. Too late. It quickly became too hot and drove her back. "Mom!" she wailed. On the other side of the fiery door, Rose Merlino gave no answer.

With a sob, Pepper ran.

The fire roared. She couldn't hear herself think. Breathing took all her concentration. She was dizzy from lack of air. She fell down the last few stairs, blinded by tears and smoke.

Scrambling to her feet at the bottom of the staircase, she heard a faint pounding on the basement door. She tugged it open. With a cry, Joe staggered up into the hallway, Billy clutched in his arms.

The windows blew out in an explosion of shattering glass.

Together the three of them battered out the front door into the coldness of the night.


# 13
## Firelight

No one in Ravenna Springs ever forgot that Christmas Eve. Soon neighbors were wandering the streets wearing winter coats bundled around their pajamas and bathrobes. Flames licked up over the rooftop of the Merlino house. A crowd was gathering, with Paul Beck at the front.

Pepper and Joe came hurtling out of the front door. Joe was carrying Billy. Paul cried out and ran toward them. He caught up with them as they stumbled away from the burning house, dropped to his knees, swept Billy into his arms.

"Are you hurt, pal?" said Paul, tearing away the twine binding his son's hands. "Did you get burned? Are you all right?"

"I'm okay, Dad."

"Billy, I saw him, too. The man in the black leather jacket." He wrapped his arms tightly around his son, as though Billy might somehow escape from him. "From now on I promise, no matter how crazy, to believe everything you say. Everything! Anything! No matter how nuts, how insane, I promise I'll believe it."

Billy put his arms around his father's neck.

After a moment, Paul Beck rose and put his hand on Joe's shoulder. "Please let me apologize," he said awkwardly. "For insulting you. For acting like a complete idiot."

"You were just being a Dad."

"A suspicious and blind one."

"Kids are worth protecting," said Joe. "Especially a kid like Billy."

"I owe my son's life to you," said Paul. He seized Joe's hand and pumped it ardently.

Billy and his father were still clutching each other in the street, surrounded by neighbors, as Joe left them in search of Pepper.

*

Firelight crackled and rippled over the depths of the ravine. The blazing deck of the Merlino house lit the creek below, as though the water had turned to molten gold in some kind of holiday miracle. Sirens wailed into the Christmas night. The first of the fire engines came lumbering around the corner.

Pepper cried in Joe's arms.

They stood in the middle of the old wooden bridge. From there they could look across the wild end of the ravine at the burning house perched on the edge, the home she would never enter again. Every time she realized that her mother was inside that house, Pepper's knees tried to buckle out from under her. When she thought about what was going up in smoke, the lifetime of familiar, cherished belongings, she felt that Joe was the only thing holding her up.

He gave her all the strength she needed.

Below, surrounded by the gleaming currents of the creek, the vine-covered log with its long-buried secret rippled with reflections of the flames. What was hidden there would remain hidden.

"The house they both wanted," said Pepper.

"Now no one gets it," said Joe. Firemen surrounded the Merlino house with shouts and leaping arcs of water. Joe took her hand. "I think Uncle Gabriel and your Mom have finally evened the score. Too bad everything they fought for is going up in smoke. Maybe that's the only way it could end."

Red and green blinking Christmas lights intersected with revolving red and blue police beacons.

"You're going to need a place to stay," he said. "I'm still looking for a housemate."

She hugged him silently.

They drew together on the bridge. Warmed by the glow of the blazing house, suspended over the firelit ravine they both loved, they wrapped their arms around each other for support in the first light of Christmas dawn.

Photo: J. Aaron Manning

**Nick DiMartino** is a Seattle native and the author of two other ghost thrillers set in Seattle, *Christmas Ghost Story* and *University Ghost Story.*

He's had 18 plays in full-run productions. His *Dracula* premiered at Seattle Children's Theatre in 1982, followed by his adaptations of *Pinocchio* and Hans Christian Andersen's *The Snow Queen.* His *Frankenstein* sold out in Honolulu, Nashville, Louisville, Dallas and twice in Milwaukee, where it was videotaped by the BBC for Globalstage in 1997. His plays include *Raven,* inspired by Pacific Northwest Indian legends; an authentic Arabic version of *Aladdin,* and a Grimms Brothers version of *Snow White.* He wrote three musicals for Bellevue Children's theatre, including *Ozma of Oz.*

His four-woman vampire thriller, *The Red Forest,* won 2nd Place at the 1987 Pacific Northwest Writers Conference. His Italian farce, *Stop the Wedding!,* was a finalist in the 1988 New City Theater Playwrights Festival. His new version of *Babes in Toyland,* with the original music of Victor Herbert, was the 1994 opening production of the new Village Theatre in Issaquah, Washington.

Since 1970, he has been the book-buyer for the HUB Branch of the University Bookstore.

---

**Charles Nitti** created the cover and illustrations for both *University Ghost Story* and *Seattle Ghost Story.* He is an internationally-published illustrator and national award winner for restaurant design, who recently re-designed and painted the interior of Seattle's popular nightclub, Jazz Alley. He created theatre sets for a presentation of Tennessee Williams' short stories for the Chicago Institute, and painted the Chicago Film Festival poster for 1985. A native Chicagoan, Nitti relocated to Seattle in 1995.

He has designed and painted trompe l'oeil and faux finishes in La Trinidad Church in San Fernando, California, as well as an outdoor mural in a drive-through museum in Venezuela and billboard art on the outsides of three 747 jets.

Enjoy other ghost stories by
# NICK DiMARTINO

☐ **UNIVERSITY GHOST STORY**

Tragic secrets haunt an English professor and a bookstore clerk whose lives become entangled with a troubled 13-year-old early entrance student and a homeless poet with terrifying results.

ISBN 0-9653918-1-7 Trade Paperback $12.95

☐ **CHRISTMAS GHOST STORY**

The quarrelling, hot-tempered members of the Rossi family learn the meaning of Christmas the hard way when they get trapped by a Christmas Eve snowstorm in their grandmother's haunted house.

ISBN 0-9653918-0-9 Trade Paperback $12.95

Buy these books from your local bookstore or use this coupon for ordering.

**Send checks only (no cash & no COD's) to**
**ROSEBRIAR PUBLISHING**
**820 195th Place SW, Lynnwood, WA 98036  (425) 776-3865**

Please send me the books I have checked above. I am enclosing $12.95 for each book plus $4.50 shipping & handling for the first book & $1.00 each additional book. Add 8.6%/o sales tax if Washington State resident.

Name
_____

Address
_____

City/State/Zip
_____

Telephone  (     )
_____

Prices and numbers subject to change without notice. Valid in U.S. only. All orders subject to availability.